FRACTURED & FORMIDABLE

THE SACRED HEARTS MC BOOK FIVE

A.J. DOWNEY

COPYRIGHT

Text Copyright © 2014 by A.J. Downey

ISBN: 978-0692448786

Edited by Barbara J. Bailey

Book design by Maggie Kern

Cover art by Dar Albert at Wicked Smart Designs

Model - Brandon Baggett

Photographer - Furious Fotog

DEDICATION

To the men and women across the country who give the time and effort for B.A.C.A. or Bikers Against Child Abuse. You are the unsung heroes and are, in part, what the spirit of the Sacred Hearts MC was modeled after, even before I knew you existed. Keep doing what you're doing; I am happy to help get your message out. It is an unfortunate reality in which we live that you are needed, but I am not the only one that is glad you are here. This one is for you.

PROLOGUE

14 months ago…

"I've got room, Red."

I looked dubiously at the man who had spoken and my mouth went dry for a second time. I'd noticed him the second he'd walked into the studio, but hadn't been introduced. I'd caught his name when he'd introduced himself to Everett though–'Zander'.

He was gorgeous. Dark hair was hidden beneath a red baseball cap turned backwards on his head. He had on a red tee shirt with the sleeves torn off and a black denim vest over it. He wore long, black-denim shorts that ended just below the knee above red canvas hi-top shoes; the kind with the white rubber toe-caps, with white socks riding above where the white laces tied off. He was remarkably well-put-together compared to the rough appearance I'd expected from him being somehow a part of a motorcycle gang... which was probably fairly judgmental of me. I immediately felt guilty for the unfair thought, but continued in my observations.

His arms were huge, one brightly-colored in fiery oranges and the other in cool black-and-white images. I couldn't discern what they were from across the studio where I stood beside my best friend. His legs were just as muscled as his arms.

His eyes, though – they're what had made my mouth go dry the first time, and my heart speed up. They reminded me of my gran's famous chocolate caramels, a lovely milk-chocolatey brown, tinged with a burnished bronze-gold hue that drew me in as they roved over me from my head to my feet. I blushed. So what, if it was exactly what I was doing to him?

"You should take him up on it," Everett said enthusiastically, adding, "It's unbelievable!"

I felt drawn to the man, who was shorter than me by half a head, though he was compact and solidly muscled. I quailed a bit on the inside and bit the inside of my cheek. He looked like he could really hurt someone, and not entirely on purpose. It was like he knew he was strong, but the way he carried himself, so nonchalant, it gave the impression that maybe he didn't know his own strength.

He gave me this devil-may-care grin, revealing a chipped tooth in the front, and with his dimples, the effect was absolutely adorable. I felt myself give an answering sweet smile as my misgivings eased. His smile said to me, *You can trust me,* and I tried very hard to trust everyone in equal measure, until they gave me a reason not to.

Everett had been my best friend since the second grade and she had never given me a reason not to trust her, even when we disagreed, or worse, fought like siblings. If she said it was something I should do or try, then it was. I chewed my lip thoughtfully, worried about what my dad would think, and caught Everett's look; she had her eyebrow raised in my direction and the look on her face that screamed, *Really? You're going to let him tell you what to do when he's not even here?* The old familiar argument, one that she always won, played out in my head. As always, she was right. If I listened to my father in my head all the time, I wouldn't have had even a quarter of the adventures that I had had with my bestie. She was a bad influence, in all the best ways.

"My car is safe here, so why not?" I finally agreed, and triumph flashed in my best friend's eyes.

"I'm Zander," he said to me quietly, and came over, holding out his arm like some old-fashioned gentleman.

"Mandy," I said, automatically linking my arm with his. The older Mexican-American man, Dray's father, (he couldn't be anything else, with how closely they resembled one another,) was speaking, and he spoke like my father did from the pulpit. He had that authority, that commanding tone of voice, as if he were a man who was used to being listened to. He was their leader, apparently, but I wasn't entirely up on how everything worked. Everett hadn't exactly had a lot of time to explain. That was partially why I was here. She hadn't called me in days, even though she'd promised to.

I let Zander escort me out into the overcast and crisp fall day and breathed deep the autumn air.

"Never ridden before?" he asked, and handed me a black half-helmet, which I took a bit dubiously. I looked at his motorcycle and cringed on the inside. It was big, and matte black, the front end long, the tires wide.

"Hey. Look at me, Red," he ordered gently, and his voice was velvet and smooth. I turned my attention away from the motorcycle and to him.

"It's okay. Do I look like a guy that'd let anything bad happen to you?" he asked with that devil-may-care grin of his. My stomach did a giant somersault.

"Um, no," I said, dubiously. Truthfully? Zander looked like the kind of man who would do bad things to me, given half a chance, bad things that would likely be so very good to have happen to a girl like me. He smiled wider, as if he'd read my mind, and stepped into my personal space. I blushed furiously and his eyes positively sparkled with good humor. He knew he was having an effect and was enjoying every moment of it! Unfortunately for me, that just made me blush harder.

Plucking the helmet from my hands, he began to speak in a low voice, mapping out his expectations and what he needed from me. I listened very carefully, terrified of doing something, anything, wrong, that might get us hurt. I tried valiantly not to be distracted when his fingertips brushed the underside of my jaw as he buckled the helmet securely onto me. They were softer than they appeared and I had to suppress a shiver at the lingering heat left behind by that touch. A small voice in the back of my mind was saying *you shouldn't play with fire; you're bound to get burned.*

Oh, how I should have listened.

Present day...

I shut the front door to the cozy little two-bedroom house that I shared with my best friend and her boyfriend. It was a bit awkward, juggling my purse and my keys one-handed, while pressing a wad of Kleenex to my nose, while also keeping my head tilted back as far as it would go. My eyes watered from the smarting pain, tears leaking down into my bright copper curls at my temples while I tried to staunch the deep ruby flow from my nose.

"Sweet Mother Mary– Mandy!" Everett, who had been in the kitchen, jogged through the dining area and living room to reach me. I dumped my purse and keys onto the loveseat beside me and sat down heavily on the thick leather arm.

"It won't stop bleeding, Evy!" I said mournfully, and she pulled my hand away from my face by my wrist, gently. She growled at what she saw.

"It's a good thing Dray isn't home. Come on, let's get you cleaned up." She guided me around furniture that I couldn't see. I couldn't tip my head downward, because as soon as I did, a red tide would gush from my nose. It was frustrating and embarrassing, no matter how many times my best friend had seen it. I dropped into the dining room chair closest to the kitchen.

Everett pulled a wad of paper towels from the roll and handed them to me. I replaced the dripping wad of Kleenex, and winced when the paper towel began to soak through immediately.

Everett held out a plastic grocery bag and I tossed the Kleenex into it with a wet splat that made me want to gag. Everett set the bag aside with a rustle and I heard her at the freezer, scooping ice into another bag. She came back over, spinning it and tying it off. Gently and ever-so-carefully she rested the ice on the bridge of my nose.

"What happened?" she asked gently.

"Same thing that happened every time he does it. It's nothing new," I muttered.

"You need to stop going over there," she said, her voice dripping with disapproval.

"I can't. You know I can't," I muttered miserably. She sighed as if her heart carried the weight of the world on it and I spiraled further down into my misery. I hated this, I hated me, for causing my best friend pain. If only...

"I ought to send Dray over there to give him a what-for!" Everett said passionately, her accent thickening.

"No! Evy, no. Please, don't tell anyone... I couldn't bear it if anyone else knew. Please, don't say anything."

She made soothing and shushing noises at me and I bit my lips together.

"I won't, Mandy, I promise, but you can't keep going over there, you can't keep letting this happen," she said gravely.

"I know," I told her. "I just don't know what else to do."

She hugged me.

"Ever the dutiful daughter," she murmured, and it sounded like she wished I were anything but. Truthfully, I wished I could be less so, too, but I was afraid, afraid of what would happen, afraid of a lot of things.

I closed my eyes.

"Just don't tell anyone," I said, ashamed.

"You know your secret is safe with me. Always has been, and always will be." She hooked her pinky finger with mine and shook my hand back and forth by it.

Sometimes, I was afraid of that, too.

1

Revelator...

I stood up straight, catching the water streaming off my face with the hand towel I pulled off the bar by the sink. I mopped the water off my face and chest and checked for any excess shaving cream. I ran a comb through my black hair; it was getting long again, but I didn't really care too much about it. It was going under a ball cap, anyway.

"Yo, Rev!" Disney called from the living room.

"Yeah, what?" I called back.

"Hurry up! We're gonna be late."

I took one or two last swipes where I still felt damp.

"Keep your panties on, Puddin'!" I yelled back to my new roomie.

He'd been moved in all of around two weeks but as far as roommates went, he wasn't half-bad. Aside from him smokin' the Ganga every once in a while, making the house reek, I didn't really have too much to bitch about. Well, I had one other gripe, but I wasn't about to tell him to have quieter sex with his boyfriend. It was none of my fucking business and I didn't want to seem like a homophobe. I wasn't, despite how much I made fun of Disney, sayin' homophobic type shit. For me, that shit was just in good fun, irreverent bastard that I am. Hell, in my world, just about fucking everything was fair game when it came to humor.

"Would you move your ass if I told you Mandy was supposed to be there?" he asked.

I ducked my head out the open bathroom doorway. That girl was sweet as fucking pie and I had it worse than bad for her.

"Is she?" I asked.

Disney scowled at me.

"Maybe."

He crossed his arms over his cut. I rolled my eyes, took one last glance in the mirror, sprayed some cologne between my shoulders and called it good. I hit the bathroom light and stepped out into the hall.

"She better be there, now, or I'ma sit on you," I threatened.

Disney grinned, a twinkle in his eye and waved his hand at me in the classic effeminate-gay-man way and, affecting that horrible accent, said, "Oh, stop!"

I laughed and went into my room and pulled on my long, light-denim jean shorts. I pulled on some white athletic socks and stuffed my feet into my red Converse.

"Seriously though, she gonna be there?" I asked. I wanted to know. The girl had pretty much been under my skin since the moment I first laid eyes on her. It wasn't just that she was fucking gorgeous, she was all fucking woman. Lush curves and soft skin, with eyes the color of autumn and hair to match. I wanted her so fucking bad, and she would be mine. Oh, yes! She would be mine.

I had just met her at a bad time to make it so right away. I had just accepted a hang-around cut and was trying to become a prospect with the MC. It was a labor of love but also really damned time-consuming and my number-one priority at the time. Finally, I had become a fully-patched member, but then my business got blowed up, and if it wasn't one thing, it was another, and I was just plain sick of all of it getting in the way now. I needed to act, stop putting it off, and really go for it. I was in it to win it, and I wanted to start as soon as possible. I was half-afraid if I didn't get off my ass and do something that I was going to miss the opportunity all together, and I would be fucked if I let that happen.

I stood up from tying my laces and pulled a black Under Armor fitted compression tee over my head and tucked it in. I couldn't get the image I played over and over, of fitting my body to hers, out of my head. God damn! All those soft, lush, curves, that silky-smooth skin, so warm and alive, pressed right up against me. Mm.

I tried to think of something else while I was threading my belt through the loops on my shorts. I was hard as a fucking rock and didn't have time to relieve any tension right now. If I stopped to take care of business, Dis was going to blow a fucking gasket. I dumped my wallet into my back pocket and snapped the leather loop at the end of the chain around my belt. I picked up my cut, shrugging into it.

"Okay, Puddin', we can go," I called.

"Thank you!" Disney called out, exasperated.

I grinned, and plucked my favorite Florida Buccaneer's hat off the rack lining the back of my bedroom door and slid it on backwards, tucking the bill at the back of my neck.

"Quit'cher bitchin' there, lover-boy. Your man-pussy will wait for yah."

I was looking forward to Dis finishing his bike so he could get around on his own again. He was waiting for some damned part that had gotten cracked in the explosion to ship cross-country, or from overseas, or some shit. I snatched my keys to my Chevelle off the hook.

"Whoa, hey! Forgetting something?" Disney asked as I pulled open the front door. I stopped and looked over my shoulder.

"What?" I asked.

He held my Browning out to me, butt-first.

"Oh, shit! Good looking' out, Princess!" I took the gun and tucked it into the back of my waistband.

"Should have fuckin' shot you," I heard him grumble, and I grinned to myself.

It was raining outside and we dashed through it, both shrugging back out of our cuts and cursing. I may have taken a touch or two longer to unlock Disney's door than I needed to. He dove into the passenger seat, cursing me out, and I laughed.

"Fuckin' douchebag!" he cried, and pushed some of his long hair out of his face, slicking it back while he laughed.

I started what I considered my real pride-and-joy up and shifted her into reverse. I'd bought her as a rusting-out piece of shit that was just this side of 'worth saving' and had spent years making her whole. I smiled with a quiet steady pride at the reflection of the waterlogged streetlight off the black vinyl dash. The weather was fucking miserable out today, a steady, constant fall of drippy rain that made me think God had a runny nose and was snotting all over us.

"What do you think they're going to say?" he asked, fidgeting in his seat.

"Dunno, what the fuck is wrong with you? Boyfriend give you crabs or something?" He punched me in the arm, probably as hard as he could, and I laughed. Didn't do much through the thick leather of my jacket.

"Make fun of me all you want, I know you don't mean it, but not Aaron. Please?" he said, and he looked uncomfortable.

"Dude, man... you know I'm just fucking with you, right?" I asked, rolling up to a stoplight.

"Yeah, man! I know," he said and shifted again.

"Disney... Dude." I scowled at him.

"Sometimes it gets to be a bit much! Okay?" he asked, and grimaced, shifting in his seat a third time. "Fucking leg itches like a motherfucker. Doc says it's because it's healing, but man! Worse than any tat I've ever had," he said, in a bid to change the subject, but fuck, I instantly felt like a douche. The wound in his leg that he was bitching about had come from flying glass from ORI blowing up.

"Dude, I'm sorry, bro."

No one felt it more keenly than me. Disney could have gotten himself dead that night and I felt wholly responsible for it. I'd called and sent him into that deathtrap. His injuries fell squarely on my shoulders. I gritted my teeth. I wanted to fuck up the Suicide Kings' world, and it looked like I was going to get my chance on at least one of them, next month.

The Suicide Kings were all sorts of dirty, and depending on how you looked at it, fortunately or unfortunately that included being in on the illegal fight circuit. That's how I'd first crossed paths with the Sacred Hearts back in the day.

I'd been in my early twenties. Young, dumb and pissed-off at the whole fucking world. A high school buddy of mine had stumbled into the area's illegal fighting world. He'd got dollar signs in his eyes and me, I was all about a good fight. I was wrestling team, all-star in three counties; state champion in my class two years running in high school. After I'd managed to graduate, I'd had little or nothing to keep me grounded, so it hadn't taken a fuck of a lot to talk me into doing it.

I'd started at the bottom rung and won a couple of fights by pure happy accident and brute strength alone. I'd risen in the ranks quickly and gotten the reputation of being pretty hardcore. That's how Unkind had spotted me. He was the old Sergeant at Arms for the Sacred Hearts. I didn't want much to do with the club, but Unkind, well, he was an all-right dude. He'd offered to train me, but I'd pretty much had thought I was hot shit, and spit on that. He'd whooped my fucking ass, and that had changed my mind in a big damned hurry.

Dude was as his name implied, a surly, nasty, bastard who didn't do 'nice'. After he'd whooped my ass, he'd then whooped my ass into shape. Hard workouts were just the beginning. Unkind taught me the meaning of discipline, taught me what it was to fucking focus all that hate and rage burning me up inside. I was pretty much unstoppable after that. I went on like that for a few years. That's how I met Trig; it was Trigger, a prospect at the time, who convinced me that there was more out there to blow my money on than nameless, faceless pussy and tying one on every night of the week. I'd mostly been spending my money on my car and alcohol and keeping a roof over my head up to that point. I was twenty-three when Trigger showed up.

It'd turned out the both of us had a talent for drawing. I'd started apprenticing for a tattoo place right out of high school, my dad's place actually, and when I caught Trig drawing and shading on a napkin, I asked him if he'd ever thought about tattooing. He helped me and I helped him.

I was pretty fucking devastated when Unkind caught a bullet the same time Dragon's Ol' Lady Tilly did.

I crawled into a fucking bottle and stayed there for weeks. Trigger stuck with me, and helped me crawl back out and rejoin the land of the living. It was about that time that I grew the fuck up and stopped playing at life and started actually living it, putting my mind towards something. My pops had kicked it around two years before Unkind was murdered; at least the son of a bitch had taught me some kind of useful skill that I could live straight with, before he went.

After Unkind, Tilly, and Rascal, the club had been in shambles. I was just a friend and affiliate at that point, and then I got too busy trying to build my business with Trig.

We opened up shop when Dragon decided to go legit.

Trig had convinced Big D that fronting the money for our own tattoo place was as good a place as any to start down the road of getting out of drug- and gun-running. By then, Trig had been voted in as the new Sergeant at Arms, and me, I was suddenly busy as fuck getting the shop up off the ground. Too busy to prospect just then, even though I'd been meaning to do it. It took everything I had to make Open Road Ink a raging success along with Trig. And Trig? Well, he had been double-timing it, building ORI up right along with me, while at the same time rebuilding the MC with Dragon, Doc, and Reave in a legit direction, butting heads with Dray all along the way.

Now all of that hard work was threatened. Hell, it was past 'threatened'. The shop was nothing but a pile of wreckage, and the club and everybody in it was in danger, and I would be damned if I was going to watch both go down the drain because of those fucking cocksuckers. I'd put a lot of shit on hold in order to reach my goals, and it felt like the wheel had turned and come full-circle and I was sitting here, marginally more successful, but at the same time, right back where I'd started.

I growled inwardly, and with a scowl, jerked my wheel to the left, powering up the drive and into the club's lot. I backed into a stall and shut her off. I'd never minded getting my fucking hands dirty to get shit accomplished before and I really didn't mind doing it now. Not for me, not for Trig, not for Dis, and not for my club, which had shown me throughout these long years what real family was supposed to be. Still, I wanted something more for myself. I wanted Red, and if I was going to be starting a bunch of shit over? Well, then, I was going to do it better than before, and that included having a good woman by my side, one who would be my partner in crime, not just a convenient piece of pussy to nail at my leisure. I had my sights set squarely on Red for the position. She'd aced the interview with one look from those autumn-colored eyes of hers.

"You know it's not your fault," Disney said, over the roof of my car.

I looked across and up at the tall-as-fuck, lanky kid. I'd almost forgotten he was with me, chasing my thoughts one after the other like I'd been. I shook my head as much to disagree with him as to clear it. It'd stopped raining and was just a fine misting drizzle now.

"I sent you over there," I said, coming to grips with the conversation that'd been initiated.

"You had no way of knowing, man, and I'm fine. Trust me, you letting my ass move in has more than made up for it." He grinned at me. I shrugged back into my cut and hunched my shoulders, making for the clubhouse door. He opened it and I stopped.

"It's great that you forgive me, but Dis, I still ain't forgiven myself, man. I don't know if or when I'm gonna. It was a shit thing I did, sending you in there." I looked up at the faded bruising on his face in the watery parking lot light and he smiled, a sad and ghostly thing.

"Fair enough, man," he said, and we went in to the much warmer and drier club.

I immediately scanned the dim interior for the bright copper curls that had been on my mind daily since the day I first saw her. I felt a surge of disappointment when I saw nothing. She didn't come around the club very often, but still, just because she wasn't in the main common room didn't mean she wasn't here. Where Everett was, that's where Red would be, and I didn't see Evy out here.

"I'll catch you later," I said, and gripped Disney by his narrow shoulders, giving him an easy shake.

He went a little off-balance and nodded absently, finding his feet. I let him go and went for the back, for the new media room, where the girls liked to hang out. The club's meeting that had been called was going to start in about a half hour, so I was pretty sure the girls were going to be settling in back, where the heavy wooden doors could be closed and we could be sure they couldn't hear a damned thing. It was even darker in the large room made for watching the big-screen TV. I let my eyes adjust, and swept my gaze across the seated girls and women, looking for my Red.

"Hey," Trig said, from where he lazed on the huge couch. Ashton was draped across my big friend's chest, her long straight auburn hair tucked behind her ears. She faced the television, but her dark lashes rested against the pale skin beneath her eyes, which when open were golden like the sun. She looked angelic and so peaceful. When I'd first seen her, I thought she was so beautiful in an ethereal sort of way. I'd had some empty space on my arm just waiting for the right face to complete an angel on my right side, and as soon as I laid eyes on her, I knew it was meant for her face.

The deep bass of my friend's greeting caused her eyes to flick open. She sucked in a tremulous breath and glanced sideways. She smiled sweetly when she saw me and it made me smile, too. I reached out a hand and she took it with the hand that she didn't have trapped between her and Trig.

"Hey, man; hey, Sunshine," I kissed the back of her hand. "What're you guys up to?"

"Mm, relaxing before I have to let him go," she murmured.

Trigger chuckled.

"Only for a little bit," he chided.

"I know. But I still miss you, even when you're only two doors away," she said. She looked exhausted; that wasn't surprising, given the amount of time and frustration she'd been expending in my garage, trying to slog through years of water-logged and half-crisped paperwork to reconstruct ORI's books, books that hadn't made it out because the computer had burned. Shit! Who could really blame her for being so wrung-out? Trig and I exchanged knowing looks. We needed to get his Sunshine girl some help.

"Up you go, baby. Come hang with us, 'til you can't," Trig said and sat up with Ashton in his arms. She giggled and finished getting up off of him on her own. We went out front and they grabbed a spot at Reaver and Hayden's table.

"Be right there. Grab me a water," I told Trig.

I hit the head, and when I came back out, Sunshine and Doll were laughing at something Reaver said. I plucked the waiting bottle of water off the table, cracked the seal and downed it in three gulps. I crushed the bottle between my hands and screwed the lid back on, setting it back on the table. Hayden and Ashton both gave me wide-eyed looks.

"What?" I asked. They burst into a fit of giggles and I grinned.

"It's impressive no matter how many times you see it," Everett said and Dray pulled out a chair for her. She smiled and leaned over to kiss him, which he returned enthusiastically. She sat down, missing it when he shook his head behind her in that way that said, *God damn, I scored and I fucking know it!* Reaver and Trig broke out into grins to match my own. Yeah, he had. Everett was both a looker and had a good head on her shoulders; that, and she'd brought Red into my life.

"You want your usual, babe?" he asked her. Everett nodded, but she was looking at me. I looked back. Dray smirked at me, like I was in for it, and stalked off in the direction of the bar, stopping to talk to a member on his way and I saw it for what it was.

Ambush.

Since when did the VP of this club get his own drink, let alone a drink for his Ol' Lady? Usually it was Everett bringing him a beer or whatever with that sexy-as-hell walk of hers, sashaying that tight ass through the tables. Well, all right, might as well cut to the fucking chase, there was only one thing this could be about.

"No Red?" I asked, mock-innocently.

"Mm-mm."

Evy narrowed her eyes at me and disapproval radiated off her. I couldn't really say I blamed her. She protected that girl like a mama tiger protected her cub.

"Why?" she asked, and her tone was icy, at best.

I shrugged a shoulder noncommittally.

Everett rolled her eyes and shook her head.

"You know, I would much rather see my best friend get involved with a guy who was serious about her," she blurted. I leaned back in my seat, tipping the two front legs off the floor. Trigger, Ashton, Reaver and Hayden all rose as one.

"On that note!" Reaver crowed.

Trigger clapped me on the shoulder.

"Later, partner. Good luck." he said, and both men ushered their women away from the potential conflagration about to erupt at our table.

I ignored them, my eyes square on the pissed-off woman across from me.

"Oh, I'm serious, Irish. Serious as a fuckin' heart attack," I said, and I winced on the inside at my poor choice of words, that was what my pops and, I think, hers, had both died from; but I didn't let it show, or back down. Everett crossed her arms and I couldn't tell if it was to hold the anger or the hurt in. Yeah, low blow, unintentional as it may have been.

Her tone, when she replied, told me all it needed to, I'd indeed hit her where it hurt.

She said to me, "You hung around for a little while, I'll grant you, but then what? You stood her up. Not a call, didn't even give her the time of day. You hurt her feelings, Zander. She thinks you pretended to be interested in her to get on Dray's good side, since he was your mentor." Everett's face crumbled into lines of sadness for her friend and I fought down a surge of fury. Touché. One low blow for another. I stopped the verbal sparring-match in its tracks.

"You know that's bullshit," I told her flatly, and she nodded, the simple gesture saying clearly, *Yes. Yes, it was.*

"I know, I get that now, but Mandy doesn't know, and that's really all that matters, isn't it?"

She had me there and with that, truce had been declared. No clear winner when it came to this match, unless you counted Red.

"Prospecting ain't no joke, I couldn't start anything with her; not when I wasn't ever going to be a fucking round," I said, and winced inwardly at what a whiny defensive cunt I sounded like.

"And now?" Everett asked, pointedly.

"Now, my damned shop's been blowed the fuck up, and I'm stuck between wondering if I should try or if I should leave her alone for her own damned good," I said truthfully.

It was something that had been weighing on my mind but at the same time, I was definitely leaning towards trying. I was pretty damned sure this interrogation stemmed from me asking Dray if Red was still single while we were hauling shit out of the burned-out shell of Open Road Ink, week before last. Everett searched my face, carefully looking me over. Whatever she saw there must have satisfied her, because she nodded carefully, more to herself than at me, I think.

"You embarrassed her," she said almost too softly to hear. "When you didn't return her calls, and now you're asking Dray if she's single? What is that? It's been over a year."

I nodded, everything she was saying was absolutely correct.

"Sounds shitty and sounds lame, but I was busy with prospecting, and you guys were busy with the shop and now, well now, I'm completely out of fuckin' excuses." I tipped my chair forward with a hard bang. Everett wasn't fazed in the slightest.

She stared me down, willing me to say more, but I had nothin'.

Well, nothin' except, "So, is she single?"

Everett let out an exasperated breath and told me exactly what Dray had told me.

"Yes." Then she added something I really didn't want to hear. "But you have some competition. I think some of the guys coming around this last week on your little protection detail," she rolled her eyes at that and I crooked a half-grin, "are sweet on her. Which, who can blame them?" She raised her eyebrows.

Dig the knife a little deeper why don't you, Sweetheart? I thought to myself. I sighed and leaned my forearms on my knees and contemplated her.

"Okay, sister. What's your end-game? Why we talking about this?" I asked. She let out a breath and threw up her hands. Her gaze, hard as steel and the color to match, pinned me to my seat.

"I see the way you look at her when she's around and she's not looking. It's the same way Dray looks at me when I am. Why do you hide it from her?" she asked, and she was genuinely curious.

"Because I didn't want to get her hopes up when I was so fucking balls-to-the-wall busy with the club. I didn't want to hurt her feelings." I swore under my breath and kicked my anger at myself back down into the deep dark hole it crawled out of.

"Mission fucking accomplished," I groused, my tone dripping with caustic sarcasm.

"Well, she's pretty well had it with waiting around, and the shop is pretty well in order once we get the numbers side of things handled..." She contemplated me for, like, a full minute.

"I'm not going to help you," she said and I felt myself deflate a little on the inside but damned if I'd show it.

"Nor am I going to dissuade you from trying." I guess I could be grateful for that, at least. She pressed on, "Just know: I am, and always will be, on Mandy's side." She motherfucking smirked. "If she calls you a son of a bitch, then you're a sorry S.O.B., you get me?"

I couldn't help it, I smiled. It was so something Dray would say: 'You get me?' He was rubbing off on her just as much as she was rubbing off on him.

Something flitted across Everett's face, something undefinable that wiped the smile off my own. It looked like a flicker of concern with a chaser of fear and I wanted to know just what that look was for where my Red was concerned, but just as soon as I opened my mouth to ask, Dray was back and setting shots down on the table.

"No thanks, man, I'm training, remember?" Dray looked at me and a flicker of dark humor slid through his equally-dark eyes.

He seized on the opportunity.

"The fuck says I brought one for you?" he asked, and downed first one shot and then the second in rapid succession.

I smiled and laughed.

"My bad, man, my bad." I stood up and looked down into Everett's lovely face and tried to communicate with my own expression that I wanted to do right by Mandy and fix whatever was busted. Maybe even break something of my own – whatever had Everett scared for Red would be a good start.

"I get you," I told her, and she nodded carefully and looked relieved.

I had a pretty full week this week, what with Trig and I finalizing shit with the insurance company, as well as staying on a regimented training schedule. I was actually pretty amped about returning to the fighting circuit, but I swore I would make time for my Red in the middle of this clusterfuck too. It sounded like, if I didn't, I had the potential to lose her all together, and I wasn't about to do that.

"I'm glad that you do," Everett said, and raised her glass before downing the shot. Something told me that something had happened. Something was really bothering her where my Red was concerned, which made me vow to instantly redouble my efforts to get to it, and get Red talking to me. This shit, this fucking hardcore attraction between me and her, had waited long enough, which was no one's fault but my damn own.

2

______

Mandy...

"Mornin', Mandy-girl!" Zeb called from the kitchen doorway. I looked up and smiled at the New Zealander.

"Good morning!" I called back. He was sweet and had been telling me all about his home country, which sounded green and lush, and beyond beautiful.

I had made the mistake, when we'd first met, of asking if he was Australian. He'd frowned at me hard and harder, before saying with great emphasis that no, he did not indeed herald from "that country full of gormless bastards", which had left me blinking stupidly at him. He'd grinned after he'd said it, and then informed me that he was something called a Kiwi, which had left me blinking even -more- stupidly.

Zeb had laughed, and then had begun to fill me in on all things New Zealand, and we'd pretty much made fast friends after that. It was almost easy to forget why he was here, that he wasn't just a new usual customer, but that he was a member of the Sacred Hearts and here to protect Evy's and my business because of some faceless, at least to me, threat, called the Suicide Kings.

Well, they weren't entirely faceless. I'd seen a few of them here or there, riding by at one point or another in my travels around town. It was a forty-five minute drive to my parents', who lived in the next county and I would go every Sunday, both for church and to have Sunday dinner with them, and that's where I saw the Suicide Kings. Mostly.

"What 'cha thinkin' about, girl?" Zeb asked, and slipped up on a stool in my ultra-modern industrial kitchen.

"I was thinking about how it was easy to forget why you're here," I said and checked the chocolate I had melting in the double-boiler. Zeb's face lost that easy grin of his, and I marveled to myself how the tribal tattoos etched into his face around his left eye and along his left cheek didn't stand out as foreign to me anymore. The blue swirling lines were just a part of him, his past and his family.

"Aww, you ain't scared are yah, eh?" he asked me. I shook my head. No, I wasn't scared for me or for Soul Fuel. I sighed. I was thinking a lot about Zander, if I was honest with myself. I knew the whole story through Everett, that Zander was okay, but I still couldn't help but feel a keen sense of loss, a deep dread over the whole thing. It'd been nearly two weeks and you would think that those feelings would diminish by now, but no... if anything they'd just grown stronger. I didn't hear Zeb get up. I'd been so lost in my own thoughts. I startled when the dark leather of his jacket edged into focus a heart-beat before his fingertips grazed my neck, thumbs beneath my jaw, gently tilting my head up to look at him the couple of inches that separated our eyes from being on an even keel.

"No! No, I'm not scared. I mean, that's why you're here isn't it?" I asked and smiled. He was a good friend to be so concerned. He smiled down at me, his brown eyes kind.

"That's right," he said. I took a halting step back and he let his hands drop.

"Rush is gone! Hey Zeb, what can I get you?" Everett called from out front. He winked at me and called back.

"Whatever that thing was that you gave me yesterday!" He retreated a few steps and with a final grin and another wink, went out front, I assumed to take up his usual post at the corner table near the register.

I smiled to myself and shook my head. It was Zeb here most of the time, occasionally a man with hair as fiery as my own nicknamed 'Duracell' would sit in, and in the evenings, there was either a very quiet and reserved brother who had 'Blue' on his vest, or an uncomfortably-flirtatious one who went by 'Grinder'. Duracell seemed unreasonably angry about just about everything. Over all I preferred Zeb and Blue to the rest.

I resumed my work with a rather single-minded determination to focus on chocolate and nothing but chocolate, thinking of nothing else. I looked up to find Everett in the kitchen doorway.

"He likes you," she said, and I scowled.

"Who Zander?" I asked without thinking. She laughed.

"Well, him, too, he said as much last Saturday night,"

I frowned, "He has a fantastic way of showing it," I muttered darkly. Everett sighed and slipped up onto the stool Zeb had vacated.

Zander... One moment he'd seemed so very enthusiastic about seeing me, dating me... then we had actually set a date and I'd wound up sitting in a restaurant an hour and more waiting for him to arrive. He hadn't. No call, no text, no response to my calls or texts. Dray had told me that Zander was a prospect and that it happened sometimes. That prospects were a lot like fraternity pledges and they were all-in until they became fully-patched members or brothers. It'd made sense, but it had still hurt, and then I had just plain gotten angry when I'd simply never heard from him again. We'd crossed paths over the last year or so but he would simply watch me, never really saying much, an odd little half-smile on his lips.

I'd asked him why. Why had he stood me up; why the silence, after expressing such a keen interest, and all he'd given me was a simple, nonchalant one-shouldered shrug and a sniffed "I got busy."

It'd been cold, and had hurt deeply. I had felt like it was high school all over again. Rejection sucked, and having the reputation of being the goody-two-shoes preacher's daughter had done nothing whatsoever when it had come to dating. Still, the darned biker was never far from my thoughts. His easy smile and his caring nature during the crisis when my best friend had been shot had gotten his name etched on my heart, and I couldn't forget him, no matter how much I wanted to sometimes.

"I know," Everett's voice was gentle, kind and sympathetic, snapping me out of my spiral of thought, but it brightened to teasing when she said, "But I wasn't talking about Rev, I was talking about Zeb."

I looked up from what I was doing and raised an eyebrow. "What?" I asked. Zeb was a good friend, he had no interest in a plain girl like me. The bell chimed above the door out front and Everett slid off the stool onto her feet.

"You need to quit selling yourself short, Sister," she said, and ducked out of the doorway and to the front to fix someone's coffee.

The door chimed again and I heard her exclaim, "Heya, lass!" and after a few more random clangs and bangs, ask, "The usual, Ghost?" which piqued my curiosity. Usually Ghost came in alone. The conundrum of Zander and Zeb momentarily forgotten, I finished up what I was doing, so I could go out and have a look at what was up out there. I blinked when I stepped out of the kitchen to see Duracell at his post. Apparently Zeb had just come in for coffee.

I wiped my hands on the old-fashioned dishcloth over my shoulder and heard Everett say,

"I can't keep up with the damned books Shelly, I need help."

I rolled my eyes and corrected Ev, who liked to think that the whole world rested solely on her shoulders. "–We– need your help." I took the last empty seat at the four-person table with Ghost and Everett, and looked Shelly over, surprised to see her here. She looked just awful, so very thin, with deep, dark circles under her eyes. Her usually so-carefully-done hair had grown unkempt. While I was studiously looking her over, Ghost stood up and made to take his leave.

I waved him off, and said that we would take Shelly home. Then Everett and I spent the next fifteen minutes convincing her that she was the right person for the job at hand, which she was, for a multitude of reasons. I watched the young lady follow my childhood friend to the back office with a heavy heart. Poor Shelly had one horrible cross to bear. I stood up and smiled at Duracell, who smiled back at me over the newspaper he had open on his table.

"Where'd Zeb get off to?" I asked.

"Think he just came in to see you," he said, shaking out the newsprint pages and smiling.

I scoffed, secretly flattered, and slipped back into the kitchen. I found myself praying for Shelly to find some solace and happiness, to heal, and while I did, set back to work making some maple crèmes for the season. The hours passed, along with the different chocolates and projects, and before I knew it Everett was at the door, with Dray just behind her.

"You okay if we go home?" he asked, eyeing me speculatively.

I smiled and nodded.

"I just want to finish these up for Hayden's birthday," I said, adding, "Don't you worry about me, my car is just out in the lot."

He nodded.

"'Kay, there's a brother out here. He'll stay until you leave." He raked me with his dark eyes. Over the last year, Dray had become quite the protective-older-brother type. Not that I minded; Everett was happy with him and he was so very good to my friend. Way better than Jerry had ever been.

I rocked back on my heels.

"Dray, it's fine, send him on his way and stop worrying so much!" I admonished and his dark gaze hardened to obsidian.

"No," he said simply.

Everett laughed.

"Shelly is still here, Reaver is on his way to pick her up since he's done with whatever he's doing."

I nodded absently and brought the molds for the starfish out of the chiller.

"Okay," I said.

"Love you," Everett said and waved over her shoulder.

I smiled at them.

"Love you guys, too!"

"Bye, Red," Dray said and I nodded, my focus on getting the starfish filled with rum out of the molds without cracking their shells, leaving them to leak.

I heard the bell above the door as Dray and Everett left and then all was silent. It was telling. I bet dollars to chocolates that it was Blue on watch. I smiled to myself.

"Hi, Mandy." The voice was right behind me, and so unexpected I bleated out a little frightened scream. Reaver laughed and steadied me, his hands on my shoulders.

"God!" I exclaimed, my hand pressed over my rapidly-beating heart. My kitchen felt like Grand Central all of a sudden.

"You shouldn't sneak up on people like that, Reaver! You scared me half to death!" I cried. He grinned and if I didn't know what a sweet guy he was I would have said it was feral.

"Sorry," he said with a shrug, but didn't sound like he was, not one bit. "Seen my cousin?"

"Office, through there." I pointed, and he nodded his thanks and looked me over. He came out a few moments later with Shelly, who looked tired but almost happy. It made me smile, and after a short exchange and one of my chocolates, they both left smiling. I heard the shop bell chime signaling their leaving and felt my shoulders sag in relief. I closed my eyes and relished the quiet for a moment as I finished up, putting the starfish into individual paper cups and nesting them into Tupperware.

I didn't see him coming, my back turned as it was. I didn't hear him either; I was just suddenly pinned flush against the kitchen counter, strong arms around my waist, his breath warm against the side of my neck where his nose was buried in my hair, behind my ear. I cried out, my hands flying to the arms that pinned me.

"Hi, Red," he said to me, his voice velvety-smooth, rich like the darkest dark chocolate you could eat and still have it be palatable. I jumped, startling hard, and shuddered in his embrace, my hands squeezing one of his muscled forearms where it went around my waist above my hips. I let out a breath I hadn't realized had stuck in my throat and swallowed hard. My heart hammered in my chest for a second time that night, and I couldn't turn around to see if this was real or if I was dreaming, even if I wanted to. He'd caught me fast.

"Hmm." He hummed out in pleasure, and placed a kiss behind my ear. I closed my eyes, awash in tingles.

"What are you doing, Zander?" I squeaked out.

"What is that?" he asked, ignoring my question.

"What is what?" I stayed rigid, stiff in his arms. *What did he think he was doing?*

"That smell? Sweet and clean, but like flowers," he asked and took a half step into me, pressing me tighter into the counter. I bent forward slightly to get away from his lips, which tickled the back of my neck when he spoke. I felt hot, flushed from his proximity and I was growing angry with my body's betrayal, even as longing and a desire for him swirled in my blood.

"I don't know what you're talking about," I said, and it sounded sullen, my voice uneven. I bit my lower lip, and shivered involuntarily when his chuckle vibrated through his chest and thrummed pleasurably down my spine. He stepped back, his arms sliding back, hands coming to rest on my jeans-covered hips. I turned to face him. It really –was– him, and I felt a wave of humiliation and hurt, of anger and loss, all these old emotions climbing to the surface from where I thought I'd locked them away.

His chocolate-caramel eyes sparkled with good humor, his dark hair was growing too long again, winging out from beneath the brim of his almost ever-present red baseball hat. I pressed back into the counter and he stepped forward, trapping me between it and him once more. His powerful thigh slid between mine and I raised my chin defiantly. He looked up at me slightly. There was about a four inch difference in our height. I was five-foot-nine, like Everett, so that made Zander five-foot-five or so.

"I've missed you, baby," he said softly.

I scoffed.

"How can you miss something you've never had... or wanted?" I asked.

He smiled a tight-lipped little smile and captured the back of my neck in one hand, stroking the side of my throat beneath my jaw with his thumb. It was a light caress that had me forcing down a shudder. *I was supposed to be upset, I was supposed to be angry!* So why was it so hard to hold on to those feelings? His arm slid around my back, a steel band at the base of my spine, crushing me to him. I didn't even realize I was letting him guide my mouth to his until his warm breath ghosted over my lips.

"You were mine the minute you agreed to get on the back of my bike, and I've wanted you since the moment I first saw you. Never stopped wanting you, Red, nothing ever changed about that. I've been a neglectful son-of-a-bitch, and I aim to fix that, starting now."

His lips touched mine, and all righteousness, all resistance drained from my body. I closed my eyes and let him kiss me, powerless to stop him or resist, but I felt a sudden and sure surge of anger, of outrage at his audacity, and that alone kept my lips in check, kept me from kissing back. That didn't seem to faze Zander in the slightest.

He pressed against my body tighter and my mind just switched off, just like watching a television screen go blank. I felt a heady rush to my head and butterflies swirled in my stomach, and longingly my heart reached back in time to a little over a year ago to the very first time Zander kissed me.

He murmured against my lips now, and my heart gave a painful twist in my chest.

"Kiss me back, sugar," he murmured. I closed my eyes and sucked in a tremulous breath, letting it escape in a shuddering sigh.

"I can't," I whispered and I felt him smile. I opened my eyes and his were warm and smiling, and so very close.

"Sure, you can." His voice was teasing and inviting, and I felt a deep, dull throb of hurt in the center of my chest.

"And if I kiss you this time? What then? You kissed me last year, gave me your number, said you wanted to see me and then left me sitting in that restaurant all alone. I won't have it Zander. I can't..." His lips touched mine again, so very softly, and I closed my eyes and fought not to kiss back, but my resolve was weakening and I think he could sense that. His tongue flicked out and tasted my bottom lip and a soft whimper ran into the back of my firmly-clenched teeth.

It was a low blow, but I needed space, I needed to think, and so I blurted out, "Are you going to make me?" He withdrew to look into my eyes and his brow wrinkled slightly in confusion.

I pressed on. "The way Shelly was forced?" I asked to make my point clear.

Zander recoiled like he'd been slapped. His warmth was just gone and I silently cursed my body for the bereft feeling it left me with, every part of me except my brain beseeching him to come back, to hold me, to kiss me, to touch me... I crossed my arms over my middle.

"I'd never do that to you, Red, don't even think it," he admonished, and the guilt swamped me sevenfold. I nodded and tried to relearn how to breathe; his departure had nearly stolen the breath from my lungs with it. I shifted uncomfortably.

"I'm sorry. You were just... You... You make it hard to think when you're that close and it isn't fair." I swallowed hard and felt the blush sweep up from my chest and go to the very roots of my hair. He smiled, his good humor at my expense back again.

"Really?" he asked dryly. I shook my head and turned; my hands were trembling as I tried to finish my task, the paper cups scratching together loudly in the quiet kitchen as I stuffed them with the little chocolates. I felt humiliated tears burn the backs of my eyes; I closed them tightly and resolutely refused to let them gather any further, let alone spill over.

I could feel Zander at my back, his intense gaze sweeping over me as he stood there. Finally I heard him sigh and the rustle of cloth shifting as he put down his arms which he'd crossed.

"Hey, don't do that, come here." I heard him take a step forward and I skirted around the counter out of reach. He cursed.

"Just give me a minute, just give me... God!" I hated how I sounded, on the verge of tears, my voice high and tight, trembling with the sheer force of will it took to force the rising tide down.

"Oh, hey, Red, no. Don't do that, sugar, don't cry. I didn't want you to cry."

He was on me before I could step away, right up in my personal space all over again. His arms went around my waist and he pulled me tightly against him and I couldn't resist this time, my hands slid over the smooth skin of his arms, my palms coming to rest just below his shoulders. He palmed my ass with one hand and I couldn't even find the will to be indignant. He pulled my forehead down to his with his other hand and simply rested them together.

"Shh, shh, shh... It's okay,"

I sniffed. No tears yet, but they were trying. This was so confusing! What was he doing here? A fine question, so I asked.

"What do you want, Zander? What are you doing here?" I demanded and held myself rigid in his embrace.

"Thought I already told you, Baby. I want you, I'm here for you."

I scoffed and wrenched myself out of his grasp. "Well, people in Hell want ice water, too!" I said passionately. "You had your chance last year. You chose not to show up or return my calls!" He looked a mix between hurt and angry and that was rich, that was rich, indeed.

"When was the last time you ate anything?" he asked, and the change in conversation was so abrupt I could swear I heard the sound of a needle abruptly being pulled across a vinyl record's surface. I frowned.

"What?"

"Food, Red. When was the last time you had a meal?"

I blinked and frowned, and thought about it before replying, "Breakfast, I think. I don't know, I don't remember eating lunch, I've been busy." I rolled my lips together, smoothing them against each other. The ghost of his lips grazing mine was still there, a slight glimmer of touch even though it'd been minutes since his lips moved on mine.

"Okay. That's too long. Finish up, I'll take you to dinner," he said gently. I shook my head.

"I'm done and I'm going home, I'll fix something when I get there."

He gave me that adorable grin, complete with boyish dimples, and with that damned chipped tooth, it made my insides melt, faster than milk chocolate in the double boiler.

"I'm taking you out. I believe I promised you dinner," he said, and I stared at the ceiling and counted to ten.

"You promised me dinner –last year–. It's been over a year now! And just how do you know I'm not seeing anyone, anyway?" I narrowed my eyes in suspicion.

"Asked your roomies," he said, with a one-shouldered shrug.

I made a disbelieving noise. I packed up the chocolates I'd been working on and put everything in its place. Zander leaned a hip against the counter, his arms crossed over his chest, his gaze following my every movement.

I hung my apron on its hook by the walk-in and smoothed my mint-green sweater into place over my hips. I brought down the sleeves from where I had them rucked back over my elbows, and tugged up on my riding boots over my dark jean leggings. Zander watched all of this, his smile slowly fading, his gaze becoming molten, liquid with heat. I gathered my purse and keys from beneath the front counter and snapped off all the lights. We'd long since been closed.

Zander followed me as I went through all of these motions, watching from a safe distance. I ushered him out the front door and set the alarm before dashing out and locking up. The parking lot was empty, except for my little blue Ford Focus and a beautiful cherry-red and white muscle car. I stopped in my tracks and stared at it. It was like something out of a magazine. My father would have appreciated it very much. He was an old car guy, though I couldn't tell you what kind I was looking at without reading the model on the back.

"What do you think? Want to go for a ride?" Zander asked and that sexy-as-sin grin of his was back.

"It's yours?" I asked.

"Mm hmm, restored her myself." He buried his hands in his pockets. "So how about a ride, Red?" he asked.

I shook my head.

"Not tonight, I'm exhausted." It was true, my day had thoroughly caught up with me and now that he'd mentioned food, I was ravenous! I wanted to go home, eat something, and go directly to bed.

"Okay, sugar. You win this time," he said and I blinked. I'd been staring into space. I colored faintly and shivered in the cool night air. I hadn't worn a jacket this morning. I unlocked my car with the little key fob, my corner lights flashing bright into the night. Zander opened my door before I could get around and reach for it myself. He held it for me. I got into the car and he leaned in; I held myself stiff. He looked me over and smiled.

"May have won this battle, but you haven't won the war," he said softly, and kissed me again, and oh God, I liked the feel of his lips on mine. I had missed it so much. I think he knew it too because he pulled back, even though I hadn't kissed him back, his eyes sparkling.

"I'm glad you like it when I kiss you," he remarked, as if he'd read my mind.

I frowned. "Who says I do?"

He grinned from inches away.

"You may not kiss me back, but you don't pull away, either," he murmured and backed out of the door, shutting it firmly on the inarticulate sound of protest that escaped me. I blinked at him and he stood smiling, a few paces away. I realized he wasn't going to leave until I had pulled out and was underway, so I started my car. He waved at me in the headlights, and, grinding my teeth with frustration, I pulled out onto the road and made my way home.

He'd conceded that I'd won tonight, so why did I feel like I was on the losing side of things? I sighed. That should be obvious: I had wanted him a year ago, and I wanted him now; I just wasn't sure I could trust that he wouldn't pull a Houdini on me again.

3

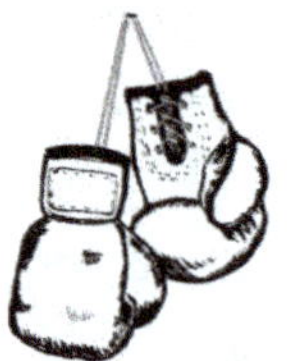

Revelator...

After I'd let her go, I thought about our entire exchange. She had been stiff and unyielding in my grasp, but she had not once fought me or tried to shove me away. I'd shot a text to Dray, telling him to make sure she ate when she got home. He'd sent one back asking if he looked like her fucking babysitter. It was geeky as fucking hell, but I'd texted back '..I.,' at him.

I got a text from Everett about twenty minutes later, a sneaky candid photo of Red at their dining room table, a large salad in front of her, her cute freckled nose buried in an e-reader as she ate. I asked Everett what she was reading, and got a text back exclaiming "I don't fucking know! Why don't you come over here and ask her? Stalker status much?" Okay, yeah, point taken.

I went home and hit my home gym to clear my head and work off my arousal. She smelled so fucking amazing. Her soft curves had yielded against me when I'd held her close. Her body was warm and supple and perfect, her lips like fucking silk...

I'd abandoned the effort pretty quickly, and, breathless, went for an icy shower instead. Not my favorite way to wrap up my evening.

The next day started with training, then a quick shower, followed by a whole lot of time working my ass off at the clubhouse putting in insulation and putting up drywall. I took myself off to my club room and cleaned up, then came out to the common area, to find Ghosty looking as lost in thought as I'd ever fucking seen him, chillin' at the bar, nursing a beer.

"Ghosty! What you thinking about, man?" I asked.

"The usual. The past, women..." Dude sighed, hard.

"You need to think about something else." I pulled a bottle of water out from behind the bar, leaning way over to do it.

"Got a lot on my plate at the moment. Life is at another cross-roads." He didn't sound entirely happy about it.

"This about Shelly?" I asked.

"Some of it, some of it's about me, too."

"Shit, you're doing some real deep thinking over here, ain't you?" I cracked the seal on my bottle and downed it, crushing and recapping it, and reached for another.

"Uh, yeah." He nodded.

"Lay it on me," I said, grinning.

"Was gonna take Shelly up into the hills to do something special for her. Take her to see something I know she'll like." He sounded thoughtful.

"What, that meteor-shower thing?" I asked. It happened every year, but typically it was overcast and hidden around here; this year it was supposed to be clear.

"Yeah, but I'm thinking I need to do something on a bit of a grander scale."

"Oh yeah? What did you have in mind?" I asked.

"I have an idea, but I'm going to need some help, and maybe a woman's touch."

"You can count me in on the heavy lifting, but if it's a woman's touch you're wanting, you should try one of them hookers over there." I gestured with my bottle of water at some of the chicks that hung around the club over in the corner, but I was really only half-assing it, suggesting it as a joke. They were easy pussy, but for something like Ghost was talking about, he needed someone with class – and we both knew who that was.

"I think I'll ask Hayden, but I'm still going to need your help," he said. I grinned. Yep, that was the particular female I'd been thinking about, too.

"As long as it doesn't cut in to my training." I shrugged and crushed my second bottle of water, and wished that it was a beer. No alcohol while training. I could drink plenty after a fight, but it was right back to training the next morning, hangover or not.

"Got a fight coming up?" he asked me.

"Next month, bottom-tier, but I should work my way up fast." I grinned, and it wasn't entirely friendly.

"Feel sorry for the poor bastard," he said, and I clapped him on the back, hard, pretty much just to be a dick. We chilled for a bit and shot the shit about some other miscellaneous boring crap before he got up to go.

"See you around, man," he said, and we clasped hands.

He left and I looked after him for a minute. His mind was worlds away and it showed. I knew the feeling. Mine was pretty much on Red constantly, now that I'd finally committed to fucking doing something about making her mine. I looked at the clock. They closed up at a regular hour on Saturdays. Red had Sundays and Mondays off. It was getting to be that time, and so I heaved myself off the bar stool and straightened my cut, going for the door. Dray fell into step beside me.

"Going to get Everett?" I asked.

"Yeah," he nodded.

"I'm headed that direction too." He stopped and I stopped with him; he eyed me speculatively.

"Look, I get why you did what you did back in the beginning there with my girl's best girl, but did you really have to be a dick about it?" he asked.

"Yeah, I fucked that one up big time, didn't I?" I asked, with a heavy sigh.

"Yah think?"

"Dragon called and I got to doin' what needed doin', and honestly, that's no fuckin' excuse; I forgot all about those damned dinner plans."

Dray scowled, "Yeah, well. She's a chick and you know how that goes. It hurt her feelings. Mandy ain't used to dudes takin' an interest. The way my girl tells it, she was kind of stuck with the stigma of being the preacher's daughter all through high school. Dudes just took her at face value of being some kind of prude. She didn't get much action, if any; only a few dates here and there and mostly on account of Em. She's shy, which doesn't help much. So you not showing up, it cut way deep."

I looked at my VP like he had grown some kind of second head.

Red not getting any play was a total fucking foreign concept to me. The girl was fucking gorgeous! I'd figured she'd be beating dudes off with a stick, which truthfully, was part of the reason I steered clear so hard. I'd figured she deserved better 'n me by a mile, especially since I didn't have any time to give her. I just really didn't want to see her with anyone else, mostly because I would've probably beat the motherfucking brakes off of any dude who tried. I thought I'd been some kind of blessed when she'd steered clear of the club, but hindsight was always fucking 20/20.

"Fuck me! She steered clear of the club because she didn't want to see me, didn't she?" I asked.

Dray looked at me like I was some kind of moron.

"You think?"

I scowled and he nodded.

"Then she just plain got busy with making her chocolates and getting shit straight with the business. She spent forever in the kitchen getting shit right with her grandfolk's recipes, doing the math to do big and bigger batches. We got her moved in, and I don't think she left the house but once or twice in the whole first month. Well, except for those damned Sunday dinners with her folks." It was his turn to scowl, and it leapt out at me.

"What's that look for, man?" I asked.

"Not sure what's up, but she goes to her parents and comes back quiet as a mouse. No smiles, no laughing, as reserved as I ever seen her. Think her pops is real overbearing, or something." He looked troubled, though, like he thought there was more to it than that.

"What's Irish say?" I asked.

"That's just it. Em won't say –anything–. She ain't happy about whatever-it-is, though. I can tell you that much."

I nodded, thinking about it.

"Think I can get a free pass on Church tonight?" I asked. Dray raised both his eyebrows and looked back towards the clubhouse. He looked me over, and looked thoughtful for a minute.

"Yeah, man. I'll see what I can do. The Pres. is in with Data, hot 'n heavy. Something's up, just don't know what it is yet. I take it whatever you got planned has to do with Mandy?"

I nodded.

"Yeah, I wanna spend time with her."

Dray nodded, saying, "Typical Saturday night for her is spent with her nose in a book or watching some TV. She's a real homebody, that one. Come by the house. She's sure to be there."

I nodded, a plan formulating.

"Good deal, be by in an hour or two," I said. Dray nodded and went for his Trans-Am while I went for my Chevelle.

If Mandy wouldn't come out and have dinner with me, I'd bring dinner to her. I wasn't a master chef by any means, but I knew my way around anything meat, and how hard was it to make salad? I headed out towards Dray's place and stopped in at the market closest to it. I found some real lean steaks and some fancy pre-made mushroom caps. I bought a bunch of shit for salad, some bottled water, and I figured I could deviate just a little, just this once, and picked up a six-pack of my favorite beer.

I drove out to Dray's with two grocery bags full of shit sitting shotgun, feeling pretty good about myself. I pulled up to the curb across the street from his place and jogged over the two lanes of asphalt, a bag of groceries in each arm. He opened the front door as I leapt the front steps in two big strides.

"She just got in the shower. We're heading out," he said.

I nodded.

"Good deal, thanks, man."

Everett looked at the bags, and then to me, dubiously.

"Good luck. But if Mandy tells you to get out, you better get. She calls me, and I'm coming back here." She gave me a baleful look.

"Not going to preemptively kick my ass out?" I asked and grinned, and she shook her head.

"I told you I wasn't dissuading you, but I'm not helping you, either. What you two do is Mandy's business, until she makes it my business." Everett gave me a pointed look.

"You hurt her again and it –is– my business. Got it?"

I nodded.

"Yes, Ma'am!"

Dray hooked an arm around his woman's shoulders and pulled her into his side. They went out the door and I kicked it shut behind them. It took everything that was in me to go to the kitchen and cook, rather than set the shit down and go for the bathroom to join her in there. I think I showed some pretty remarkable restraint.

I started doing my thing, my heart doing a little leap in my chest when the water shut off. I wanted to see her so damned bad, to make everything up to her. I studiously kept cooking. The steaks were seasoned and the broiler was on. The mushroom caps, stuffed with all sorts of good stuff, were in there and I was nearly done with the salad when the bathroom door opened. I heard her give a gusty sigh.

I replaced the mushrooms with the steaks and called out, "Hope you aren't comin' out here naked. You do, and I'm not sure my self-control will take it."

I figured it was only fair, warning her I was here, seeing as I'd snuck up on her last night, and that hadn't exactly gone the way I'd had it mapped out in my head.

Mandy slowly crept into view in a deep, forest green silk robe with golden-orange flame-colored leaves around the bottom and edging the sleeves. Her red hair was twisted up into a knot and care-fully pinned at the nape of her neck. She was fuckin' heart-stopping.

"What are you doing?" she asked. She was a whiter shade of pale, her freckles standing out on her face, fresh and clean without makeup. Her autumn eyes seemed larger somehow, without all that crap around them. Not to say that she did her makeup badly; she did awesome. But I really liked her this way, too.

"You wouldn't have dinner with me last night," I said.

"Where's Dray and Evy?" she asked.

"Club."

"Did they let you in here?"

"Yeah."

"What are you doing?" she repeated herself.

"You already asked me that, and the answer is, 'I'm making you dinner'."

"Why?"

"Because I really want to make it up to you, Red," I said gently, and she softened a bit.

"Give me a minute to get dressed."

"No need," I told her, and shrugged, while I used the back of the knife to scrape the chopped veggies into the salad bowl.

"I beg your pardon?" She looked affronted, and I couldn't help but chuckle. Man, I sure knew how to put my foot in my mouth when it came to her.

"You just got home from work, and you should stay comfortable." I gesticulated with the chopping knife, "'Sides, I like this. Looks good on you."

She blushed a deep crimson, and with the green robe it suddenly looked like Christmas. I grinned.

"I should probably find something more modest," she stammered. I set the knife down with a scrape and a clack and leaned both hands against the kitchen counter and stared her down hard.

"Why?" I asked her.

"I, um... It's not proper..."

I stopped her stammering by coming around the counter.

"By whose standards?" I asked.

"I, uh... society's?" she murmured.

I stalked towards her and she backed into the wall.

"Society in here?" I asked.

"No..."

"Then, stop fuckin' worrying about it, and relax."

"Kind of hard to do when you're invading my space and intimi-dating the heck out of me!" she blurted, and clapped both hands over her mouth. She looked fuckin' terrified for a split-second.

I was just inside arm's reach by now. I grasped her gently by the hips and stepped in the rest of the way, looking up the few inches into her lovely eyes, which were fixed on my mouth. She wouldn't make eye contact, but that was okay.

"You want me to kiss you, Red?" I asked.

She lowered her hands, startled.

"What? No! Um, why would you ask me that?" She looked a little lost, like her poor mind was overloading.

"You're staring at my mouth," I said.

Her eyes snapped to mine, widening.

"I'm sorr-!" she didn't get to finish. I brought her mouth down to mine and kissed her softly, and this time I think she forgot because it was as sweet as the fucking first time.

Her lips parted with very little urging, and I cradled her against me, my tongue plunging past her teeth into her sweet hot mouth. She gave a little moan, her eyes slipping shut; I went from zero to rock-hard in my jeans in point-zero-three-seconds flat. Too soon, she came to her senses and jerked back, her lips slightly reddened from my kiss, and I smirked.

"I missed you too, Red."

She stepped out from the wall and I gave her some space so she could sink, breathless and a little shaky, into one of the dining room chairs. I smiled to myself and went back to finishing up dinner, checking on the steaks in the oven.

"You always this heavy-handed with everything you do?" she demanded.

I looked up from the oven.

"Go big or go home," I said, with a shrug.

A weird look crossed her face.

"You know, this might go a lot better with me if you said you were sorry!" she crossed her arms over her chest and her legs at the knee.

She wore a long cream satin nightgown under the robe, her legs safe from my prying eyes, but the way that material clung to her figure... well, my brain went out to dinner without me for a second.

She gave an exasperated sigh.

"You know, saying you're sorry doesn't mean that I was right or that you were wrong... It means you care about our friendship. That it's more valuable than your ego." She fixed me with an unwavering look.

I blinked. I'd never considered what she was saying. Truth was, I wasn't much for apologies. Shit happened, you did something wrong, a few words wasn't going to fix it. You had to do better, try harder. In my world, actions spoke louder than words ever could. I regarded her, sitting there so very serious, the hard set to her shoulders, the tightness around her eyes slowly blurring and fading into lines of weariness and hurt.

"You should probably just go," she said uncertainly.

"Not going to happen," I told her as I pulled the steaks out of the oven and ditched the pan on the cooktop, switching off the broiler. I came around the counter and crouched in front of her, putting my hands on her knees, resting them there lightly. She met my eyes and I held hers fast with my gaze.

"I'm sorry," I said and she looked past me, over one of my shoulders. I cupped her face gently between my hands and forced her to look at me.

"I screwed up. I forgot about dinner, and I got wrapped up in the club, and being a prospect. I was doing club business and couldn't answer the phone. When I picked up my messages I felt like a world-class douche, but then you wouldn't answer my calls, and that pissed me off and..."

Her voice stopped me. "It doesn't matter."

"Why do you say that, sugar?"

She shifted uncomfortably, opened her mouth, closed it, and opened it again. She looked to be on the verge of spilling it but her eyes held such a pleading look, begging me not to make her say it, that I had to know, so I pressed her.

"Talk to me. Not going anywhere until you do," I said firmly.

"I thought, when you didn't show up, that something had come up. I waited, and when a half hour went by, I tried to call you, you didn't answer. I was embarrassed. I waited in that restaurant over an hour. When Evy explained that being a prospect was a lot like being a fraternity pledge, I..." She pursed her lips and rushed the rest of it out. "I thought you'd never really been interested. That one of the guys put you up to it, or that you were just leading me on to impress Dray and when you figured out you didn't have to, you just stopped bothering."

"What do you mean?" I scowled. I was fixated on the last bit of what she'd said.

High spots of color appeared on her cheeks. She gave a harsh and exaggerated sigh.

"I figured you got wrapped up with one of the girls at the club. That I was just a passing fancy and that you weren't really serious about me. I didn't answer your calls the next day because I was hurt, Zander." She looked defeated. She stared at her hands in her lap for a long minute. I was fucking floored, silent, because I couldn't believe what I was hearing. I'd had no freaking clue.

She took a breath. "I know I'm not pretty, like Evy or Shelly. That compared to them, I'm, um – "

"Red, stop. Just stop." I shook my head, incredulous. "You're fucking gorgeous, and I don't ever want to hear you put yourself down again. You hear me?"

She swallowed hard, her autumn-colored eyes so very wide, and nodded. I was fuming, but not at her, more at me and whoever had put those craptastic ideas into her head. It wasn't lost on me that someone, somewhere, at some time or another, had done something really shitty to Mandy, to have her believing any of that horseshit.

"It wasn't either of those things," I told her, "you know that, right?"

Her lips thinned down, and regret and heartache flashed across her pretty features in equal measure. I swore, low and heated, and she stopped breathing, freezing in place.

"I just realized that I couldn't give you the attention you deserved at the time, babe. Patching into the club was a really big deal to me and a long time in coming. When I set my sights on something, I just, I don't know... I get real focused." I sighed, defeated. I wasn't sure how to explain it. I stood up, my knees cracking in a bit of protest, and moved around the kitchen, finishing up dinner, plating it before it got cold.

"I had no idea you thought any of those things. I feel like such an *ass.*"

Mandy sat for long moments, thinking, before finally rising and asking, "What can I do?"

"You can just sit down and relax, let me make you dinner. Let me try to fix this. I never meant to hurt your feelings, Red. Believe me."

I brought the plates over and set them down, contemplating her. She looked like she really wanted to do something, anything to help, rather than just sit there.

"On second thought, where's the silverware at?" I asked. I knew damned well where it was, but she was sitting there just looking so uncomfortable and wringing her hands. I could tell this was –way– outside her comfort zone.

Hadn't any guy ever taken care of her?

She finally smiled and got up to get the utensils, returning with them and a couple of paper towels to use as napkins. I held her chair for her and pushed her in. Never saw the fucking point of doing that, really. All it did was bang the chair into the backs of her knees, but it was worth it to pretend to be a gentleman, if only to watch the warm glow that suffused her cheeks and across the bridge of her nose when I did it.

"Thank you," she murmured.

"You're welcome, sugar."

She bowed her head over her food and closed her eyes, murmuring a prayer and I took the opportunity to look her over. She had a long graceful neck. I'd never noticed it before, with her hair always down. An errant curl draped artfully along the side of it, the end just teasing her pulse point. It was probably one of the most provocative things I'd ever seen and I was hard to the point of aching from it.

"I'm really sorry, Mandy. I really suck at apologizing, but I'm trying here," I said, when we'd been silent a touch too long.

"I can see that."

"Ouch," I said dryly, and smiled.

"Oh no," she said abruptly, "I meant, that I can see that you're trying!" She looked horrified and I couldn't stop the laugh if I had wanted to.

"Relax, Red. I knew what you meant." I took a bite of food and looked her over. She was fucking beautiful when she blushed like that, and I just kept making her do it.

"So, what were you planning on doing this evening?" she asked, cutting her steak into dainty bites with such a lady-like precision. I chewed through my own bite of meat.

"Keep blushing like that, you," I said simply, with a roguish grin. I bounced my eyebrows at her and she scoffed and laughed incredulously. She blushed even more deeply, which made me grin more broadly, and she took a bite of her steak. I think I'd rendered her speechless.

She looked slightly more comfortable, which I claimed as a small victory, but she still sat back straight and shoulders stiff. She cleaned her plate; I could appreciate a girl who wasn't afraid to eat, but after she'd finished, which was before me, she simply sat there solemnly, eyes fixed on a point on the table.

"What were your plans for the night?" I finally asked her, picking up where the conversation had left off while we ate.

"I was going to catch up on a television series I've been watching," she murmured.

"Oh, yeah? What one?" I asked, expecting something completely girly to come out of her mouth.

"Um, *Sons of Anarchy*," she said, and blushed again, rushing on with, "Everett and Dray got me hooked on it. I'm trying to catch up."

Well, color me impressed.

"No shit? I dig that show. Where you at with it?" I asked.

"I'm a couple of episodes into season two."

No sooner had I pushed my plate a couple of inches away from me then she was up and clearing the dishes. I considered as I watched her move around the kitchen. She did all of the cleanup, loaded the dishwasher, covered the salad bowl with saran wrap and stashed it in the fridge. She moved around the kitchen with sure efficiency and startled when I came into it.

I went to the fridge and grabbed a beer, twisting off the top. I took a drink and watched her.

I recognized it. Everything she was doing.

My mom had been the same, right before she ditched me with my old man, who was a real fucking winner, let me tell you... I kept my seething anger below the surface, where Mandy couldn't or wouldn't see it. I was keeping the poor girl on edge enough as it was. She drifted past me, and I reached out and captured her hand. She startled and her eyes flicked to mine again, wide and beautiful, but with that glint of fear in them that I was really beginning to hate.

"I don't bite, Mandy. I'm not going to hurt you," I said.

"Oh! I know that! I apologize, I..." She looked like she was heading into a state of some real discomfiture, so I tugged her into my arms.

"Always been a shy girl, huh, baby?"

She nodded mutely.

"I make you that uncomfortable?" I asked, and she gasped, her autumn-colored eyes, like leaves turning from green to winter-brown raised from where they'd been fixed on my chest.

"Oh, no! No... at least you didn't before... I just, I guess... I don't know how I should feel."

I nodded and thought for a second. She looked so unhappy.

"Close your eyes for me, sugar?"

She looked apprehensive for a second but then complied, her eyes drifting shut. She was rigid in my embrace.

"Now, do me a favor, think back to the hospital; remember?"

She relaxed marginally.

"Yes."

"Then, after that, at the club, remember then?"

She nodded.

"I'm the same guy who was there for you back then, Red, same man. I'm sorry I dropped off the face of the earth, it was a dick move, and it's not gonna happen again," I whispered, and I kissed her.

And this time, she was so beautifully responsive, her lips parted beneath mine and pressed back soft and sweet. I flicked my tongue against her lower lip and with a soft little sigh she let me in, her tongue finding mine, stroking. I pulled her tightly against my body, she was so warm and soft and *Christ, what was that fucking phenomenal smell?* Whatever she wore drove me absolutely fucking crazy! It was such a pure, clean, and delicate floral scent.

Her hands drifted to my chest from my shoulders and she pressed a little. I pulled her tighter against me, God, I wanted her so bad it hurt! No, really, I was so fucking hard in my shorts, I thought I was gonna split my foreskin. –That– image cooled me off just a bit, along with a more insistent shove from my Red. I let her break the kiss, her impassioned gasp twisting me up inside.

"I need a little room to breathe, please," she said and patted her hands where they rested on the chest of my thin, sleeveless Misfits tee, an old favorite of mine. I took a step back, my hands coming to rest on her hips and gave both of us a little breathing room.

"Sorry, sugar, too easy to get carried away with you," I told her honestly.

I took her by the hands and she followed me in to the living room only a little reluctantly. I sat down on the couch; well, laid down really, propping my head on the arm, one leg resting along the back, the other bent, foot planted on the floor. I pulled her down to sit between my legs, swept the remote off the coffee table and propped it on my knee.

"Come here. No play tonight, I just want to hold you."

I took a hold of Red's hands and gently tugged, guiding her to lay down. She shifted her hip to make sure she wouldn't crush the family jewels and laid her legs sideways on the expanse of the couch, twisting her upper body, her ear resting over my heart. I smiled, one hand on the nape of her neck, massaging. The other, I smoothed up and down her silk-clad back.

"I like this," I murmured, and switched on the TV. Truthfully, the only way I'd have liked it more is if I'd been smart enough to sweep off my shirt before getting her against me. It felt like too much material was between us as it was. I switched the television over to the Blu-Ray player and brought up Netflix; I'd spent enough time over here as a prospect while the girls were out doing girl things to know what was up. Although, now that I had more perspective, Red bolting for and shutting herself into her room as soon as they came home made more sense.

"Me, too," she said after a minute. Her voice was timid, like she expected judgment, or for me to ravish her, or –something– and it derailed my train of thought completely.

She was a bit stiff in my arms, but slowly began to unwind. I got things picked up where she'd left off in the series I tossed my hat onto floor by us; the bill had been digging uncomfortably and the damn thing didn't want to stay on with my head laying against the arm of the couch. I held on to her through the mild fidgeting to get comfortable, one hand continuing to rub the tension from the muscles in her neck, the other smoothing up and down her back until, with a soft, gasped-out little sigh, she relaxed completely. Sometime later, I pulled the throw on the back of the couch down over the top of her to keep her warm. I don't think it was long after that both of us were out like a traffic light.

Having her down against me like that was pure epic bliss.

4

———————

Mandy...

I came back to myself slowly, the daylight coming through the living room windows muted by deep gray clouds. It looked to be a chilly and damp Sunday, but it was so very warm and safe lying here with Zander. The TV was still going, the Netflix hooked up to it having auto played through who-knew-how-many episodes while we'd cuddled and apparently, slept. I let my eyes close again and listened to the cadence of Zander's heart, the rhythmic deep breathing of his sleep, and I smiled. His intensity frightened me sometimes; he could be so bossy, bossy like my...

"Oh, no!" I bolted upright and looked at the clock. "No! No, no no no no!" Zander's hand grasped my arm above the elbow and I jerked.

"Red, what's wrong? What's wrong, sugar?"

I searched his alarmed face and desperately put a lid on my burgeoning fear.

"I overslept! I'm late!" I cried and stood. He let me go and I bolted around the corner into my room. I swung the door shut and heard him go into the bathroom; I needed that myself, but clothes! I had to find clothes! Something appropriate for service! I ripped open my closet door and pulled down a conservative cotton dress. It was a deep, earthy forest-green turtleneck with long sleeves and I threw it on the bed so I could rip off my robe and nightgown.

"Hey, Red, you okay?" Zander called through the door.

"I'm fine!" I called out, which was a lie, a total lie, I needed to go! I slapped a hand on my alarm, the music shutting off. I hadn't heard it from the living room. I pulled on bra and panties, and the dress was just falling to cover my legs, when my door swung wide. Zander leaned a muscular shoulder against the inside door frame and crossed his arms. He crossed one ankle over the other, the white rubber toe of his red high-top burying itself in the carpet, and he raised his dark eyebrows. I pulled on some socks and zipped up my brown leather riding boots to the knee.

"Where's the fire, sugar?" he asked, kindly.

"The church, if I don't move it!" I cried. I snatched a wide leather belt, a brown to match the boots, off the inside of my closet door and fitted it around my waist.

"I'm sure God will forgive you for being a few minutes late, darlin', you're human." He smiled and his chocolate-caramel eyes danced with a sparkle of amusement. My mouth went dry, and I nodded but didn't slow one bit. I pulled my hair from its pins and sloppy bun and gathered it, pulling it into a tight twist.

"It's not God's forgiveness I'll need," I said dubiously, and twisted my hair up in the back. I snatched a copper hair basket in a Celtic knot work design that Evy had bought me for Christmas one year and held it to the back of my hair, jamming the matching metal stick through to hold it in place. My eyes watered as the stick caught and pulled in my hair, yanking some at the roots. I sniffed and the smarting soon went away. I snatched up my purse.

"I apologize, Zander! I will make it up to you, I promise I–" He stepped into my room, my space, and he took up so much of it with both his sheer size and force of personality.

"Shh, easy, sugar. No need to apologize to me, just slow down a little. Not sure I like the idea of you driving all worked up like this."

I blinked twice as his words registered. He was worried about me? I was speechless. I nodded, my eyes a little wide, and Zander put his hands gently to either side of my face, cradling it softly between his rough and calloused hands. I forced down a shiver even as I felt the room grow hotter, or was that just me?

He brought his lips to mine and kissed me gently. I covered his hands with mine and kissed him back, but my need to get out of the house and to my father's church overrode just about everything right now. I pulled back, heat dusting my cheeks, and Zander smiled at me with the devil's own grin. I smiled back and swallowed hard.

"'Kay, that's better. I'll lock up, I still got a key," he murmured.

I nodded mutely and he walked me out to the living room. He kissed me one more time at the door and breathed deep just beneath my ear, the warm current of his breath radiating through my body sending gooseflesh in a ripple down my back.

"God I love that smell!" he exclaimed in a harsh but soft voice. I smiled and went out the front door.

"I'll see you later?" I asked, dashing down the front steps.

"I promise, Red. Not going anywhere this time," he called after me and I stole one last glance as I shut the car door behind me and started it. I pulled away from the curb, Zander's shiny red-and-white muscle car parked across the street, and drove quickly, but safely, in the direction of the highway and, ultimately, my father's church.

I pulled into the first available space when I got there and speed-walked to the building. I was over twenty minutes late. My father was up at the front in his pastor's robes, my mother in the front row, as always. I slipped inside quietly and walked up the side of the sanctuary, attempting to be as unobtrusive as possible. I slid into the pew beside my mother, who took one of my hands in both of hers and patted the back. Her face was impassive, but her brown eyes were so very worried. My father didn't miss a beat and preached on, but I didn't miss the hard look, the icy glare he gave me at my late arrival.

If I were lucky, he simply wouldn't speak to me; middle of the road, I would receive a lecture. I really hoped it would be one of those things. To be sure, this Sunday dinner would be an uncomfortable one; not that it was ever filled with the warmth I found at Dray's table with Everett. I bowed my head in prayer with the rest of my father's congregation, going through all of the motions as a dutiful pastor's daughter.

Meanwhile, the inside of my head, the inside of my heart, was a raging tempest of emotions and 'what-if's.

What if he asked me why I was late? What would I say? *Gee, I apologize, Dad, I spent the night on the couch with a tattooed heathen biker who I'm pretty sure has never set foot in a traditional church. What? Oh, no. We haven't had sex, I'm still a virgin. No, Daddy, I'm not a whore!* I grimaced. I'm pretty sure that if I hadn't already, that would be the point I would get a taste of the back of his hand. Whether it would be for what I had done with Zander, or for disagreeing with him would be up in the air. I squeezed my mother's hand and she squeezed mine back twice with both of hers.

She smiled pleasantly at me and I smiled serenely back, even if I was sick with wondering, with fear at what my daddy's reaction would be. There was really nothing I could do but wait and see how he would handle things. He was such an exacting man, everything had to be just so and appearances, well, appearances meant everything. I had long since given up hope of ever pleasing him, of ever having my father be proud of me for anything. No. The only reason I came back here, the only reason I continued to silently endure, was gripping my hand with both of hers until her knuckles became mottled and they shook, trembling in my grasp.

We rose together and sang the selected hymn our voices strong and unwavering. Still, I felt incredibly tired despite what a warm, safe, and good night's sleep I had had the night before. I flashed back to the hospital waiting room, the morning Everett had been shot while my father preached about doing good works, about selfless acts of kindness. I'd gotten to the hospital as soon as I could. I'd left my parent's home, my old room, in the wee hours of the morning. My father had been upset about being woken.

I'd like to believe that at his very heart, he was still a decent man in some ways, just, not where his family was concerned.

I'd told him and my mother it was Everett, that the hospital had called and that she was in the emergency department. Everett had signed papers when she'd made me her emergency contact, after her father had died, telling the hospital that it was all right to tell me what she had been admitted for, so when I'd told my parents it was a gunshot wound, my mother had cried out in dismay and hugged me, and my father, well, he had held my coat for me to shrug into. It was the nicest thing I think I can ever remember him doing.

I'd arrived and spilled through the emergency room doors and straight into a hulking pile of biker muscle, in the form of most of the Sacred Hearts local charter. Zander had stepped out of the crowd in his black denim vest, and the look of raw sympathy flashing in the chocolate-caramel depths of his eyes drove me dodging around the lot of them and towards the back, where I called for my best friend. I'd found her tearstained and bloody in a hospital bed, Dray hovering at her side like an angry, dark shadow, an avenging angel if I'd ever seen one, and I felt the fear constricting my heart ease. She was out of it, but she was alive, and seeing her let me know she would be okay.

Zander's hands had descended on my shoulders and I'd startled, but their weight was a comforting thing as he'd gently pulled me back, steering me towards the waiting room. He'd taken care of me, been a comforting presence at my side and someone solid that I could lean on while the implications of what could have happened sunk in. I'd almost lost the only person I could ever count on, my rock in an otherwise storm-swept sea. Everett had been shot. She could have died, and I would have been cast adrift without anything or anyone to anchor me like she had since we were kids.

A paper cup of hot coffee had been thrust into my hands, murmuring voices had filled my head, but Zander hadn't wavered, hadn't moved from my side. He'd sat beside me, one hand on my knee, the other rubbing up and down my back for as long as I had needed him to stay. That had been the last time I had felt anything like that – until last night.

The congregation rose and I followed suit, just a touch behind the rest, so lost was I to the memory. I stole a glance at my father, who hadn't noticed my daydreaming, thank goodness, and looked over my mother's shoulder at her hymnal to find the right page in my own.

Mrs. Patterson began to play the old electric organ and our voices rose in an old favorite of my mother's, which made me smile. We sang, voices lilting, retaking our seats after my father asked us to be seated. He gave his closing thoughts and the final prayer, and we rose. A short time later, we took our places at the front door to shake hands and well-wish as his flock left the sanctuary, and eventually the church, to enjoy the rest of their day.

Only a bit longer and my mother and I would find out what kind of mood my father was be in. We waved goodbye to the last of the congregation as they pulled out of the lot and my father turned. I flinched but all he did was fix me with a steely glare, his mouth compressed into a thin line of displeasure, before he marched back into the church. I let out a breath I hadn't realized I'd been holding. My mother studied me with a worried gaze.

"What happened, Baby?" she asked me.

"I slept through my alarm," I said miserably. It was the truth, and she didn't need to know the why of it. Neither of them did. I was too afraid of disappointing them both. My mother took my hand and tucked it into the crook of her arm while we waited for my dad to come back out and lock up. She and I murmured back and forth about dinner plans and some baking she wanted to accomplish before Thanksgiving. We both fell silent as my dad locked the front door. He turned, gave me death's own glare and stalked to the car without a word. I breathed a silent sigh of relief, and my mother did, too. It was to be the silent treatment then, no cutting remarks, no verbal flogging, no slaps or cuffs or hits.

"I'll see you at the house, baby girl." My mother hugged me and dashed towards my father's car, getting into the passenger side. He looked at her and barked something, and my mother shrank in on herself. I huddled miserably in on my own self and made for my car. He pulled out of the lot and I got into my little Focus and followed. I pulled up to the curb in front of my parent's little bungalow-style house and joined my mother on the front walk. My father stalked inside without a single backwards glance, and I figured it was fifty-fifty on if the silent treatment would endure or if I would receive a dinner-time lecture on what it means to be on time or about appearances.

Well, there was a third option, too, now that I was contemplating it as I moved about my old familiar kitchen with my mother. He might go the passive-aggressive route and just make some sort of cutting remark during the meal time prayer. Those were always fun. Usually, it was something snarky and if I looked at him or made a defensive remark, it would just get me back-handed. Sometimes that was preferable to the seething anger or crushing hurt those remarks left behind, making me feeling three inches tall.

It was a wonder I hadn't gone completely homicidal or suicidal by now where my father was concerned. I think that was mostly due to Everett. She was the glue that held me fast when my father was hell-bent on tearing me down or apart depending on his mood for the day.

"So?" my mother murmured briskly when we heard the television turn on to whatever football game happened to be going on that day. My father was a die-hard Patriots fan. I looked at her and she smiled guiltily and captured her bottom lip between her teeth, shrugging her shoulders. I smiled conspiratorially, and went for my purse.

"So, I tried making Nanna's white-chocolate, pumpkin-spice-filled maple leaves this time." I murmured and brought out the tiny box. My mother peeked into the living room, and I handed her one and took one myself. We both popped them in our mouths at the same time. Her eyes rolled up in bliss and she nodded rapidly.

"You did it, m'girl!" she whisper-cried. We knew better than to disturb daddy's football game.

"Melinda!" he called.

My mom quickly chewed and swallowed the rest of her chocolate and called back,

"Yes, dear?"

"Bring me a root beer!" he called.

"I've got it, Daddy!" I called.

He shouted back, "Is your name Melinda?" I bit my lips together and my mother sighed and gave me a sad smile. I nodded and handed her a root beer from the fridge, the good kind, in the bottle. My mother opened it and took it and a glass out to my dad.

"I don't want that!" he said irritably, and my mother returned with the glass.

I swallowed, my mouth dry, and we set to work fixing dinner. If my dad knew about the chocolates before dinner... holy crap. He would have gone off. My father, in addition to being a pastor, had antiquated notions about how things should be in his home. No sweets before dinner, dinner always served by six, homework done by seven, and everyone in bed by eight. It's how it had always been. Exceptions were rarely, if ever, made.

My mother and I set to work in earnest, fixing a decadent Sunday dinner of glazed ham, biscuits, salad, green beans, and mashed potatoes. We always, –always– ate at the dining room table. The television was off. The table must be set precisely one half hour before any food came out. Not a thing was allowed out of place, the house was immaculately kept, to the point it looked as if it came from a magazine spread.

We all took our places at the table that would normally seat six, my father at the head, my mother to his right, and me to his left.

We bowed our heads and my father began the meal time prayer.

"Dear Heavenly Father, we would like to give thanks this evening for the food we are about to eat, for the health of our family, and for my congregation. Thank you Father, for gifting me with eloquence and allowing me to speak your word to so many this morning." He paused and I thought to myself, *Here it comes* and sure enough, "Father, I would ask that you teach my willful daughter obedience, so that she may attract a proper husband, and gift her with the intelligence to read and understand time, so that she may not be late to partake in your teachings, in the future. Amen."

I cringed inwardly and squashed my inner voice, which at the moment sounded a lot like Everett screaming, *Why don't you just trade me for six goats and a cow while you're at it Dad?* I bit the inside of my cheek and clenched my jaw firmly shut on the notion of saying any such thing to my temperamental father and instead quietly said 'Amen' and unfolded my napkin in my lap.

"Why were you late, Autumn?" he asked. I swallowed hard and rolled my lips together, smoothing them, and suddenly wished for some lip balm. That was crazy, I had to answer him, my thoughts just didn't want to. I decided on the truth, which was rarely, if ever a good idea, but I tried hard to do as my father bid me, and he bid me constantly to be honest.

"I slept through my alarm, Daddy. I apologize, it won't happen again." Short and sweet, I didn't even try to argue my case. There was no saying anything about long hours in the shop I shared with Everett, nothing about staying hours after closing to perfect this or that recipe, or to make sure there were enough chocolates to stock the display case for the upcoming holidays. My daddy was an exacting man. With a hard twist in the center of my chest, I painfully realized just how much I missed Mr. Moran, Everett's dad. It broke my heart that my father couldn't, or wouldn't, love me like Mr. Moran loved Everett and even me.

"Sloth is one of the severest sins. The church is holding a fundraiser just before the holidays. I expect you there to help," he said.

"Yes, Daddy." I nodded and he banged a fist on the tabletop, causing the flatware to jump, and myself and my mother along with it.

"Don't use that sullen tone with me, girl!" He raised his voice.

"I apologize, I didn't mean for it to sound that way, I just meant that, of course, I would be there to help!" I stared at my father wide-eyed, and held still. He stared at me with an unfriendly gaze and my mother interjected quietly.

"Jim, darling, I'm sure our Mandy-girl didn't mean for it–" My dad's hand flashed out and caught my mother in the mouth in an open-handed slap. My mother cried out and pressed both of her small hands over the red print left behind and pressed her lips together, her shoulders hunching, her eyes downcast and subservient. I did the same, casting my eyes to my plate. The silence was the loudest I had ever heard it, all of us tense.

"Eat your dinner. The both of you," my father ordered, and with shaking hands, my mother and I automatically began to shovel small bites of food into our mouths. There were no tears. We didn't cry. My father had no use for tears and all they did was make him come unglued even harder. We finished the meal in tense silence and waited patiently for daddy to get up and go back to his football game. As soon as he did, my mother and I travelled, wraithlike, between the dining room and kitchen, clearing the plates.

I was on the final trip from the dining table to the kitchen when I caught my mother at the kitchen sink. She gripped the edge as one side of the two-basin sink filled with hot, sudsy water. Her fingers were turning white from her death-grip on the counter. She bowed her head and her shoulders shook with silent sobs. I went to her and hugged her from behind. My mother always tried to draw his ire off of me; sometimes, like today, it worked. Other times, not so much. I hugged her from behind and Everett's words from two weekends ago came back to me.

For the first time ever, I contemplated it. I really did. I wondered what the look on my father's face would be, if he opened the front door to see Dray or even Zander standing on the stoop with vengeance in their hearts. I swallowed hard and closed my eyes as my mother sobbed at our kitchen sink. I prayed really hard for forgiveness, and that my father would realize what a bastard he was and would come to his senses, would seek out some help... I'd been praying for those things for as long as I could remember, and they hadn't happened yet.

"Why do you stay with him?" I whispered, and my mother patted my hand with hers.

"You wouldn't understand, Mandy-girl. You wouldn't understand." She sniffed and wiped beneath her eyes and thrust her hands into the hot water filling the sink. She was right, I didn't understand. I don't think there was anything that would ever make me understand.

She washed, I dried. It was how it had always been; our kitchen didn't have a dishwasher. When everything was in its place, and everything sparkled and looked perfect, as it should, I gathered my purse from the kitchen chair under the wall-mounted telephone, another testament to my father's outdated and antiquated way of thinking. The house had a landline and he wouldn't hear anything of carrying a cellphone.

"I love you, Mom," I murmured and hugged her close.

"Oh, I love you too, Mandy-girl." She hugged me tightly.

"Daddy! I'm leaving!" I called.

"Drive safe, Autumn," he grumbled from the living room, but I didn't mistake it for being a sweet gesture, no. He just didn't want to pay higher insurance premiums or for any damage done to my car. I'd been amazed that my mom and dad had bought it for me upon graduation in the first place, but had later found out that Mr. DelBene, a congregant who owned a dealership, had suggested it and that he had given them an incredible deal on the car. My father never missed an opportunity to look good, like an upstanding pillar of the community, or like a doting and loving father. He believed in leading his flock by example. If only his flock knew what an utter farce his examples were.

I left quietly and drove home. My mood, as always after a Sunday spent with my family, was sullen and borderline morose. I pulled up to the curb in front of the house I shared with Everett and Dray in our quiet little neighborhood and felt mentally- and emotionally-drained, like I had no energy whatsoever. I dragged myself up the front steps and let myself into the house, and found Dray slouched down low on the couch.

"Hey," he said, his dark eyes sweeping from my booted feet to my face, where they stopped cold and his eyebrows came down in a crushing frown.

"C'mere," he ordered, struggling to sit partway up. I sighed and complied, dropping onto the couch a cushion away. I knew Dray was a sweetheart deep down inside by the way he looked at my best friend, by the way he treated her, and yes, even me, but he was still a deep and dark and brooding soul on a good day and intimidating as could be.

"Talk to me." He leveled that dark and thoughtful gaze of his at me.

"Nothing to really talk about, had a nice visit with my folks–"

He snorted, cutting me off.

"That's bullshit!" he called me out. I bit my lips together. He looked me over thoughtfully.

"Where's Everett?" I asked.

"Dance studio. Don't change the subject. You go over there every Sunday, and come home looking like someone just kicked your favorite puppy."

I flinched inwardly and hoped like heck it didn't show on the outside. I fixed Dray with my best wide-eyed-innocent look, which pretty much doubled as my deer-in-the-headlights look, which is really how I was feeling. He sighed out and raked his fingers through his hair, pulling it back from his face, when I'd been silent too long.

"You gonna make me ask?" he demanded and gave me a hard, flinty look. I nodded mutely and his mouth cracked wide into a grin.

"You can be a royal pain in the ass, just like Em, you know that?" he demanded, and my shoulders dropped.

"You guys have an argument?" I asked.

He gave a shrug that could mean nothing and could mean everything, his face impassive. I sighed and got to my feet.

"We aren't done. Something is going on with you, and Em won't break your guy's bro code, so..." He raised his eyebrows and willed me to fill in the blanks.

I smiled wanly.

"Just, a lot to do, for the church and the upcoming holiday fundraiser." That was the truth, just not all of it. "I'm off to read and relax; I have a lot to do tomorrow for both it and the shop. You really shouldn't worry so much, but it's very sweet that you do."

I kissed Dray's cheek and he gave me a crooked grin.

"Okay, Mandy-girl." He used the nickname my mother and Everett had been using on me since the dawn of time. "I'll let it go for now, but don't think Zander will go easy on you. He's a right pain in the ass if you present him with a mystery." He winked at me and I stiffened.

"You didn't!" I gave him a considering look and his face said it all, he most certainly –had–. My shoulders dropped. "You did." I chewed my bottom lip and Dray's overall look softened. He sat up the rest of the way and pulled me into a hug.

"You're my Em's family, which makes you the entire MC's family, Red. It's been a year you been living here, and that's an entire year of Sundays, watching you come home half-wrecked, and watching it take the better part of the week for you to put yourself back together." He pursed his lips and, when he didn't get anything from me, huffed out a harsh sigh and continued. "And for what? For you to go over there and have the damn cycle repeat itself?" He sat back and held me by my elbows and searched my face.

"Now, as your honorary big brother, I am obligated to kick some-one's ass for making my baby sister..." He frowned, "You never cry, but you get what I'm sayin' here."

I nodded.

"Really, Dray, you're making something out of nothing, nothing at all," I smiled and it was equal parts sad and tired. "I'm grabbing a shower and bed. Tomorrow's horizon is a lot closer than I'd like it to be, and I have a lot to get ready for."

He let me go.

"Night, then," he said, and sounded more frustrated than happy about it.

"Goodnight, Dray," I went past him and into my room. My bed was still made from the day before, seeing as I hadn't slept in it, but my robe and nightgown, which I had carelessly discarded that morning on the floor, were neatly laid out on the bed for me. There was a note on the robe, written on the back of a discarded envelope.

Hey, Red,

Text me when you get home. I'm kind of missing you already. Last night was real nice. Wow. Awkward. I wish this message would self-

destruct once you read it. It makes me look like some kind of pansy. Anyway, here's my number. Hope I hear from you.

-Revelator... Zander.

He left his number under his signature and I couldn't help but smile to myself. His handwriting, for a guy's, was actually lovely, a looping, flowing script that made my cursive look positively terrible by comparison. I went to my dresser and tucked the envelope between the frame and the silvered glass of the mirror, right below the first picture ever taken of me and Everett, from the second grade.

I frowned and picked up my small ampule of Lily of the Valley perfume oil from the varnished wood top. I set it back in its place beside my deodorant on the silver tray that held all my perfume, makeup, and toiletries. I couldn't for the life of me recall if I had put any on this morning, and simply set it back on the dresser top instead of where it belonged in my rush to get out the door. I looked over everything and satisfied it was where it belonged and the perfume was the only thing out of place, began to change for bed.

I read my Kindle, a Christmas gift from Everett two years ago, for a while, before my uncontrollable yawning forced me to tug the bead chain on my bedside lamp and set the Kindle aside for the time being. Dray was right, visiting with my parents really did take it out of me.

5

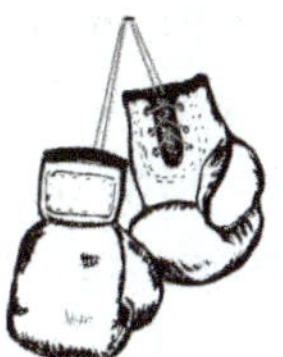

R evelator...

As soon as Red was out the door, her small blue car pulling away from the curb, I went back inside. I finished cleaning up the kitchen from the night before, which really just means I put soap, which I conveniently found under the sink, into the dishwasher, and ran it.

That done, like a total fucking creeper, I found myself back in her bedroom. Everything was perfect and neat in here, like something out of a magazine or some shit, except for her robe and nightgown which lay in a puddle on the floor.

I stared for a long time at the creamy pool of satin lying there against the gray carpet and all I could do was picture it sliding down my Red's alabaster skin, those freckles of hers spattered across her lush curves and smooth skin like the stars across our universe. Goddamn, the girl was under my skin!

I was miserably hard in my shorts and I had already had a deep and abiding ache in my balls when she'd pushed off of me that morning. I picked up her robe and nightgown and laid them out side by side over her crisply-made bed.

She had everything tucked and creased with military precision, and when I picked up the edge of her comforter and peeked, I half-expected her sheets to be folded into prison corners.

I'd spent enough time in Juvie, and later, in County for assault & battery and the occasional drunk & disorderly, to know what those looked like. Hell, I used them myself on my own bed at home.

Her bedroom was done in soft greens and creams. The furniture was white and done all classic rustic-farmhouse. The walls were a light mint. Her comforter had subtle ivy patterns on it, and her sheets, from what I could see, were matched to it.

She had the full bed pushed flush against the wall on one side and at the head, tucked neatly into the corner of the room. On the one nightstand rested a reading device in a green leather cover with a giant oak tree on the front, some Celtic thing. A glass of water stood by if she needed it, and a really nice stained-glass lamp, with lily pads, water lilies and jewel-bright dragonflies, presided over it all.

I decided I'd better leave a note or something; I didn't know if she still had my number or not. I looked around and found an empty envelope, slit open at the top, just chillin' on top of some other miscellaneous trash in her wastebasket by the dresser. I picked it off the top and pulled a pen from a cup of 'em on a shelf built under the drawer on her bedside table. I was smoothing the envelope flat on the dresser when a little glass tube caught my eye. It had a matte gold top and a pastel label in pinks, yellows, greens, and blues. I picked it up and smiled to myself. The purple script on the label said "Lily of the Valley Perfume Oil".

I twisted off the cap and breathed it in.

Yep. That was it. The clean, delicate, flower scent that drove me fucking wild every time I caught it lingering in the air near where she'd been, or when I held her close. Only it wasn't quite the same. It was a funny time to remember it, but I recalled some bitch I was banging back in the day asking me how something smelled on her when we were out at a shopping mall. She'd said that perfume smelled just a touch different on everyone, that no two people wore it exactly alike or some shit. I could believe that, that some of the smell that twisted me up and turned me inside out was just purely Red.

I recapped the vial, twisting it tight, and set it down on the dresser. I needed to get the fuck out of here. I was pretty sure I was square in the middle of being a creepy-ass stalker fucktard, so I wrote out a quick note with my number at the bottom, laid it on her bed and returned the pen to where it belonged. Then I got the fuck out of her room and locked the place up tight behind me.

I drove home, put in a brutal morning workout, showered, ate, and spent a decent chunk of time at my drafting table, drawing up some random tattoo designs to stay in practice. Couldn't tell you why all of them were girly as fuck and along the same damned theme. I ended up with any number of crosses surrounded by ribbons and lilies, and even spent some time plucking out some random inspirational Bible quotes for some of them. I figured if anything, with as many of the small drawings I put to a single page, they would serve as some decent flash art for the walls of whatever new place me, Trig, Dis, and Ash opened up. Like a phoenix, Open Road Ink would rise from the ashes at some point. Might as well be ready for it.

Huh.

Phoenix.

Not bad.

As soon as I was done with the Christian flash, I started on a mythical creature set, starting with a phoenix. I must have been at it for hours. It was a good way to kill time on a Sunday. Around four in the afternoon I started stealing glances at my phone, which was chillin', dark and lonely, on the edge of my table. Around four-thirty, I found myself willing the damned thing to light up. Around five I willed it to ring, and by seven, I was getting seriously fucking agitated, my knee bouncing of its own volition, expending nervous energy.

I hit the gym for a hard evening workout to burn off the rest, docking my phone and using it to blast music in the home gym. I don't think I took my eyes off it as I went through rep after rep, building chest, arms, and upper body. This was fucking ridiculous, man! I was like a teenage fucking boy all over again! I ain't been a teenager in a long damned time, and this shit was like living some of the worst fucking parts of it that I'd never actually had to live before. I had never wanted for pussy. Not then, and to be honest, not fucking now, either. I could have any club whore I wanted writhing underneath me in the space it took me to grin at 'em, but that was the giant problem here.

I didn't want a random piece of pussy. I wanted Red. And Red didn't operate like any other girl I had ever known. She didn't care about looks, she didn't give a shit about what kind of car I drove, or how much green was in my pocket. I dropped the hand weight to the floor and sat for a long minute, chest heaving, sweat cooling and gelling into place on my skin.

"Hey, Disney!" I yelled and waited, and waited some more. Shit. Not home. I got into a shower and let the hot spray ease the tension between my shoulders. It was almost eight-thirty and still no call or text. I closed my eyes, and every time I did, I couldn't help but picture Red's angelic face, smoothed into lines of utter, contented, –peace– as she'd rested against my chest the night before. I'd spent fucking hours last night, memorizing the moment. Every line, every detail, while SoA had played on mindlessly in the background. God, I was hard again. Only this time I was in a position to do something about it, and so I did. Still, jerking it in the shower was a frigid comfort and one shitty consolation prize.

I thought about going over there, but I held myself in check for the moment. I dried off and pulled on a pair of comfortable basket-ball shorts to wear around the house. I checked my phone again and was surprised to see a text from Dray.

Dray: She came home around six. Something's got her down, she went to bed pretty much as soon as she got here.

Me: Should I come over?

It felt like fucking forever before my phone buzzed in my hand with a return message. My breath whooshed out, and I shook my damned head over the fact I'd even been holding it.

Dray: Naw man. Let her sleep but might not be a bad idea you took over watch at their shop if you got time.

Me: Anything you say VP.

Dray: Not telling you this as your VP dude. Tired of watching that girl come home missing pieces if you get me. It bothers my girl and what bothers my girl always bothers me in the end.

Me: I hear you. I'll find out what's up. When is the next time she's supposed to go over there? Sunday?

Dray: No. Thx Giving this Thurs. dude. She's spending it with her folks.

Me: Copy that.

Dray: Later douchebag.

Me: Later dick-cheese.

Dray: Fuck. You win.

I chuckled at Dray, then sighed and tossed my phone to the side and scrubbed my face with my hands. If it was enough to get Dray involved, then it was high past time for me to be involved. It was definitely time for me to do some sleuthing, figure some shit out and what was going on with my girl.

I had a busy couple of days up ahead. Trigger and me were supposed to go scouting around town for a good location for a new shop, which was a lot harder than it sounded. We'd already been turned down by two spots because of the explosion.

The insurance company was supposed to settle with us on Tuesday, before the fucking holiday, and with as much as they'd been dicking around, we were gonna see what this latest offer was, and if it was shit like the last two? Well, we weren't afraid to lawyer-=up. We just didn't want to drag it out any further than we had to, and we sure as hell didn't want to resort to his woman's money. Ashton had done way more than enough, between the club and opening up Soul Fuel with Ev and Red.

I dragged my ass to bed even though my mind was restless as hell. Part of staying fit and in prime fighting condition was to get the requisite amount of sleep. Still, every damned time I closed my eyes, I was assaulted with the vision of the season personified. Red was a fucking goddess, and I wanted so fucking bad to make her mine in every way.

6

———————

Mandy...

I felt incredibly guilty. I'd programmed Zander's number into my contacts but I never called him or texted him and I hadn't seen or heard from him either. I had been completely slammed the last three days, what with the approaching holiday, and now having to plan for the fundraiser and make sure I had enough of everything, including the money it would take to purchase ingredients. I'd figured out that I wouldn't be doing anything fun for the next two, three months or so, if I were going to make my penance for my late church arrival doable.

I'd worked on Monday, my other day off, to make absolutely sure that I was ahead of the holiday shoppers we were anticipating for Friday, and to plan all this church fundraiser business out. I wasn't about to defer the cost of my mistake to our business, however, I was going to make this a prime free-advertising venture by slathering every box of chocolates I made with the shop's name, address, phone number, and logo in hopes of getting something out of it.

Hopefully, my scheme would go unnoticed by daddy and everyone would win. He'd look good, Soul Fuel would look good, and the church would receive the donations it was seeking for both itself and this year's fundraising cause. I didn't even know what it was this year, but it was one thing my father let my mother do, so whatever it was, knowing my mom, it was good. Last year it had gone to a local homeless shelter, the year before it had been in the name of Saint Francis and had gone to the local animal shelter.

I had a couple of binders full of photos and descriptions of different chocolates and packaging ideas, ranging from contemporary to fall to Christmas holiday. I was hoping that my father would be in a good mood and I could sit down with him and make him a part of things as Thanksgiving dinner cooked. It was probably way too idealistic of me to think so, but stupidly, I still held out hope that daddy and I would reach some sort of understanding on something that didn't involve me, or my mother, getting cracked in the mouth and us just doing whatever he told us to do, in order to keep the illusion of peace and harmony in place.

I pulled up to the curb in front of their house, which was lit from the inside by a deceptively cheery glow. The clouds hung low and gray, and threatened rain, the sky ominous and drear... or maybe it was just me. I sighed. The older I'd become, the worse my father became. Still, it was Thanksgiving, and while last year Everett had been here to cushion things a bit, this year she was spending Thanksgiving with Dray and their motorcycle club family. They had tried hard to talk me in to doing the same, but I just couldn't leave my mom. Not for the holiday.

I went up to the door, one arm burdened with my purse and two binders and knocked. It opened and my mother blinked at me, surprised.

"Mandy-girl! You don't need to knock!" she cried, and stood aside. I smiled and glanced into the living room. My father was in his recliner, the game on, as always.

"Hi, Daddy!" I called.

"Autumn," he drawled. I sighed. My father always called me by my first name and he sounded dour as he'd done it.

I forged ahead anyway.

"I brought some sample photos and descriptions for the

fundraiser, packaging ideas and that sort of thing. I thought maybe while dinner was cooking I could sit down with you and look things over." I waited, my breath held, but all he did was grunt noncommittally.

I sighed and my mother gave me a sympathetic look. We went into the kitchen together; the turkey was already in the oven and we set about making a modest amount of sides for our small, broken family of three.

When everything was in the ovens and the dishes from cooking were caught up, washed, dried, and put away, I sat at the kitchen island on the high kitchen stool with the binders and a notepad.

"Okay, baby, show me what you have." My mother leaned on the counter and I showed her everything I made for the shop or planned to make for the shop in the future. All of the recipes were her parents', my grandparents', and my mother's brown eyes shone with pride. She tucked some of her graying chin-length brown hair behind her ears and turned pages, pride written clearly over her features, etched in her smile.

My mother, unlike me, was small. I think I got my father's genes when it came to build. I wasn't quite as tall as him, but I was certainly closer to him in build. We don't know what recessive gene caused the ginger in me. We weren't one-hundred-percent on where my hazel eyes had come from, either. My dad's hair was brown like my mother's and his eyes a pale watery blue. My mother had a light smattering of freckles, but not like my riot of them. I took after her in the looks department, through and through. Same nose, same ears, same shape of the face.

"Hey, Daddy, did you want to see these?" I called.

"I'm watching the game!" he called back, tersely. My mother and I exchanged a look and I rolled my eyes. She put a hand over her mouth and suppressed a laugh.

I set the table before the appointed time could arrive and couldn't help but feel sad that it was only three places I set. I sighed silently, and wondered what Zander was doing for Thanksgiving, and realized he was with the MC along with Evy and Dray. I didn't think he had any other family. At least I'd never heard of any.

My mother had put together a beautiful centerpiece of candles and colored leaves to reflect the holiday. The candles were unscented and off-white with just a hint of a golden hue. It made me think of almonds for some reason. I dug around in the kitchen junk drawer and found a lighter for the three candles, lighting them as my mother brought the turkey out of the oven. I helped her get the bird onto the serving platter and the sides out to the table.

"Daddy! Dinner!" I called and smiled, suffused with a quiet pride at my mother's accomplishment. The television clicked off in the living room and my father, who was a big man, tall with broad shoulders, lumbered into the dining room. He was dressed comfortably in a blue button-down shirt and khaki pants. My mother wore a gray pair of slacks and a cream-colored blouse. I wore a comfortable pair of fitted jeans and a thick, cream-colored cable knit sweater that fell to just above my knees. I'd completed the outfit with a brown belt and brown riding boots and added a brown suede headband to hold back my copper corkscrew curls. I thought I looked quite fashionable for the holiday.

Leave it to my father...

"Jeans? You couldn't dress appropriately for the holiday? It's Thanksgiving, Autumn." He was both demanding and chiding in equal measure and I stared at him a moment, wide-eyed. My mother, as always, tried to draw his fire.

"Oh goodness Jim, let her be comfortable! I think she looks lovely!" my mother said and plastered a false smile on to her face. It didn't keep the worry or the fear out of her eyes though. I held my breath to see how he would respond... fifty-fifty as always.

"Nice spread this year, Melinda. You've outdone yourself," he grunted.

Hallelujah! He picked up the carving knife and fork, and my mother and I took our seats and let him portion out the turkey.

"Light or dark meat, dear?" he asked my mother.

"A little of both, please?" She smiled up at him with affection and

I felt a wistful pang and wondered how on Earth she could do it, after all these years and just... everything. But there it was, she still loved my father.

"Autumn?" he asked.

"Light, please," I smiled and asked if he wanted some green bean casserole. He chuckled, actually chuckled, and said of course, like I knew he would. My mother's green bean casserole was his favorite. I had ever-climbing hopes that this was actually going to be a pleasant experience this time. I mean, they did happen, they had just become rare as of late. We made it through the mealtime prayer without any snide or cutting remarks and began to eat our meal.

"Oh! Mandy! You absolutely must show your father your ideas for the fundraiser packaging! Jim, our daughter has really outdone herself with her new business. You should really be proud of her!" My mother glowed with enthusiasm, but it was the wrong choice of words.

"Woman, you don't tell me what I should and should not be proud of."

Mom and I both paused.

"I... I'm sorry..." my mother stammered, caught off-guard. I closed my eyes. His fist came down on the table.

"What did I tell you?" he demanded. 'We apologize in this house. We don't say we're sorry'. I'd heard it a million times growing up. My mother and I never understood why my father had something against the phrase 'I'm sorry' but we were almost always corrected to say 'I apologize' instead. It was a mark of how flustered my mother was, that she'd forgotten such a detail.

My dad cut into his turkey, sawing into the tender white meat savagely, all the while an endless, insulting diatribe issued forth out of his mouth against my mother – my mother, an impossibly sweet woman who, despite what an utter asshole my father was, still loved him, still stayed with him, and still put up with him.

I clenched my teeth as a seething anger took hold, lighting me up from the inside out. My hands, which I kept clenched in my lap, shook with how hard I gripped them, and I kept my eyes fixed on my half-eaten plate.

My mother sat across from me, meek, and I raised my eyes to meet hers. She shook her head imperceptibly, a pleading look in her soulful brown eyes, and something inside me just snapped. I stood up abruptly, my chair scraping back against the hardwood floor.

"Sit down!" my father barked, and I stared down at him for several heartbeats. I wanted to scream at him. I wanted to scream at my mother, I wanted to shake them both and demand of them, did they not see how broken this was? How sick, and twisted, and just wrong our family had become?

I marched into the kitchen and swept my purse, binders, and keys into my arms. My mother and father rose, and he reached out to grab my arm as I went for the front door.

I wasn't going to do this, not today! This was utterly ridiculous!

I didn't know exactly what had gotten into me. Maybe it was Dray's talk the last time I had come home from my parents'. Maybe it was how hard he and Everett both had tried to convince me to spend Thanksgiving with them, rather than here. Maybe it was even a little of Zander. It felt like he'd disappeared on me again, and even though I had to admit that he'd left me his number and I hadn't exactly reached out to him either...

Gah! I had just bottled all of it up in the same godforsaken bottle, and for whatever reason this, now, today was the time and place that particular cork decided to go flying.

I ripped open the front door and started down the walkway, my parents hot on my heels.

"Autumn Amanda Price!" my father shouted and I froze. I turned just in time for him to grab me, shaking me by the shoulders.

"Get your hands off me!" I shouted at the same time he was screaming something about me being ungrateful and disrespectful. I shouted back, giving no quarter.

"Me, disrespectful? How about you? Up there, preaching God's word every Sunday, but do you actually practice anything that you–"

His hand flashed out of nowhere in a wicked open backhand that caught me right in the mouth. I let my head snap to the side with the blow. You went with it and it typically left just a red handprint; it's when you braced against it that you got bruised.

"Jim!" my mother cried, dismayed, and jumped back, her eyes fixed over my shoulder.

My dad looked up, and he turned several shades darker red than he'd already been.

I turned, too, to see Zander striding up the sidewalk and across our grass, the devil's own fire in his eyes, his car parked down the block, the driver's door swinging wide.

"Zander, no!" I cried. Dropping my binders to the walk, abandoning them to the grass, I put both hands to his chest and pushed, but it was like trying to stop a juggernaut once it was in motion. He stopped, though, his chest heaving, and stared my dad down over my shoulder for a minute before turning his eyes on me. My expression must have been frozen into one of sheer desperation, because his look softened.

"Red, you okay, baby?" He cradled my face in his hands, his thumb gently grazing my lip. I jolted at the raw sting of it and his expression darkened.

He pointed at my dad.

"You touch her again, –I will fucking break you–!" Zander snarled. My dad drew himself up to his full height, which was taller than Zander, of course, but then again, I was taller than Zander.

It hit home for me just then: *Zander was here. On my parent's front lawn,* and I blurted "Zander! What are you doing here?"

He returned those warm brown eyes to mine, and his mouth compressed into a thin line. He pulled me into the shelter of his arms, my hands still pressed flat to the slick leather of his motorcycle vest, the name patch that read 'Revelator' rough beneath my fingers.

"I told you, Red, I am not disappearing on you again." He gave me a watery version of that devilish grin, the chip in his tooth both endearing and menacing at the same time, but he'd lost some of the tightly-coiled rage when he'd taken me into his arms.

"Just who are you?" my father demanded.

Zander turned a rough look in his direction.

"I'm the guy who's gonna fuck up your entire world if you ever lay a hand on your kid, or your wife, again," he said.

My father gave him an imperious look and looked me straight in the eyes before he said,

"I don't have a child. Autumn isn't mine."

I blinked at him stupidly.

My mother gasped, horrified, and cried out, "Jim!"

"Baby, Red, get your things, sweetheart, we're leaving," Zander's voice was quiet. He was so serious, the most serious I'd ever heard him, as my father and I both stared one another down.

I looked at my mom.

"Mom?" My voice sounded both wounded and unsure. She stared back at me, a mix of pity and horror on her lovely face.

"Mandy, baby, come on. Get in your car, we're leaving," Zander insisted sharply.

Tears coursed down my mother's face.

"Come with me," I said, but she shook her head.

"I can't."

I gave an inarticulate cry of rage and scooped up my belongings off the grass. I let Zander lead me to my car, my parents looking on. He unlocked and opened the door for me, and I got in.

"Drive to the club," he ordered.

I shook my head.

"I'm going home."

"Please. Red, for me? Go to the club. I'll be right behind you."

I looked up into his eyes, which were beseeching, and nodded. Everett was at the club and I really wanted to see my soul-sister. Zander leaned down and pressed his lips to mine in a quick, chaste kiss, and shut the door. I started the car. My father stood where we'd left him, his hands balled into fists at his sides. My mother, standing just behind him, hugged herself, watching me pull away, her eyes wide, her makeup smeared by her tears.

I didn't stop, but started to drive away, leaving Zander on the walk between me and them, a living shield. I glanced at my own, completely-dry, face in the rearview and couldn't bring myself to feel sorry for my dad, even knowing what Zander might do. I was surprised to see him say something to my parents, his breath fogging the air, and then turn, the Sacred Hearts emblem larger-than-life on his back as he strode up the sidewalk and back to his car.

Just as he'd promised. He was right behind me.

7

Zander...

"You better listen, and you better listen good! I swear to fucking Christ, you hurt either of these women again, I'm going to – end– you, old man! You get me? You see if I'm fucking lyin'!" I told him, just after Red pulled away. She was fucking outstanding! Didn't shed a single tear; tough as nails and I would so be making her mine.

"Just who the *hell* do you think you are?" her father demanded.

I spit on the ground in his direction.

"I'm the guy that's gonna marry your daughter," I said with a shit-eating grin, and flipped him the double bird, before addressing her mother.

"He touches you, you call Mandy!" I told her, and she nodded dumbly, her eyes wide and frightened.

"I mean it!" Her head bobbed more rapidly.

I strode up to my Chevelle and left twin strips of rubber, peeling out in front of their house. I wanted Pastor Dickwad to remember me for a while, and painted in front of his driveway, where he'd see it every time he stepped out to go somewhere and every time he came home, was as good a place as any to leave the reminder, even if what I wanted to do was leave it on his face for him to look at every time he looked in a fucking mirror. Tire tracks would last longer than the bruising, but were a lot less satisfying to me. *Fucking self-righteous prick!*

I'd trailed Mandy since that morning, content to spend Thanksgiving with her, whether she knew it or not. Stalker status much? Yeah.

But also necessary, according to my Pres. All the women attached to the club, and by 'women', what I really meant was 'Ol' Ladies', had a twenty-four-hour detail, which really wasn't saying much, considering they were with their men most of the time. I'd straight up assigned myself to Red, when she wasn't at her shop under guard with Everett anyway. She wasn't an Ol' Lady, wasn't technically a part of the club, but Dray had made things clear as day to me and given me the go-ahead to watch her when she wasn't with Ev or at home, absolving me of any assignments elsewhere so I could do it. Thank God, he knew what was what. The girls didn't. We were keeping all of this on the down-low with them.

I followed Red through streets that were almost eerily deserted because of the holiday until she pulled over, out of nowhere, into an empty grocery store parking lot. I pulled up next to her, expecting to see her in some kind of full meltdown. It surprised me when I jumped out of the car to see that she was parked, both hands on the wheel, her chest rising and falling with deep, even breaths, as she kept her composure. Damn. Not a single tear. Most girls would be a mess after something like that. I tried her door handle. Locked. She hit the switch and I opened her door.

" 'Sup Baby?" I asked her.

She looked up at me, her face unreadable and set in stone. "I don't know if I want to go to the club; I don't know if I want to be around all of those people. I don't want to have to explain…"

I fell into a crouch by her open driver's-side door. "Shh, don't you worry about that, sugar. You just let me do all the talking. Okay?"

She locked eyes with me.

"Why were you there?" she asked.

"Didn't want to spend Thanksgiving without you," I said; it was the truth, just not all of it.

She searched my face.

"So you parked outside my parent's house and waited, like some kind of creeper?" she asked.

I grinned.

"Actually, I was waiting for you to leave. I brought you flowers, was planning on being some big, sappy, romantic dope and everything."

Her eyebrows went up.

"You're not serious?" she said.

I stood up and opened the passenger door to my car. There, wrapped in white butcher paper was a bouquet of fierce trumpet-shaped flowers in a riot of fiery oranges that reminded me of her curls; nestled between them were little white bell-shaped flowers. I picked up the flowers and brought them over to her. She sat stunned and I smiled to myself.

"Lily of the Valley," she murmured, smelling the little white blooms. "I don't understand... lilies aren't even in season! It's too cold." She looked up at me and seemed so lost.

"Nothing I wouldn't do for you, sugar. Found a greenhouse that forces 'em, dropped a decent bit of cash, but it was worth it for the way you're lookin' at me right now."

She unhooked her seatbelt, got out of the car and wrapped her arms around me. –Then– the waterworks started. All that fucking bullshit, her dad backhanding her a good one, and she fuckin' cries over some goddamned flowers. I held her close and breathed her in.

"Why would you go through all this trouble?" she sobbed.

"Because you're worth it, Red," and wasn't that the God's honest truth?

"That and I feel like an ass for not getting in touch the first part of this week. I got wrapped up with Trig dealing with the shop and helping Ghost do some heavy lifting. I wanted to show you I wasn't disappearing again."

She settled down and wiped a few stray tears, and I got her to agree to come to the club through a little bit of fast talking. She got back in her car with her flowers and spent a couple minutes fixing her subtle makeup with some shit from her purse before pulling back out onto the route to the club.

The gate was closed when we got there but one of the new prospects opened her up for us. I'd never seen the lot so full and I was glad that the whole damned holiday didn't go to waste. Red got out of her car with her purse over one shoulder, the flowers grasped in her hand like they were some kind of treasure. Some of the guys were out back popping off rounds, no mistaking that sound. I opened the clubhouse door for her and she went into the common room to several cheers.

"Hey, hey! Look who it is!" Dragon cried. He got up from his place at the table and came up to crush Red into one of his bear-hug deals. She squeaked as he lifted her clear off the floor and set her down.

"Mandy!" Everett called, surprised, from the doorway; the girls were all coming out with empty pie plates from somewhere in the back.

"Yeah, waited outside Red's parent's place 'til they all got done with dinner, had to make sure she saw all her family on the holiday." I stretched and shot her a wink and she gave me a grateful look. I got the impression she didn't like to lie, and I was more than cool with that, and with lying for her in this particular application.

"Pretty flowers!" Chandra exclaimed.

Mandy beamed at her and nodded.

"I need to put them in some water."

Dray came in from the back and grinned, "Hey, you!" He winked at her and she blushed harder. Everett steered her in the direction of the kitchen, saying something about water and finding a vase, but her steely gaze was fixed on Red's lip. Good. Hopefully she would get some ice on it. It wasn't swelling or bruising, which was good, but it did have a small but healthy split in it. Enough to make a visible line, to show something had gone down. I nodded to her and she went with Ev. Dray came over and raised his eyebrows. Dragon looked me over, considering, at his son's look.

"She come tearin' out of the house like her ass was on fire. Her old man grabbed her and is shakin' her up some, but she was givin' as good as she got. I think she had enough or somethin', anyway, he backhands her and I intervened. Didn't touch him, couldn't do that with a fight comin' up. Gotta stay clean." I put up my hands. Dray and Dragon exchanged a look.

The thing about illegal fights is that you can't go popping off on Joe Citizen. That gets you the kind of attention that the underground circuit likes to stay far the fuck away from. If I got arrested, they'd pull my card from the running, and truth be told, I needed the fucking cash, now that I had no legal means to earn. That meant staying out of trouble so I could get in to trouble. Bass-ackwards right?

"Trust me. I want to take care of it. I want to take care of it bad, but between Red and the fights, I got every reason to be a pious little angel." I gave my Pres. and VP a feral grin and received twins of the same from father and son.

"Naw, I get you," Dragon said, and patted, then gripped, my shoulder.

"Reaver?" Dray asked.

"Naw! Reaver's a bit much for this, don't you think?" Dragon asked and Dray lifted his shoulders in a blasé shrug.

"Not from where I'm standing," I said coldly.

Dragon barked a laugh.

"Yer a cold-blooded motherfucker, after what you saw him do," he commented dryly. I gave my president a blank face. He nodded.

"I know you got a thing for the fire... hair," he changed what he was about to say at the last second at my baleful look, and Dray looked impressed.

"You trust us to get it handled? We won't do you wrong, brother." Dragon shook me back and forth by the shoulder and I nodded.

"Thanks for having my back."

"Our pleasure," Dray said. "I been living with her for the last, almost year. So, seriously, I'd do it myself, but, yeah..." He looked over his shoulder and made some thoughtful nonsensical noises as he scanned the room.

"Duracell!" he called.

"Yeah, VP?"

"You gingers like to stick together, yeah?" Dray asked.

Duracell frowned from where he was sitting.

"The fuck you talking about?" he asked.

Dray gave a wolfish grin and went over. Dragon chuckled and I shook my head.

"Thanks, man." I held out my hand and he clapped his into it. We clasped hands and shook on it.

"Happy Thanksgiving, brother," was all he said. We let go and I went off in the direction of the kitchen. I leaned a shoulder just inside the doorway and buried my hands in my shorts pockets.

Red and the rest of the girls were around the center kitchen island. Everett was fixing her, and it looked like maybe even me, a plate. Hot damn! Someone had found Red a tall cylindrical heavy-glass vase and she had the flowers out on their wrapping and unbound. She was clipping the ends with some hand-held garden shears, the fuck if I knew where those came from, and was artfully arranging both lilies and greenery as she talked with the girls.

"Where in the hell did you find lilies this time of year?" Chandra asked me, lighting the cig she had pressed between her lips.

"I told you, I'd have to kill you," I said. She snorted and smoke came out her nose.

"Classy," I commented dryly. She flipped me off and I grinned, pushing off from the wall. I took a seat on one of the stools the girls had brought in from the bar as the microwave went off. Everett slid a steaming hot plate of food in front of me.

"Thanks, Irish." She smiled and handed me silverware and a napkin. "Ashton cook this?" I asked with my mouth full.

"Yes, you barbarian," Sunshine said from the sink and I blinked in surprise. I had the flowers between me and her and she was so damned small I had completely missed that she was in here!

Just to irritate her, I talked with my mouth full again, "You think I'm gonna stop eating your cooking just so's I can talk? Pffft!" A meaty smack landed on the back of my head, the blow cushioned a bit by my favorite Buccaneer's hat.

"You got a bunch a ladies in front of you, asshole." I grinned, unrepentant, up at Trig.

"Whoa! Those are nice!" he exclaimed for Mandy's benefit. She smiled and it was the sweetest thing... I didn't think I would need dessert after that, but fuck that if it was Ashton-made pie.

"Ash, you make the pie?" I asked.

She shook her head. "Mandy made them all for us." I looked over at my girl who was suddenly very focused on her flowers. She had made enough pie to feed the entire MC and everyone attached to it, knowing she wasn't even gonna be here. I smiled. I loved her for that.

She finished putting all of her flowers in their water and slid up onto a stool next to me to eat. She gave a little secret smile at her flowers while she chewed thoughtfully, and I wondered what was chasing around in her brain under all those fiery-red curls. Whatever it was, it looked to be good.

I was a lefty and she was a righty, and unfortunately, we were sitting on the wrong side of each other for it to benefit us, which was both a blessing and a curse. A blessing because the dudes wouldn't be able to call me a pussy, but a curse because I really wanted to hold her fucking hand where it rested idly on the countertop by her plate.

The crowds in the kitchen and the common room were thinning out as dudes hauled their Ol' Ladies off to fuck and other dudes hauled themselves off to just plain take a nap. Red covered her mouth politely to yawn, herself. She'd had a rough day so I was pretty sure it wasn't the turkey kicking in. She stood and cleared our plates, and I stood too.

"C'mon, Red," I said, and held out my hand.

"What should I do with..?" She indicated her flowers. I smiled.

"They're fine where they're at,"

She took my hand and slung her purse over her shoulder, and I led her quietly through the back to my room. She went inside first and I shut the door behind us. She set her purse on the black leather recliner I had in the corner. That was pretty much it in here. The recliner in the corner with a lamp behind it. A queen-sized bed with drawers in the base for some spare clothes and a bedside table. I had a couple of framed drawings up on the walls, mostly scenes I'd imagined from some books I had read. Cool shit.

Mandy looked at them, her eyes roving over the one above the head of the bed. It was a scene out of Dante's *Divine Comedy*, complete with the canto in its original Italian. Her eyes studied the image for long moments.

"Is this in Latin?" she asked.

"Italian."

"You know Italian?" she asked, surprised and I smiled.

"No. I know what it says though." I couldn't stop smiling.

"What does it say?" she asked, the question of course, inevitable.

"Says 'Do, in me, preserve your generosity, so that my soul, which you have healed, when it is set loose from my body, be a soul that you will welcome.' It's from the thirty-first canto in *Paradiso*."

Mandy turned back to the drawing of a ravaged Dante in his Beatrice's lap as she lovingly bound one of his wounds. I studied her face as she studied my drawing.

"What are you thinking?" I asked softly.

"It seems so sad," she murmured.

"Do you know the story?" She shook her head. "It's an old poem, about a man who travels first through Hell, and then through Purgatory, to reach Heaven and find his lost love who was taken from him."

She hugged herself as her eyes roamed over Dante, who I had drawn pretty much in as wretched a state as anyone could get. He looked to be on the verge of death in my version, which was kind of the point. He was on the edge, too soon to tell if Beatrice could pull him back from the brink, but at the same time, his expression was beautiful and at peace, utterly content at being reunited, even if she couldn't save him. I don't know why I'd drawn it that way. I just had, and it had come out pretty bad-ass, so I'd framed it and put it up here, so I had something instead of nothing on the walls. She turned reluctantly from the drawing and faced me, her eyes searching.

"I apologize for what you had to see today," she started and I went to her. She seemed just, fractured… in need of some healing. I pulled her into my arms and placed my fingers over her lips, shushing her.

"Shhh, no need to talk about it anymore today, sugar. You're safe with me. You know that, right?" I trailed my fingertips from her lips, grazing her cheek. Her eyes closed and she seemed to relish the little touch. She sighed out and nodded faintly. God, she was beautiful. So soft, so sweet, and I couldn't imagine anyone treating her like anything less that the fucking magical creature she was.

"Kiss me?" she asked and I smiled. I couldn't think of anything I would do. I leaned in and brushed her lips lightly with mine, so softly, in a barely-there caress. She sighed out and leaned into the kiss, pressing her lips to mine, parting them in invitation and I didn't need any further urging than that. I swept my tongue past her lips and slipped it into her mouth.

Her arms slid along my shoulders and twined around my neck. She pressed her body the length of mine, and buried her fingers in the hair at the back of my head, pressing me closer. The action knocked my hat off, but fucked if I cared. It was just the first of many articles of clothing that I planned on making the floor their new home.

I held Red around her waist but I wanted skin, I wanted my hands on her smooth skin so bad. I slid my hands around to her front and worked at the wide decorative belt she had on. She took a half step back with her lower body but kept us firmly pressed up top. She wanted it, was letting me do it. *Yesssss.* I felt giddy, excited, I dunno, like I was on top of the world. The belt dropped to the floor and I gripped her lush ass and pulled her in to me.

God I loved her hot, soft mouth on mine. Her kiss was sweet, and honest, and so pure. A wild thing, she didn't think when she kissed, she felt, and it was so raw, so real, and so fucking good! I rucked up her sweater until I reached the hem and slid my hands underneath it, sliding them ever upwards until the denim of her jeans gave way to smooth, soft, silky heated skin. She moaned into my mouth at the contact and I couldn't stand it anymore. I had to be inside her. I needed to be inside her. That tiny, soft little moan had me completely undone.

I broke the kiss and lifted the sweater off of her, over her head. I dropped it to the floor and the camisole she had on underneath it joined the sweater in short order. She wore a satin-and-lace nude bra and I couldn't wait to see if the panties matched, but first... I shrugged out of my cut and tossed it at the recliner. It landed, leather on leather with a slap and Red jumped. I pulled my shirt over my head and dropped it to the floor, and pulled her by her denim-clad hips tight up against my chest, skin-on-skin and good Christ, it was almost enough to make me jizz in my pants.

She kissed me, her mouth becoming more insistent the more comfortable she became. I could feel her heartbeat pounding, throbbing steady and sure where my hands smoothed up her ribcage. I curved one arm around her back and held her against me. The other I ran up her body to cup one satin-and-lace-clad breast. I gave the lush globe a squeeze and she moaned again. That sound was officially my new very-favorite sound in the fucking world. I turned us, putting her back to the bed and broke the kiss. I searched her face and found it flushed, her eyes hooded with desire and lust. And yeah, I could totally say the feeling was mutual. So very mutual.

I grinned and gave her a shove. She yipped out a short laugh and tumbled onto her back in the middle of the bed, the down comforter fluffing up and nearly swallowing her. Her red hair turned fiery against the black backdrop. I knelt and she started to sit up. I planted a hand on her chest, between those glorious tits of hers, and pressed her back down.

"Lay back, I'm gonna get your boots." She relaxed after a heartbeat or two of consideration and I knelt, lowering first one zipper and then the other, easing off first one boot and then the other, divesting her legs of the socks she had on while I was at it. I reached for her waistband, keeping eye contact. She bit her lower lip uncertainly, almost shyly and it was the most erotic damned thing.

I slipped the button free of its loop and lowered the zipper slowly.

Holy God, the panties matched, and I think I about died and went to heaven. Yep. I was pretty sure I was dead and this was heaven, because I had the most perfect fucking angel in my bed. *How did I get so lucky?*

I knelt on the bed between her legs and kissed her. She captured my face between her hands and kissed me back and there was a low level need to it, an urgency, and a barely-controlled frenzy this time.

I unbuttoned and unzipped and shoved my shorts to the floor, taking the boxer-briefs down with them.

I fumbled at the laces of my high-tops and got them loose, toeing one after the other off as I lowered my body over hers.

I wanted her skin against mine. She was so warm, and I loved it. There was an awkward couple of half-seconds, while I reached back and ditched my socks, which left her laughing nervously. I shuddered, my erection pressing over her mound... She was soaked through her panties, so hot, and wet, and ready, and she smelled fucking amazing! Like her lilies and all woman, her sex delicately perfumed the air.

I kissed the side of her neck and she must have liked it; she must have liked it a lot because she cried out and she writhed underneath me. The feel of all that silky soft body pressing up against mine, oh, yeah, oh, God, I needed in her. I needed in her, right now. I slid my hands under her back, my lips still working that sweet-spot on the side of her neck, and unclasped her bra. It wasn't the smoothest unhook of my sexual career, but the girl was driving me nuts with the beautiful, soft little whimpers she was making, and her nails digging lightly into the back of my neck where she held me to her.

The bra joined the rest of the textile wreckage on the floor. I disengaged from kissing her reluctantly, but I wanted so badly to see. I cupped her breasts in either hand, the full weight of them so incredibly sexy and alluring. Her nipples were perfect, a soft shell-pink and standing like perfect, beaded pearls. I looked up her body as I took the first one into my mouth. Her back arched so beautifully, her eyes fixed on me, so deep and dark and lovely with the heat of her passion. I rolled the delicate tissue of her nipple between my tongue and my teeth and she cried out. Her eyes closed as she relished the sensation, and she was so beautiful doing it, my heart gave a sharp ache at just how exquisite the vision was.

I hooked my fingers in the waistband of her panties and whisked them off her legs, quickly re-covering her body with my own. I kissed her, our tongues playing against each other, our bodies pressed hot and close, intertwined.

She broke the kiss with a gasp.

"Zander!" My name spilled from her lips an impassioned plea, a siren's call, and I didn't even care. I lined myself up; I would put a condom on, but first, God, I just had to feel her wrapped around me just once, just for a moment, without. I know! It was a selfish, dick thing to do, but I couldn't resist, I couldn't not do it.

"Zander!" she cried desperately and I thrust forward. I felt some unexpected resistance, heard a slight pop, and Mandy cried out – and it wasn't in passion, oh no, I knew the difference. Something was wrong, that was pain. One of her hands was pressed over her mouth, the other against my stomach. I froze, seated deeply inside my girl, and didn't move.

"Oh, shit! Oh, baby, oh, Red, no... Why didn't you tell me, honey? Huh? Why didn't you say something, sugar?" I said in a panic, as I smoothed her copper curls back from her frightened face and felt the worry crease my own.

My girl, my beautiful angelic Red, had been a virgin.

8

Mandy...

"Oh, shit! Oh, baby, oh, Red, no... Why didn't you tell me, honey? Huh? Why didn't you say something, sugar?" His voice was strained tight over his panic. My eyes watered and the moisture slicked down my temples. He smoothed my hair back from my face with gentle hands.

"I was trying to," I whimpered and he closed his eyes. It had hurt, briefly, a flash of pain then nothing. Now I simply felt full and wet, and I swallowed hard, half-afraid there might be something wrong with me. Everett had always described it as something so magical, so full of bliss... We were both so still. Zander searched my face but then he dropped his forehead to mine, closing his eyes, overcome by some unnamed emotion.

"I'm so sorry, sugar. I would have made this so much better, been so much more careful with you, if I'd known," he murmured, his breath warm and gentle against my lips. I pressed my hands to either side of his face and forced him to look at me.

"You know now," I said gently and he nodded.

"I promise, baby, I'm not gonna leave you like this. I promise I'm going to make it good for you." I smiled tremulously at this and nodded.

"I'm gonna move now, okay?" he asked and I nodded again and, oh my God, he moved.

He withdrew from me slowly, searching my face for any signs of discomfort, and finding none, eased his way back in. The sensation of it, the feeling, was as if my body was awash in a tingling wave, as if the most pleasurable electric current gently hummed through me.

My eyes drifted shut as I let the sensations take over. Zander felt so good. His hard body warm against mine, caging me protectively in his embrace. He tenderly moved above me, inside me, and kissed me so sweetly... but too soon, he stilled, and, with a gentle kiss or two, murmured for me to stay put.

"Where are you going?" I asked, startled.

"I need a condom, baby; you're not on birth control."

I blinked.

"Yes, I am." I colored deeply, and he frowned in confusion. "I have been since I was fifteen; it helps keep my periods regular." I felt myself blush an even deeper shade of crimson.

"I guess I just never figured a virgin would be on it," he murmured. "Still want me to get one?" I thought about it and shook my head. I knew there was still a risk, but the moment called for this, for us to simply be, and I was okay with that. Zander looked relieved and started that slow rocking of his hips that was driving me crazy! I smoothed my hands down his body and gripped his ass, urging him on, and he groaned, and it was such a sound! It coiled things low in my abdomen tight and tighter, until I simply couldn't stand it. I knew something had to give, that something should give. I had had orgasms before, through pleasuring myself, but what happened next... there were simply no words to describe it.

The world imploded. It was as if my body had become a bottomless black hole. Every sensation known, hot, cold, soft, sharp, tingling, rough; all of them filtered through me all at once! White shining starbursts, fireworks of passion and beauty and grace went off at the edges of my vision and I bowed beneath him. He held me fast, grounding me in the moment, keeping me protected and safe as pleasure coursed in a rapid-paced closed circuit, over and over again, through my body from my head to my toes. I was vaguely aware of my echoing cry bouncing back from the ceiling at me before his mouth closed over mine in a greedy, desperate kiss.

Zander swallowed my cry, and too soon, the ride was over and I fell limp and quiescent beneath him. He smiled at me and kissed the tip of my nose. I laughed, which twisted into a throaty moan as the pause he'd taken to let me come down ended, and he stroked into me once more.

"Oh, God, Red!" He closed his eyes, the cadence of his breathing becoming ragged and uneven, and with a final violent jerk of his hips, he withdrew from my body, the hot wet splash of his release coating my hip and lower stomach. He held himself up from crushing me and I cradled his head against my breast, smoothing my fingers through his sweat-damp hair, lightly scratching his scalp with my nails, which made him groan, his eyes slipping shut in pleasure.

"Move in a minute, Sugar, just give me a second," he panted.

"No rush," I said, my voice husky from my cries, "I like this."

He pressed his lips against my shoulder in a reverent kiss that made me smile.

"We are definitely doing that again, and soon. Christ, woman!" He propped himself up on his brightly-colored arm depicting all the scenes of Hell, and I looked down between us. Zander grimaced and tipped my chin up, capturing my eyes with his.

"No, don't look," he said.

"Why not?"

"There's a decent amount of blood, baby," I nodded.

"Um, it was my first time. Isn't that normal?"

He smiled.

"Speaking of your first time, c'mon, up you go! You gotta go pee."

I laughed and raised my eyebrows,

"Wait, what?"

"I'm serious. Come on, sugar, let's get you cleaned up." He plucked his briefs off the floor and tugged them on. I managed not to grimace; he was right, there was definitely blood.

"How did we go from 'amazing first-time sex', to 'I need to pee'?" I demanded, and Zander laughed.

"It's a girl thing, figure no one told you," he shrugged. "Either pee right after sex, or run the risk of a real nasty UTI."

My mouth dropped open.

"And just how do you know that, Dr. Zander?" I asked, amused.

Zander had the grace to look embarrassed, but he was honest with me. "Was your first time, baby, but not mine. Not by far, and aside from loving you, I've fucked some real classless chicks." He shrugged, "I've also fucked some real honest ones." I swallowed and nodded. I didn't really want to think about him with anyone else, but Zander was a gorgeous man, it would be silly to think he was... inexperienced.

He opened the closet and held out a robe for me to shrug into, but not before he wiped the worst of the mess off with his discarded black shirt, which he then pitched into a laundry bag in the closet. I peeked into the hall and followed him quietly into the bathroom; he shut the door behind us and locked it.

"You are too fucking cute," he said with a laugh.

"Why?" I asked, grinning.

"Sugar, nobody cares that you just had sex," he said, shaking his head. He took the robe from me, it was gray and warm and made out of sweatshirt material. It had a hood on it and looked like something a boxer would wear; with his wide breadth of shoulders I simply swam in it.

"Besides that, with how you came, I'm pretty sure everyone already knows."

I felt myself color and he pulled me tight against him laughing. He kissed my throat and smacked me on the ass which made me give an indignant yip.

He started the shower and got in saying, "Go pee and get in here," before snapping the black shower curtain closed. I did what he asked and was surprised that I didn't feel weird or uncomfortable about it. I mean, it was kind of hard to feel embarrassed when we'd just done what we'd done, right? I slipped into the tub behind him and he grinned at me, the water cascading over his shoulder and down his chest.

I reached out and traced a line of black flowing script with curious fingers. It was tattooed along his ribs beside the arm covered in demons and hellfire.

"What does it say?" I asked. I couldn't read it with him moving as he was. He stilled and turned so I could read it. "*Through me you go into a city of weeping; through me you go into eternal pain; through me you go amongst the lost people.*" I murmured aloud. I looked at him.

"It's Dante," he said, with a shrug.

"Why this particular line? Why here?" I asked, tracing the small, delicate script with my finger again.

"I'm a southpaw, you know what that means?" I gave him a blank look and shook my head. "It's a boxing term, means I'm left-hand-dominant." He sniffed and turned me under the shower spray, which ran hot and delicious down my back.

"Okay…" I said slowly, not quite understanding.

"It's the kind of fighter I am, sugar," he said softly. I read the line again, '*Through me you go into a city of weeping; through me you go into eternal pain; through me you go amongst the lost people.*' I swallowed hard and suppressed a shudder. When he put it like that, well… I think it was one of the most formidable things I'd ever seen or heard.

I focused on his right side, tracing a curve of an angel's wing near the crook of his elbow. "And this?" I asked, letting my finger trace another line of script along his ribs on that side.

"Milton, from his book *Paradise Lost*."

I read it aloud. "*I sung of Chaos and Eternal Night, Taught by the heav'nly Muse to venture down the dark descent, and up to re-ascend…*" I smiled, "It's beautiful."

He pulled me tight against him.

"No, you're beautiful," and he kissed me, drowning any further thoughts or questions in my body's very visceral reaction. We stayed in the shower for a long time, washing each other clean, kissing and touching, just generally exploring one another for a time.

"Come home with me tonight," he said as he dried my body, and giggling I tried to return the favor, when really, all we were accomplishing was getting in each other's way.

"Oh, I wish I could," I said regretfully. "Tomorrow is Black Friday. It's all 'hands on deck' at the shop. I've spent weeks getting ready for it."

He stopped toweling me off and pulled his robe off the hook, holding it for me.

"Then, your place it is," he said, with that endearing, devilish grin. I laughed and wrapped the robe around me. He wrapped one of the towels around his lean hips and tucked one end. The other he threw over his broad shoulders.

"I need to sleep, you know!" I cried, as we padded barefoot across to his room.

"I know!" He smacked me on the ass and I jumped, another girlish yip coming out of my mouth, which I clapped my hands over.

"Why does it matter so much?" I asked suddenly.

"Red, I just made love to you for the first time. I don't want or need you thinking that it meant anything less than the world to me. You tell the guys, I'll deny it, but my sappy ass wants to sleep with my woman in my arms tonight. That cool with you?" He raised his eyebrows and rubbed the towel he had over his shoulders over his black hair briskly.

I rocked back on my heels and looked him over and finally nodded. "Okay," I agreed. I turned the possibilities and implications of what he was saying over in my mind. Finally, I couldn't help myself, I blurted, "Does this mean we're boyfriend and girlfriend?" I immediately colored at how incredibly and humiliatingly junior-high I just sounded, but it was out in the ether and there was no taking it back so... I shifted on my feet and waited until Zander finished howling with laughter at me.

"Yeah, sugar. Yeah it does," he said, and immediately started howling again, with a great side-splitting laughter that he couldn't breathe through, and that I couldn't help but join, with a titter of laughter of my own.

Okay, I was a dork, but apparently I was his dork now. I kind of liked the sound of that.

9

Revelator...

Mandy's bed sucked. I couldn't get comfortable, but it didn't much matter to me when we were pressed, close and warm, between her crisp cotton sheets, her head cradled on my shoulder and her delicate fingertips tracing patterns on my skin, well, tracing the letters of some of the script across my ribs. It was dark, but it was still early yet. Only like, seven, which I guess was late for my Red, because she had been fighting back yawns for about twenty minutes now.

"What's your real name?" she asked me quietly.

"John Marcus Alexander."

I felt her lips curve against my chest before she said, "I knew it was a nickname, too. 'Zander' I mean. 'Mandy' isn't my name, either," she confessed.

"No?"

"Mm-mm. 'Autumn Amanda Price'."

I laughed softly and she smiled wider, I could hear it in her voice, when she asked, "What?"

"That's how I've always thought of you," I admitted. "Between your eyes and hair, I always kind of thought of you as the embodiment of the season, my goddess of Fall. My girl with eyes the color of turning leaves, and hair to match." I kissed her forehead as she laughed at me.

"Really?" she asked, when I didn't join in.

"Really."

We were silent for the longest time and I thought she might have fallen asleep, but then her voice crept out into the dark.

"Not sure I deserve that," she said, but her body told me how much the sentiment meant to her, her leg coming over mine, her soft form pressing closer in the dark. I put my hand on her nude thigh just above her knee, and brought it up higher, to rest more comfortably on my body. I loved how she twined around me like ivy.

I didn't dignify what she'd said with a response, instead I simply smoothed my hand over every place on her I could reach, and stroking over her satiny skin until her breathing fell off, deepening and evening out with sleep. I didn't think I would be getting much myself, her bed was a serious piece of shit, something meant for a guest room, and not for a grown-up. I mean, shit, it was a full, for one thing, and a coil mattress, for another. My bed back at the club was too, but at least I had thrown a memory-foam pad on it, which did a hell of a lot more than I realized.

She'd tried dressing for bed, but I'd won that veto and her nude body against mine. Damn, I wanted her all over again, but I was betting she needed a day or two before I took her. I tried not to think too hard about the blood. There had been more of it than I remembered from the last time I'd popped a girl's cherry. Everybody was different, I suppose. I still couldn't believe she was mine, and only mine. There was something incredibly appealing about that when it came to my caveman brain, that mine was the only cock that'd been in her.

I drifted off eventually, the cadence of Red's breathing a soothing sound, like waves on a shore, or rainfall from the sky. I jolted awake to her moving around in the dark the next morning.

"What the hell? Come back to bed, Red," I groaned.

She giggled.

"I can't, I have to go to work." She bent over the bed and zipped up her boot. She kissed me, a quick press of lips in the dark, and I reached for her, but she dodged. I sighed and it wasn't at all happy.

"Fucking retail holiday," I cursed, and she huffed a quiet laugh in my direction.

"Sorry I woke you up. Go back to sleep and come see me later?" she asked.

"I'll bring you lunch," I promised, and she made a soft noise of agreement. I was glad she liked the idea of it.

I turned over in her bed and closed my eyes, trying to go back to sleep, but her bed sucked and it was weird being here without her. I lay still, and I guess it hadn't been as weird as I thought, or I was just that tired, because the room was lit with a watery gray light through the curtains the next time I opened my eyes.

I groaned and got up, stretching.

I pulled on my boxer briefs and some cargo shorts. I wore shorts year round, even in the snow; at most I would put some long johns on under 'em. Don't ask me why. Just been doing it since I was a kid. Once I figured I was decent, I went to take a leak. I ran into Dray in the hall when I came out of the bathroom and he eyed me blearily, rubbing the sleep from one of his eyes.

"You fuckin' Mandy?" he asked by way of greeting. I grinned and he frowned, "Be out in a minute. Go make some coffee or something."

I went into the kitchen. Not because he'd told me to, but because I needed a hit of caffeine myself. I listened to Dray take a piss and the toilet flush, and shook my head at how paper-thin the walls were in his old, but well-kept, house. He washed his hands, the blast of water from the sink taking a while, probably he was waiting for it to heat up some.

While he went about his business, I went about mine, measuring out coffee from the canister into the French press next to it, all the while looking around for the coffeemaker. I figured it must be an Everett thing, because there wasn't one in sight, even though I knew he'd had one. I started up the burner on the gas stove and filled the old fashioned whistling teakettle at the sink. Dray came around the corner as I put it on the cooktop over the licking blue gas flame.

"What happened to the coffeemaker?"

Dray made a face.

"My woman. Don't change the subject."

He placed his palms flat against the countertop and leaned in, fixing me with his dark eyes. I raised an eyebrow and a funny look crossed his face.

"What're you looking at me that way for?" he asked.

"Did you know she was a virgin?" I asked him, and he looked surprised.

"No shit?"

"No shit."

"I knew she didn't get much play, but I thought she had at least had some. Now, I really want to know what you're gonna do." He crossed his arms.

"Dude, relax. I know you've known me a long time, and I know I haven't exactly been the committed type either, but Red's different. She's not the kind you love and leave." I crossed my arms too, which was a bit awkward with how big I'd gotten.

"She's like a sister to Em and I'm not gonna lie, after her bein' here almost a year, she's like the little sister I never had. She's a sweet girl and deserves good things." He fixed me with a hard stare as he spoke and held it long after he'd finished. I didn't intimidate easy, so the whole hard-assed routine was sort of lost on me. In this particular case it was a totally wasted effort; we were already on the same page.

"I didn't know about the whole virgin thing either; had I known I would have done a hell of a lot better than my fuckin' room at the club. I have no intention of one-and-done with Red, she's not disposable pussy, man. Never was, 'n never will be. I'm surprised she let me, to be honest." I shook my head and ran my hand back through my hair.

We had a tense standoff for a few seconds. Well, Dray did, anyway. The teakettle started shrieking into the silence. I was caught between wanting to reassure my friend and VP that I had nothing but the best intentions where Red was concerned, and wanting to knock his teeth in for suggesting anything otherwise. I settled for taking the damn kettle off the stove and pouring the hot water into the damn glass carafe of the French press.

"Got any plans for tonight?" Dray asked and the tension eased marginally with the subject change.

"Promised Red I'd bring her by some lunch. I figured I would see if I could get her to come home with me tonight. I want to spend some time with her." I rolled my eyes at the look he was giving me. "I want to get to know her, asshole! Talk about what happened at her folks."

"Yeah. Had a talk with Em about that last night. She filled me in, reluctantly and only a little bit, but it was enough," Dray sighed. I pressed the coffee and poured two cups. Something about using a French press made it come out richer, the coffee taking on a velvety texture and whatever the shit was that Irish bought, it was fuckin' good! It was also a kick in the pants. I was awake, for sure.

"What do you eat for breakfast? Ain't you training?" he asked. I nodded and rattled off my morning diet.

"You're on your own. That's disgusting," he stated flatly.

"And that's why you'll never be as cut as me," I said, saluting him with my coffee. He snorted and I sat in long contemplation of the flowers I'd bought Red, which rested on the kitchen counter between us. We'd forgotten them at the club altogether the night before. I felt a wicked smile curve my lips as I thought back to why it was so easy to forget about 'em.

Dray's voice interrupted my thoughts. "We got something going on tonight. Take Red home with you, keep her at your place," he said.

I felt an eyebrow go up.

"The way you say that sounds like an order from my VP."

"It is," he said and took another swallow of his coffee. "Me and some of the guys are going out for a little retribution for your place of business."

"In that case, oh, hell no, you ain't going without me!" The coffee mug in my hand made a sharp sound against the counter when I set it down.

"You need to stay clean for the fight next month. Trigger is in on this, you stay home with your woman where she can front you an alibi if the cops happen to come sniffin' around. We both want and need you in that ring." Dray gave me a pointed look and I felt suspicion take hold.

"Why? What you got riding on this fight?" I asked.

Dray grinned.

"Club needed some revenue after membership was on life-support for so long; Dragon took a vote. We're placing the last few months of dues on a bet on you, my man,"

I looked over, amused.

"That so?" I asked.

"Yep. So stay clean, fight hard, and don't fuck up. Whole club is counting on you." He gave me a shit-eating grin.

"No pressure," I grumbled, but felt a matching grin of my own take over my face. "So, what're you guys up to tonight, anyway?" I asked.

Dray shook his head. "Plausible deniability, bro," he said and I nodded. Yeah, I knew the drill. I didn't have to like it, though. My memory shifted, drifting back to the summer lake run and of Shelly, her pale and haunted face, lip busted wide open, lap draped in a random sheet as she shivered with shock in the cabin's small dining room. The tortured and torn look on Ghost's face as he realized what was what, and the incredible guilt that had swamped him as he'd taken the blame all on himself. I shook my head to clear it.

"Whatever you do, make it count," I said, and locked eyes with Dray. "Make it hurt."

He nodded and nothing else needed to be said.

I went back into Red's room and felt a fine burning rage take hold in my chest. I ripped my shirt over my head and onto my body, and pulled on my All-Stars. I needed to hurt something.

My anger was out of its box and burning me up from the inside out and only one or two things would take the edge off it at this point.

I needed to plow my fist into another dude's face, or work myself out so hard my limbs felt like overused rubber. There was a third option, back in the day, and that had been some hard and punishing sex, but I wouldn't do that to Red, and I wasn't ever going to be the man to satisfy that particular urge with anyone else ever again. The nameless, faceless parade of sluts and the occasional hooker was a thing of the past, now that Red was in the picture. I just didn't want 'em anymore. I just wanted her. Her, and to hurt every last motherfucker in a Suicide Kings cut that wanted to beef with me or any one of my brothers.

Yeah. That sounded about right.

10

Mandy...

I was half-afraid Zander would stand me up. The possibility of him disappearing after last night... Well, I tried valiantly to banish the thought from my head, but the anxiety just kept creeping back in. I was hard at work in my kitchen, and Soul Fuel was incredibly busy! As soon as the first hour had gone by and I saw what we were selling the most of, I immediately started in making more of them. Just when it looked like we were going to run out of the truffles, I completed a double batch, which was really a double batch of a quadruple batch of my grandparent's original recipe.

"Mandy-girl!" Zeb called from the doorway, in his rich and melodic accent.

"Yes?" I asked, looking up from the marble countertop I was scraping fine curls of chocolate off of, for decorating purposes.

"Someone to see you, girl," he said and my heart leapt. I felt my breath catch in my throat as he stepped aside, and, where I thought I would see Zander, my mother stood wringing the strap of her handbag between her hands.

"Mom!" I cried, astonished and wiped my hands on my apron.

She rarely went anywhere without daddy, and I ran my tongue nervously over the slight split in my lip from yesterday.

"Oh, um, I'm here by myself," she said and asked, "May I come in?"

"Of course!" I stepped around the counter and pulled two stools out from under its top. I got up on one while my mom hopped up on the other.

"Are you okay?" she asked me quietly after the silence had dragged out for a moment or two. I smiled.

"Absolutely."

"That boy who came to the house yesterday..." I smiled in spite of myself.

"Zander? He's not a boy, mom; he's, like, ten years older than I am!"

She searched my face, worried.

"Is he in a gang?" she asked.

"Nope, the Sacred Hearts is a club. Not a gang."

My mother and I both turned sharply at the sound of Zander's voice from the kitchen doorway. He stood in his typical long shorts and sleeveless shirt under his black leather vest, a couple of full brown paper bags in his large hands. He padded into my kitchen on those soft rubber-soled red canvas high tops of his and set the bags on the counter between me and my mom. One of his massive arms circled my waist and he stood hip to hip with me, turning those chocolate-caramel-colored eyes of his on my mother, searching her face.

"He touch you after I left?" he asked her, and my mother blanched and shook her head. I put a hand on my mother's arm.

"It's okay, mom. Zander's a good guy," I smiled a reassuring smile.

"John Alexander," he said, holding out a hand to my mother.

"Melinda Price," she made to shake Zander's hand but at the last second, he turned it in his grasp with that devil-may-care smile of his and kissed my mom's knuckles like some kind of old-fashioned gentleman.

"Oh my!" My mother laughed and smiled, and put a hand to her chest, flustered.

"Mom just got here," I murmured.

"Want me to come back later?" he asked, eyeing us both. I smiled and shook my head, my mother smiled too.

"No, that's all right, John. Please stay." She shot me a questioning look and Zander grinned.

"Look, I'm real sorry we had to be introduced like this after yesterday going down the way it did." He had the grace to look embarrassed. "But, I'm not sorry I said anything that I said to your husband. And I mean it: he touches you or Mandy again, I'll be there."

I fixed my eyes on my mother's wedding set where it sparkled under the kitchen light.

"Jim's not normally like that... I think he was..."

"Mom, stop! It's okay, you don't have to make excuses for him anymore!" I rubbed my forehead. "I'm not, anyway... Dad's been like that my whole life, and the older I get the worse he gets. I just wish I knew why he hated me so darn much."

My mother looked positively heartbroken in that instant.

"Oh, Mandy-girl, oh, baby, he doesn't hate you, Honey... he hates me." She took my hands in hers.

"Why, Mom?" I asked, desperate for an answer to the question that had been plaguing me since I was a child. "And why would he disown me like that?" I stared at her and let the pleading look on my face finish doing the talking for me.

My mother's face collapsed into lines of sorrow, and the din from out in the shop lessened by half. We turned, Everett was leaning on the inside of the closed kitchen door.

"Hello, Everett, dear," my mother said, ever so polite.

"Hi, Mrs. Price." Everett smiled, but it was watered-down.

"Perhaps some privacy would be best for this," my mother tried, but failed.

I shook my head.

"Mom, Everett is family, as sure as anything, and Zander..." I looked at him and he gave me a crooked smile.

"Mrs. Price, I've loved your daughter for a while now, and I'd really like to be here for her, if it's all right with you," he said and my mother's look softened.

"You have to understand it was a long time ago," my mother began and sniffed. Everett went over to the paper towel dispenser and ripped two out, bringing them over to my mom.

"Thank you," my mother said, and dabbed at her eyes.

"Mom, just tell me, please?" I pleaded.

She took a fortifying breath and let it out slowly.

"I'm so sorry, Baby girl. I cheated on your father, before you were born, and the man I was unfaithful with..." she rolled her lips and I blinked and swallowed hard.

"You what?" I asked, and my voice sounded hollow. Zander's arms tightened around me where I sat. I stared at my mother in stony silence while I tried to process what she was saying.

"He was a high school sweetheart of mine. Your father and I, our marriage was in trouble and... He was a member of our church and a good man. When we all three saw what it was doing to Jim and I's marriage, when the guilt became too much... David left, and then I found out I was pregnant and we couldn't be sure, and then you were born and..."

Everett put her arms around my mother, heck, our mother, and hugged her as she dissolved into sobs. I swallowed hard, unsure how to feel right this second, but no matter what mistakes were made, and by whom... I slipped off the stool I was perched on and Zander let me go, my arms going around my mother.

"I love you, mom." I sniffed and held her tight. I would not cry.

"It's okay, we'll figure it out somehow," I murmured, but I wasn't sure how you figured something like this out, I mean... holy geeze! Wow. I looked at Everett over my mom's head and I think she looked as poleaxed as I felt. Zander's hand was a warm, comforting weight at the small of my back as he lent me silent strength from behind.

"I think your whole family needs to talk, Red," he said and my mother nodded emphatically.

"Come on Sunday?" my mother asked, hopefully.

"Daddy doesn't want me there," I said, exasperated, playing our last exchange over in my mind.

"No, he does, I'm certain of it. He went to the church after you left, to pray for guidance. When he came home we had a good talk. At his heart, your father is a good and decent man Mandy – "

I scoffed, I couldn't help myself, and I stared up into one of the kitchen light fixtures.

"He is!" my mother insisted, and I dropped my eyes back down to hers.

"I need to think about all of this," I said and she nodded.

"If she does come, she's not going alone," Zander said firmly. My mother nodded.

"I'll go with her," Everett told him, and I cut in.

"I'm here, I'm right here! And if I decide to go, you'd best set the table for six, because I'm not coming without Zander, Evy, and Dray."

I shook; I loved my mother, I loved her very much, but this was a lot to process. I would never in a million years have suspected that what my father had said the day before was something he meant literally and not just figuratively. I stepped back from my mom and wiped my nose with the back of my hand.

Whatever. My dad was a jerk at home. I'd known this for a very long time, and now it all made sense, the tumblers all falling into place now that I had the key bit of information to turn in the lock that was the whole mess. Still, so many questions ran through my mind, and before I could stop them, some of them came pouring out of my mouth.

"Why did you stay with him? How could you let him do that to us?" I shivered and Zander stepped in front of me and pulled me against him. He was so warm; I felt chilled. I stared at my mom from over his shoulder and felt a couple of tears get loose.

"I stayed because I made a commitment to your dad under the eyes of God, in the house of God, baby. I took my vows seriously..."

I scoffed again, and my mother flinched, and I instantly felt bad. I wanted to be angry at my mother and I was, but most of the anger, and yes, even hatred, that twisted in my heart was reserved for my... I didn't even know what to call him anymore. A sob tore from me and Zander clutched me tighter against his chest.

"You should probably go," he said. "We'll be there on Sunday to sort this shit out; right now she needs time to get through all this,"

I let him hold me and I let him handle it. I didn't want to handle it anymore. My mother was silent and cried as Everett took her out of the kitchen. Zander sat me back up on my stool but kept his hold on me. He leaned back and palmed the side of my face gently, smoothing his thumb through a track of moisture on my cheek.

"God you got a brass pair," he muttered and pulled me into a hug with a sigh.

I rasped a laugh and asked, "What?"

"Takes a whole lot of shit blowing up in your face to make you cry, and even then, one or two tears and you're done." He kissed the side of my neck through my hair. I sniffed and wiped under my eyes.

"Crying, in my house growing up, was just something you simply didn't do," I said honestly, and it was as if my heart gave a sigh of relief at the burden that was lifted from it. No more secrets, thank God. Everett came back in the kitchen.

"Hey," she said.

"Hey. Who's got the front?" I asked.

"Don't worry about that right now, okay? How are you doing?" she asked.

"I'll be okay," which was true; there were worst things in life weren't there? I went to the sink automatically and washed my hands.

"Brought lunch," Zander said dryly, but he was watching me intently.

"Not very hungry now," I murmured and he nodded. Lexie, one of our part-time counter girls, pushed through the kitchen door.

"Sorry, Everett, need some help, another rush just came in. It's either you or Zeb." Her long blonde ponytail slipped over her shoulder, her blue eyes uncertain at the mention of the Sacred Heart brother out there.

"I'm coming, Lexie," Ev said with a smile, and then she turned her steely blues on Zander, jabbing a sharp finger in his direction.

"You take care of my girl!" she crowed.

"Plan on it," he said dryly, but he was talking to the swinging kitchen door. He turned contemplative eyes on me. I sighed and shook my head.

"It'll be all right," I said and he gave me that smile, suffusing me with warmth.

"That's my line, sugar." He sat up on the stool I'd vacated. I tried to make light of things and stuck my tongue out at him.

"Well, consider it stolen."

I returned to curling chocolate shavings with my painter's knife from the marble countertop, to Zander's booming laughter. I smiled faintly to myself but I could feel the tension between my shoulder blades and in my upper back as I reeled on the inside from the implications of what my mother had told me.

Before I knew it I found myself praying on it, struggling to come to terms with an entire childhood... twenty-one years... of lies. I missed my daddy from when I was a child. The one who held my hand as we crossed the parking lot. The one that rode the teacups in Disney World with me, laughing, when I was six. I missed my dad when he was a dad. Before I started to grow into my own, and I guess he started to see more of this David person in me than himself.

Large, gentle hands plucked the knife from my shaking fingers and Zander pulled me into a gentle hold. He murmured soothing things against the side of my neck while I stared sightless at the hardening chocolate. I let him sooth me a moment more and pulled back gently.

"I need to finish before it gets too hard for me to curl."

"Okay, babe. I'm going to make a quick call out front, that cool with you?" he asked. I nodded, smoothing my palms over the rough canvas of my apron.

"Yeah."

"Okay, back in a minute." He kissed me, a quick soft press of his mouth to mine and one I gratefully returned.

"I apologize!" I blurted when he opened the kitchen door.

He froze.

"For what?" he asked.

"For leaning on you so hard the last few days, that you've suddenly found yourself tangled up in all my problems, when I know you're still dealing with your business and the club and all of that." He let the door close.

"Sugar, there's no place I'd rather be than here helping you. I'm glad I showed up when I did... both times." He smiled, his eyes so warm and sweet as they looked me over.

"Thank you," I murmured. He nodded.

"Be right back." He gave me one more long, considering look.

"Dis is stayin' at his boyfriend's place tonight. Come home with me," he said abruptly. I thought about it a second and nodded.

"I'd like that, I think."

"Good. Settled, then. Back in a sec." He disappeared through the door and I hoped that Everett would understand. A half-second later, she slipped into the kitchen as if my thought had conjured her by magic.

"Going home with Zander?" she asked and I nodded. She smiled. "He's been there for you and been good for you the last few days," she stated.

"Yes, he has." I blushed furiously and she smiled wide. We'd had the entire sordid girl talk about my first time in the car on the way in this morning. Everett hugged me close and I hugged her back.

"I know you almost as well as I know myself," she stated dryly. "So are you feeling what I'm feeling about your da'?" she asked.

"Almost relieved?" I asked.

She laughed, "Certainly explains a lot."

"Yeah it does," I said.

Everett knocked her shoulder lightly in to mine. "I think it's a good thing you want to talk to Zander rather than me about this one. I'm close to the situation. I know your da' and how it's been and all of that. All I could tell you is what you already know and from the same perspective. Zander might have something different for you."

I sighed and said the thing that Everett and I had fantasized about for years. "Why couldn't my mom…"

She picked up and finished with me

"…and my/your da' have gotten together when we were growing up?" We laughed lightly together.

"My da' loved my mum… so much. I wish I had more than just the one picture of them together. I wish I had some kind of journal or something to know what she was like," she said wistfully.

"I just wish my dad loved me. Saw me for me and could be proud of me." I leaned my butt against the kitchen's sink.

"I know that look," she said and crossed her arms.

"What look?" I asked.

"The one written all over your face that spells out regret but also says you're going to forgive him and keep trying. I've seen it a thousand times before." She rolled her eyes. I pursed my lips.

"Shows you don't know everything. I wasn't thinking about my dad just then."

Everett's eyebrows went up.

"Your mom?"

"It's the first time she's ever let me down, and it's just so big." I sighed.

Everett snorted. "Bullshit! Your mom has been letting you down your entire life! Every time she let him hit you, or her, without standing up to him." Everett shook her head. "I love you, Mandy, but it stops here. I won't be silent anymore. I can't be silent anymore."

I nodded. "It wasn't fair of me to ask you to keep such a big secret anyway," I admitted and Everett softened.

"It all had to come crashing down at some point. I'm just glad Zander was there to protect you when it did," she said. The kitchen door opened and the man of the hour stepped in.

"I'm glad I was there, too, but Red had it handled. I'm pretty sure she was going to serve him a mean right hook any second." He put up his fists and went through some boxing movements and I smiled, but it wasn't exactly easy or a comfortable one.

"Violence isn't Mandy's thing," Everett said, "Never was and never will be,"

Zander straightened up.

"I know, that's why it was funny, and it's one of the reasons I love her like I do." He quirked that grin that made the butterflies in my insides lift off.

"Me, too," Everett said.

I finished with my chocolate curls and laid them artfully over the top of the chocolate ganache-coated fudge cake and slid it towards Everett. She picked it up and took it out to the display case, carefully backing out the kitchen door.

Zander retook his seat at the counter and sat quietly, watching me move around the kitchen, cleaning up and moving fluidly on to the next project. After another hour I joined him at the counter, where we quietly ate our lunch.

I was appreciative of the fact that he didn't feel the need to fill the silence; that he gave me time to sort through the things in my head.

It was nice to have a presence other than Everett in my life that didn't tell me how I should feel, or react, or how to handle things, but at the same time I was feeling a little lost at not having these things spelled out for me. What did that say about me?

I did what I was raised to do in these situations, I practiced what my father preached, and I silently prayed for guidance and for some kind of answer to the conundrum that was the whole situation.

With any luck, God would be listening.

11

———

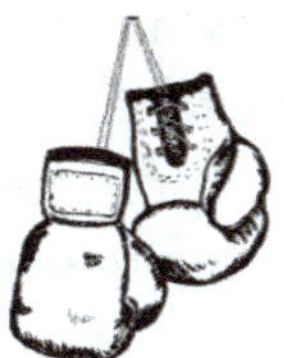

Revelator...

I'd called Dray and asked if the thing with Red's dad had been gotten to. He said he'd check and would hit me right back, and he was dependable like that, so I waited. My phone buzzed in my hand less than two minutes later.

"Nope, not yet. Why?" he asked.

"Hold off," I'd told him, and laid out what had just gone down in my Red's kitchen. Dray was silent for a minute.

"What're you thinkin'?" he asked.

With the image of Red's too-solemn face still burned into my brain, I'd said, "I'm thinkin' that it's time to break the cycle for her, but that it's also time to send a message to her daddy that he'll never forget."

"Oh? And how do you propose we do that?"

So I sketched out the idea I had forming in my brain. I could almost hear my VP grin through the phone.

"You know what, brother? I think you're onto something, and I think that it might be good, not just for Mandy, but for the club, too. We been back-sliding into some gnarly-ass shit with the Suicide Cunts. This might just be a good reminder that there's something out there other than blood and violence and blowing shit up that we could be doing. Let me run it by my pops."

"Good deal. I gotta go, man. I got Red to agree to stay at my place tonight."

"Good times. Talk to you later, bro."

I ducked back into the shop and found Red, with Irish at her side, saying she was glad I'd been there when the shit went down. I tried to lighten the mood, but failed miserably, so I just tried to content myself with being near Mandy while she worked.

"Why are you looking at me that way?" she asked, around an hour later, when she seated herself at the counter with me. She pulled a burrito out of the sack I'd brought in with me. She started to unwrap it but I stilled her hands.

"You're going to make a mess," I laughed. "Let me show you how these are done." I brought out the plastic knife and fork from the bag and cut into the thing with surgical precision, squishing the two ends together to open it up more. I handed her the fork for the neat little foil-and-flour-tortilla bowl.

"Seriously?" she asked.

"What?"

"This is not how you eat a burrito!" She laughed at me.

"It is, if you don't want to wear it." I shrugged and she dug in, humoring me.

"This feels so wrong, but it tastes so good!" she said a few bites in, and I laughed, working on my own, which was –so– not on my meal plan, but I would work it off as soon as I got home. I was human and allowed to cheat every once in a while. Of course, come weigh-in, I'd probably be kicking my own ass for the burrito but you know, whatever... Nature of the beast.

"Thank you for being here," she said quietly a few minutes later. "I'm sure you could be doing any number of things right now."

"Yeah, but I really want to be doing you," I winked, and she blushed and laughed, giving me a gentle shove.

"Pervert!" she declared.

"You have no idea, but no worries, Red, I'm gonna show you." I winked at her again, and she got seven different kinds of flustered.

"I um, worry about that, you know?" she confessed.

"About what?"

"My inexperience, I mean I... um... and you, well..."

I chuckled. "What, the fact that before I met you I could be qualified as a top-ranking member in the male-slut hall of fame?" She really blushed at that and fixed her eyes on her burrito.

"I wouldn't put it like that," she said weakly, and I grinned.

"I know, that's why I did it for yah. And to answer your question, I'm not worried about it in the slightest, but I can see you are, and I'm telling you right now, you ain't got no reason to worry."

She met my eyes reluctantly. "Okay," she said quietly, I could tell she didn't quite believe me, but that was okay. I had her to myself all night, tonight.

"What time are you out of here?" I asked.

"Three more hours, we close at our regular time. I think it might be quieting down out there."

We finished our food quietly and she went back to moving, wraithlike, through her kitchen. I fucked around on my phone for some of it, when really what I wanted to do was take us both the hell out of there and back to my place.

The clock ran down slower than the pregnant cow on methadone crossed the field, but finally, with a gusty sigh, my girl undid her apron and hung it neatly on a hook set in the wall by the big freezer thing.

"'Bout ready?" I asked her nonchalantly. She gave me a wry smile.

"Just about," she said, and with my arm around her waist, we exited the kitchen. "Need a ride, or is Dray coming?" she asked Everett.

"Ride, Dray is at the club, I'm supposed to meet him. I was going to ask if you could drop me off there."

"Tell you girls what. Let's head to your place so Mandy can get an overnight bag and drop off her car, and I'll give you a ride to the club, since it's on the way to my place."

The girls both nodded.

"Sounds great. It'll let me throw some things together for tomorrow, too," Everett said.

They went through the motions of final clean up and shutting down.

"When did Zeb take off?" I asked.

"When it was clear you weren't going anywhere, I told him to go; there wasn't any point in having both of you here," Everett stated flatly.

"Surprised he went," I said.

Everett scowled and Mandy laughed at her.

"He didn't listen to her! I know that look anywhere."

Everett menaced Mandy with the cloth she was using to wipe off glass cleaner from the front of the display cases.

"You're right, damn you. I had to call Dray and he had to tell him to go."

"Yeeeeah," I drawled, "the new guys may be fully-patched but they still act like prospects sometimes."

"Except for Grinder; he probably would have just gone," Mandy observed. Everett rolled her eyes at his name.

"Problem with Grinder?" I asked.

"He's just a big damned flirt and doesn't know when to turn it down a notch," Everett declared. Red shifted.

"He make you uncomfortable?" I asked her, eyeing her carefully.

"Depends, are you going to do something stupid?" she asked, which was pretty much all the answer I really needed.

"Stupid how?" I asked, grinning.

"Like punch him or something?"

I laughed. "Does he make you uncomfortable?" I repeated the question.

Mandy paused in her sweeping and shook her head, "No."

"You suck at lying, sugar."

She looked up, alarmed, as Everett started to howl with laughter. Red frowned at her best friend and stuck out her tongue. I laughed, too.

I followed the girls home and waited while they threw some of their shit together. Mandy paused at her flowers I'd brought her the day before and smelled them, a slight smile curving her lips, before she shouldered her small gym bag and turned to me, ready to go. Irish came out right behind her.

"All set," she declared, and after locking up the house, we trooped out to my Chevelle.

Mandy got in back. I frowned.

"What're you doing, babe?" I asked.

"Everett's getting out first; I'll switch then." She smiled warmly at me.

Everett sighed.

"This isn't high school anymore, Mandy," she chided.

"I know." Red smiled brightly at her friend, and Everett got in. I filed the exchange away for later and drove us to the club, letting Ev out in front. Mandy switched into the front seat after handing her BFF her bag and giving her a hug. Everett waved over her shoulder before disappearing inside. Red fastened her seatbelt and looked up at me, running straight into the kiss I had waiting for her.

I kissed her carefully, leaned way over the center console, which didn't exactly make things comfortable for an extended make-out session. I pulled back and smiled at her and she smiled back, almost shyly in return. Good. She had an idea of what we were gonna be up to then.

I shifted the car into first and pulled out, headed for home. The car ride was silent, Red looking out at the scenery, but not really seeing it. When I pulled up in front of the house, she looked at it without comment.

"Not much to look at. Was my dad's-dad's place. He was a son of a bitch, so was my pops." I let my gaze roam the dilapidated one-story rambler. The yard was overgrown, choked with brown, dried-up weeds. The tan-and-brown paint was peeling off the sides of the house.

"You don't pull into the garage?" she asked.

"It's full of shit from the shop right now," I told her, and a cloud of some unnamed emotion passed over her face. "You okay, Red?" I asked.

She unhooked her seatbelt. "I'm fine, it's just..." she trailed off, staring sightless off into space.

"Just what, sugar?" I kept my voice low and soft.

"It scared me. That level of violence." Her hazel eyes met mine and searched my face. "What if you'd been there? Or Disney had gone inside?"

I trailed a fingertip down the silky skin of one of her cheeks.

"I wasn't, sugar, and he didn't. Let's go inside. I'll build us a fire and we can take some time out to relax."

"I'd like that."

"Kind of figured you would."

We popped open our doors and I came around to her side, taking her bag out of her hands and slinging it over my shoulder. She put her free hand in mine, my keys lightly spiking into our palms, as we walked to the front door. I keyed us in and hung them on the hook by the door.

"Hey, Disney! You here?" I called out.

"Yeah!"

"Got company!" I called, just in case he decided to wander out here in his Fruit of the Looms or some shit. He came around the corner, fully dressed, slinging on his jacket and cut.

"Hey, Mandy!" He beamed at my girl and she smiled.

"Thought you were out with Aaron tonight," I grunted.

"He's on his way now."

I nodded and stepped past him.

"Gonna put your bag in my room, sugar. Make yourself at home." She smiled at me, and Disney started chatting with her as I made my way up the hall and towards the back. I set her bag on the foot of my bed and tried not to feel too self-conscious about the outdated, rundown nature of the house. I mean, shit, she was used to living in places that looked like something out of a magazine, if Dray's place was anything to go by. I'm pretty sure her folks' place was nice too, judging by the outside of it.

My house, though? The thing had been built in the late sixties, early seventies, and aside from a few coats of interior and exterior paint throughout the years, not much else had been updated about it. The carpet, where there was carpet, was old and shabby; the linoleum and cupboards and bathroom fixtures were all shit that had come with the house; hell, even the range and fridge were older than I was.

It wasn't much to look at, but it was mine, and it had the potential to be nice with some serious remodeling.

I switched out of what I was wearing and into some gym clothes. I had to put in an evening work-out, keep on an even training schedule. It'd only take me an hour, hour-and-a-half, tops, with a shower. I'd get Mandy set up on the couch and a fire going in the grate, pound it out, and we'd be good to go for the rest of the evening. A soft knock on my bedroom's door frame had me wheeling around.

"Dis leave?" I asked.

"Mm-hm."

"I need to hit the gym, stick to my training. Let me get a fire started and get you comfortable first, though."

"Okay." Her voice was so soft and sweet, like her; it made me smile. I walked back out into the living room with her. The house may be rundown and old, but the furniture was decent in the living room. A black leather couch and love seat, and a fifty-inch flat-screen TV took up most of the space. Red sank down onto the couch at my urging, and I started working on starting a fire in the old-ass grate.

"You don't have to do all that, you know."

I smiled to myself. "I know, sugar. I want to. You're a treasure and I want you to be comfortable." I shrugged haphazardly and shoved some newspaper under the logs.

"Zander, really, it's just nice to be here with you."

I lit the paper and sat back on my heels. I looked over my shoulder at her, and when I was sure that the Presto-Log in with the rest of the regular ones was gonna catch, I slid across the open expanse of carpet between us. I placed my hands on her knees and looked up into her face. Her hands covered mine.

"I want good things for you, babe," I murmured.

"I know, thank you." She was quiet for a moment. So was I, as we studied each other.

"When will you be back?" she asked quietly.

"Not going anywhere, baby, home gym in the back. It'll take me an hour, hour-and-a-half. You good?" She nodded silently. I reared up and kissed her forehead.

I pulled the remote off the TV stand and handed it to her.

"Make yourself at home; I mean it."

She nodded and I tore myself away, as much as I didn't want to, and headed for the back room. I would have skipped it if I could have but I couldn't, so...

Damn.

12

Mandy...

Music started up a few seconds later in the back of the house. Hard-hitting and loud, the suddenness of it was startling. I set the remote Zander had given me off to the side and instead pulled my Kindle from my purse. The fire was catching and starting to throw some warmth out, beating back the slightly damp chill that was pervasive in the house.

I hadn't any idea what to expect coming to Zander's home, but this... this wasn't at all what I'd envisioned. I don't know why, but I had always pictured him as an apartment-dweller. A nice two-bedroom with uniform white walls. I'd been surprised when he'd pulled into a neighborhood full of houses.

I took in the shabby interior of the house. It was dusty, but relatively neat. It wasn't even close to the sparkling perfection I'd been raised in, but then again, I'd had the impression from before that Zander's upbringing was nothing like mine, except, maybe, in one aspect. I'd heard comments alluding to the fact that Zander's father had a volatile temper, something Zander had apparently inherited, though I'd yet to see it. I rose to my feet and chewed my lip in indecision. He'd said to make myself at home, but I couldn't, quite.

I sat back down and tried to read, but after the fourth or fifth time of raking my eyes over the same line or paragraph, I realized the effort was futile, at best, so I put the thing away. I took off my shoes and padded down the hall in my thick wool socks, thinking that maybe, if I changed into something more comfortable than my jeans...

I paused outside Zander's bedroom door and looked into the lighted doorway across the hall from it.

'Home gym', indeed! This was the nicest room of the house, and by all appearances had been the master bedroom. The walls were a crisp white, and the far left-hand wall, as you went through the doorway, was floor-to-ceiling mirrors. Windows took up the back wall, but white cloth shades were pulled from ceiling to floor over them. There was a darkened doorway to a small bathroom in the far right corner, and the rest of the room was filled with various weight equipment, the hardwood floors gleaming beneath black rubber mats on which rested the shiny white and chrome equipment.

Zander straddled a bench, his back to me and the doorway, gripping a bar that was attached to a cable at its middle, turned down at either end and capped in black rubber handles. His head bowed, he pulled the bar to the back of his neck across his powerful shoulders, the muscles coiling and bunching beneath his tattoos, the flames of his left arm dancing, the clouds of his right arm boiling as he pulled and eased off, pulled and eased off. I swallowed hard, struck by the fluid grace with which he moved until he reached the end of whatever count he'd been holding and with a metallic clack let the weights rest back in their place. I was frozen in my place, watching him, and blushing furiously at how inappropriate it must be. The thought broke me out of my locked status and I ducked into his room and sat heavily on the edge of the mattress beside my packed bag.

I didn't regret having sex with Zander; not at all. In fact, I was pretty sure I was ready to again and I knew he felt the same, from the heated looks and constant nearness. Still, I felt incredibly guilty at times for going against my father's, and the church's, teachings on the subject. That felt a little ridiculous now. My dad and my mom were nothing but big fat liars, it seemed. That hurt, that hurt, incredibly so, and I really didn't want to think about it. I didn't want to feel these things, I simply wanted to be here, with Zander, where I felt safe and cherished – and that was the heart of it, really.

Zander made me feel special. Every time he looked at me, every time he touched or kissed me, he made me feel like he'd been waiting for so long just for me to come along and that was the sweetest thing anyone had done for me, no matter whether it was conscious or unconscious on his part. I'd never been in love before, but I was pretty sure that that was what this was, the feeling that stirred in my chest, just beneath my breastbone whenever I thought of him, or whenever he smiled at me. A feeling like I weighed nothing at all overtook me until I felt as light and insubstantial as the air I breathed.

I listened to the rhythmic click and clank of metal against metal, at odds with the music pounding from speakers I hadn't noticed in the room when I'd been surreptitiously watching him. The music cut after a few moments and I heard him sniff and cough. I ghosted to the door to his gym, but he had disappeared. The darkened rectangle that I had assumed was the bathroom was lit and the water in the shower was cranked on.

I had never been a brave or wanton girl. I had always done what was expected of me and stayed neatly within the boundaries, however restrictive, that my parents had laid down for me. But after today, I was sick and tired of being who my family wanted me to be, especially after finding out that neither of them were who they presented. Perhaps it was wrong of me, I mean they were human and all humans were prone to mistakes, but I wanted this. I wanted to be close to Zander, to have him hold me, to have him kiss me and to replace all these ugly feelings with something beautiful for a time and so before I knew what I was doing, I found myself threading my way through his weight equipment and stepping through the bathroom doorway.

He was in the shower, behind the opaque curtain, and so, before I lost my nerve I slipped my sweater over my head, shivering in the cool air of the bathroom. Warm steam puffed out from behind the curtain as I let the rest of my clothes fall, and after quickly rearranging my hair with the basket and stick to twist it all up off my neck rather than only half-up the way I'd had it before, I boldly and bravely pulled back the curtain and stepped into the bath, before I could lose my nerve.

"Hey, sugar." Zander smiled appreciatively and leaned back into the shower's spray, water coating his chest and running down his body, magnifying the delicate black script along his ribs.

"Hi," I said, softly.

"C'mere." He reached for me and I gladly went into his arms, our lips found each other and we kissed slowly and sweetly. He was so warm and I pressed my body to his, his hands roaming freely over my skin causing me to heat up from the inside. He turned me in the close space, so that the water hit my back and I gasped into his mouth. It was hot, just this side of being too hot. I squirmed in his arms and he chuckled, low and bass, and the sound thrummed through me turning my gasp into a sultry moan I didn't even know I had in me.

The sound that emitted from my throat had Zander pressing my body even closer to his. He palmed the outside of my thigh and pressed me back against the shower wall. His kiss became an urgent and wild thing. He broke the kiss, his chest heaving with desire, and pressed his forehead to my chest, just below the hollow of my throat. I smoothed my hands up his solid physique and buried my fingers in the thick wet hair at the back of his head, tugging gently. He tipped his head back, his chocolate-caramel eyes darker, somehow, with the base things he wanted to do to me.

"What's wrong?" I asked.

"Nothing, sugar. I just want you. Want to love you, but shower sex, as awesome as it is on TV, is just about completely impractical." I laughed and he smiled.

"So, take me to the bedroom," I said, and he blinked as if he hadn't expected me to suggest such a thing. Truthfully, I surprised myself with it, too.

"Oh, I intend to, but first…" He picked up a bar of Dove soap and I giggled. "What's so funny?" he asked.

"Same soap I use," I murmured.

"Gotta take care of your skin when you're inked, or the tats start lookin' like hell," He soaped up his hands and glided them over my skin. I sighed out, my eyes slipping shut.

"Pun intended?" I asked, trailing a finger down his fiery arm.

He chuckled, "No, but it was a pretty good one," and then we were silent as I grew relaxed under his soap-slicked palms gliding over my skin. He washed every inch of me and almost, himself, with how he pressed our bodies together. I gasped when he slipped his hand between my legs, teasing at the sensitive folds, paying extra attention to the top of my sex.

He let me return the favor, let me wash him and explore him just as thoroughly with my fingers while the water slowly began to grow tepid. We were both fairly pruned, our fingertips wrinkled by the time we finished our explorations and he shut off the tap. He snatched a towel off of the bar outside the curtain and gathered me to him, drying me gently and wrapping me in the thick terrycloth material. He wrapped another towel down low around his hips and, his hands on mine, turned my back to his front and guided me out through the shiny metal equipment, across the hall and into his room.

He shut the door behind him, batted my bag to the floor and tugged the towel away from me, letting it fall to the floor. I shivered in the bedroom's cool air and he pulled my body tight against his, backing me up against the foot of the bed. I tugged the tucked corner of his towel while we kissed, and let it fall to the floor, wrapping my hand around the burning hard length of him. He sighed out against my mouth and thrust me back by the hips, I tripped over the end of the bed and, secure that it was behind me, let myself fall.

I tingled, down there, hungry for his touch, for him to fill me and kiss me and move above me like before. He stood over me with a dark grin taking hold of his lips as he looked me over and instead of dread, which I had felt a time or two when Grinder had looked at me the same way when I was fully clothed, I felt nothing but want and need and a fine burning desire for Zander.

"Make yourself comfortable, Red," he commanded in a low and even voice. I put my palms against the mattress and pulled myself back, up towards the head of the bed. Zander watched me, so carefully, a hunger in his gaze that my body matched. He devoured me with his eyes and fisted his erection, stroking himself slowly. It was probably one of the most erotic things I had ever seen, even though admittedly I hadn't seen much, just imagined plenty when I was alone in my bed late at night when the rest of the world was sleeping.

"God, I love it when you look at me like that!" His voice was low and impassioned but what he said, it made me smile.

"Like what?" I asked.

"Like I'm some kind of wonder, makes me feel like a fucking superhero or something."

He crawled up the bed, over me, and I willingly parted my legs so he could get between them. He pulled open the drawer on the nearest bedside table and brought out a foil packet, tucking it beneath the pillow. He kissed me and pulled the stick and basket from my hair, setting them both off to the side. He combed his blunt fingers through my hair until it uncoiled and hung more naturally.

"God, you're fuckin' beautiful!" he exclaimed and kissed across my jaw, finding that spot on the side of my neck, the one that made me break out in a pleasurable wash of tingles over every inch of my skin. His big hands roamed my body as freely as his mouth as he kissed down my chest. I loved the silky soft feel of his hair, which was already almost dry, as I wound my fingers through it. He took one of my nipples into his hot, wet mouth, grasping it lightly between his teeth as he sucked, teasing me with his tongue. I arched beneath him, a deep ache starting between my thighs, my body growing needy, and way past moist.

His fingertips grazed my mound and my legs jerked from the still as yet unfamiliar touch. His body was in the way of my ability to snap them closed which filled me with yet more heat. He tipped his head and I met his eyes as he continued to tease my breast with his mouth.

Whatever he saw on my face must have reassured him because he broke the suction he had on my nipple and moved to give the other equal attention, his fingertips lightly grazing over my vulva in a feather-light touch that had me moaning.

I let my head fall back to the pillows and I couldn't help but writhe at all of these beautiful, new, and enticing sensations he was eliciting from my body. He took his mouth from my breast and kissed his way down my body, firmly palming my sex, his hand rubbing broad strokes over it, a press and grinding motion that was driving me wild. He stopped his mouth just above the line of my pubic hair and checked on me with his eyes.

I had no idea what he intended to do, but at that point, I would have let him do anything he wanted, anything at all. He stroked my folds one more time and, with a glance in my direction, plunged one of his fingers inside of me. I cried out and he smiled against my skin, stroking the digit in and out of me in a fluid glide. It felt amazing, his hands on me. The other he stroked across my stomach in a firm caress before stretching the skin. Cool air caressed my nether region and before I knew what was happening his hot mouth licked over that sensitive bundle of nerves before he sucked the delicate nub of tissue into his mouth.

My body went wild. A fine burning, shining wave of pleasure swept over me and through me. My back arched off the bed, my hands clutching the covers by my hips. Zander used the hand on my stomach to hold me down, his arm a bar across my hipbones as he pressed me flat, working me expertly with his mouth and fingers until white starbursts went off at the edges of my vision, ever-expanding towards the center until I was drowning in light and sensation and gasping desperately as I tried to writhe beneath him.

My vision came back in stages, and I trembled as Zander carefully climbed my body. He propped his chin in his hand, his elbow resting against the bed above my left shoulder, his other hand lightly stroking up and down the skin of my arm. I shivered, and wanted to slap the smug look off his face, but I couldn't form words, let alone move. He had effectively rendered me a useless puddle of Mandy in the center of his big bed.

"How you doing, Red?" he asked, his voice low and teasing.

"Good," I answered faintly and I could feel the ludicrous grin overtake my face. Zander laughed.

"Mind if I join you?" he asked.

I felt myself frown, and reading my puzzlement clearly he lifted his body slightly from mine and his free hand drifted down between us, slicking his erection up and down between my folds, teasing the head of it against my clit. I moaned, my head falling back, my eyes slipping shut, and I heard him smile.

"I'll take that as a yes."

I heard the crinkle and tear of plastic as he retrieved and tore open the condom. A brief moment went by and I opened my eyes and met his so-very-serious expression as he eased his way carefully inside me. I cried out, my voice an alien thing, the sound emanating from my lips a full, throaty, and sultry moan and something belonging entirely to a wanton sex goddess, not little Mandy Price, the well-behaved pastor's daughter.

I loved that. In fact, I loved it so much, I twined my legs around Zander's lean hips, my arms going around his neck, and, looking deep into his eyes, I captured my lower lip between my teeth and moaned, arching my hips to meet his careful thrusts. His eyes widened and he groaned, and it was such a sexy sound, all deep and full and like a man on the brink and he thrust harder, which didn't hurt; it didn't hurt at all, in fact, it did just the opposite.

I gasped, "Oh yes!" and Zander growled, a deep, and bass, and supremely satisfied sound.

"Tell me how much you like it..." he demanded, and I smiled, no coyness, no shyness.

"I love it!" I cried, and I arched into him. I had thought this rhythm was intense, but it had nothing on what he did next. He drew back and surged into me so deeply, so powerfully, and set a punishing cadence, so hard, so fast that each thrust was punctuated with the sharp report of our flesh coming together in a heated slap. I felt things low in my body tighten, and by instinct alone I squeezed down on him.

"Oh, shit!" he cried, but it wasn't alarmed, not in the slightest; the expletive was a surprised, happy sound instead.

"Christ, you feel so fucking good!" he growled, and that was it, my world blanked out again behind those white hot flashes of light that were burning me up from the inside out with pure shining pleasure, so intense that I swore our bodies blurred together and we melded into one being.

"I love this!" I gasped out when I could finally find my voice again.

Zander chuckled and kissed my shoulder, a hot press of lips against my freckled skin.

"I love you," he murmured and I stared at the ceiling, blinking, completely unsure of what to say back. His proclamation had caught me completely off-guard.

13

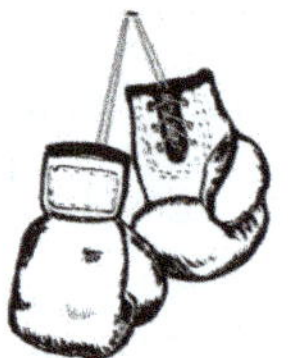

Revelator…

I switched on the bedside lamp. Red lay flat on her back, her eyes fixed on my ceiling, a myriad of emotions chasing one after the other, after the other, across her pale face. It had been too soon, but it was also too late to take it back. Not that I wanted to. I kissed her shoulder, planting soft kisses to her skin while she processed.

"I… I don't…" She always stuttered when she was uncomfortable.

"Shh, don't expect nothin' from you, Red. Sorry I just blurted it out like that, but at the same time, I'm not. You been on my mind, and in my heart, under my skin since the first day I saw you."

She searched my face, a fine wrinkle of concentration between her sweeping golden-red brows.

"It's a foreign concept," she admitted finally, and swallowed hard. I could see how much the honest comment cost her. She was so used to having to hide how she felt, and I knew how that went.

"My old man was a piece of work too, baby. Takes time to work through that shit. You ain't hurtin' my feelings none." I smoothed some of her fiery curls back from her face and I could see something in her eyes ease.

"I'll be right back, get us cleaned up, don't you go away," I kissed the tip of her nose, a quick peck.

She laughed softly and the tension between us disappeared. "Like I could walk if I – oooh!" Her head fell back and her back arched a little, thrusting those perfect tits up at me like a goddamned offering as I pulled myself out of her hot, wet, grasping cunt. She was fucking perfection and I suddenly had no desire to leave the room, even for just for a second. Nope, instead I found myself discarding the used condom and replacing it with a fresh one, to slip right back in her and drive her right up and over the moon all over again.

I made her come at least twice more, maybe three times, I couldn't quite be sure, before taking my satisfaction myself.

When I came back with a warm, damp cloth to clean us up, she looked at me with baffled wonder.

"What?" I asked her.

"I'm not sure I'm ever going to be able to walk again after that," she commented dryly.

I laughed and pulled the blankets out from under her. She yipped in surprise and I fell into bed beside her and covered us up. She snuggled into my side, her head on my chest, looking down our covered bodies. I couldn't see her face, but the way she relaxed against me, that she was satiated and spent was all I really needed to know.

"Zander?" Her voice was soft in the dim room.

"Yeah, Sugar?"

"Is it all right that I don't know how to feel?" she asked quietly. Her voice sounded brittle, like she was on the verge of tears, but I knew better. If I looked, her eyes would be dry, crystal-clear, and as perfect as ever.

"Babe, you've had a lot of emotionally heavy shit happen to you in the last couple of days. It doesn't surprise me at all that you don't know how to feel." I kissed the top of her hair. Poor girl was probably all mixed-up and inside-out from all of this.

"I can't tell you 'I love you'. Not yet, but I can say I've never felt the way you make me feel."

"Yeah? How's that?"

"Safe, and loved. I think I'm falling in love with you, I'm just not quite there yet." Her words made me smile.

"Fair enough. I'm just going to keep tryin' over here, so do me a favor and just let me know when you get there, okay?" She snorted and laughed a little and I chuckled too.

"You can be so full of yourself! But, deal."

"You gotta work tomorrow?" I asked.

"You know what? No. I worked on Monday and I think I've earned a three-day weekend," she murmured.

"Atta-girl," I said, and gave her a little squeeze. She yawned. "Sleep, babe, you've earned a nap."

"Mmm, I'm hungry though."

I blinked. Shit, yeah, we hadn't eaten since lunch.

"Got some shit in the kitchen. You pack your robe?"

She nodded.

We got up and I gave her one of my tee shirts that was a little big, even on me. She put her robe over it but, damn, the sight of her nude, in nothing but my shirt, had me wanting to bend her over the counter and fuck her from behind. So far, I'd made love to her, and we'd only done missionary, but I had every intention of introducing her to every position in the Kama Sutra, and then some. I also intended to find out her take on some downright dirty, porn-worthy sex in the near future. There was so much shit for us to do that if she didn't like something, I could find plenty of things that she did.

I made us a couple of sandwiches and kissed her until she was languid in my arms and I could go for a round three. Instead I let her go and we ate in front of the fire, which I added wood to. We talked until late, and I told her things about growing up, shit I hadn't ever told anyone else, and she told me some shit that I packed away in my angry-box to fuel me in my next fight. If I couldn't beat the fuck out of her dad, I'd let loose on the poor bastard I was up against in the ring, not that I felt too sorry for him. Word was, he was an up-and-comer on the underground fights circuit –and– a Suicide King. It'd be my pleasure to take him apart, even if it was only because he chose the wrong set of colors to sport on his back.

When we finally went to bed, Mandy coiled around me in the dark and dropped off almost immediately into sleep. Even with her warm, silky-smooth, nude body tucked close to mine I wasn't far behind her. The poor girl was emotionally and mentally exhausted, because I managed to get up, go through my morning workout routine, shower and eat, and she didn't so much as move from the position I'd left her in. I wanted her to sleep. I had no designs for the day other than to spend it with her, so I figured I could fix her whatever she wanted when she woke up.

I stood in the doorway of my bedroom. The morning light, gray and watered-down by the rain and cloud cover outside the house, didn't do my girl much justice but hell, she was beautiful in any light. She lay on her stomach, one arm and the long line of her back down to her hip exposed.

I smiled to myself and went into the smallest of the houses' four bedrooms, which I used as my art space.

I pulled the marker case off its shelf on the underside of my drawing table and unzipped it. Nearly every color of Sharpie permanent marker known to man was lined up neatly inside. I used them for clients that were unsure about a tat. If I had time, I'd draw an approximation on 'em and let 'em wear it for a day or two to decide if it was a permanent decision they wanted to make. I couldn't resist breaking them out when I had such a beautiful canvas laying in the next room. I just wanted to play for a little while. Besides, you could scrub 'em off early if you wanted to, it just took some soap and a little determination.

I stared at her in wonder for a few more minutes, mostly that she was actually here and would let me touch her, would let me love on her so thoroughly. I really hoped she would let me show her something else new today. Truth was, she'd shocked the hell out of me, climbing into the shower with me the night before, but damned if I didn't like it. I liked it a whole hell of a lot, actually.

I got up onto the bed and laid the markers out next to me selecting a brown one first.

I knew exactly what I wanted to do. Hopefully, she wouldn't be too pissed at me, but you know what? She was sexy as fucking all-get-out when she was mad, so a little part of me kind of hoped she would be. Guess there was only one way to find out.

I uncapped the pen...

14

Mandy...

Tickling against my arm. I sucked in a breath and moved. It stilled, but it started up again a few seconds later, a light touch that tickled across my skin and was driving me nuts. I moved again and it stopped, but started up again just a few seconds later. Ugh!

Zander chuckled and my eyes snapped open, which is when I saw the tip of the felt pen moving against my shoulder.

"What are you doing?" I burst out.

He smiled and it was so incredibly boyish and cute it made my heart give a twist in my chest, and things much lower in my body give a pleasurable throb.

"Couldn't help myself, Red. You were laying here just so perfect and inspiration struck... Had to do it."

I started to sit up, but he pressed his palm to my back, warm between my shoulder blades, and pushed me, gently, but insistently, back into the mattress. The pressure of his hand gave my back a delicious little stretch and I groaned out in bliss.

"You going to let me finish?" he asked, sounding amused.

"Please tell me it washes off?" I said dryly, when, truthfully, I was kind of delighted in not only the sensation, but the fact that Zander would take the time and care to put some of his art on me. I loved the way he drew. I wished I had such a talent for it.

"In a day or so, no problem, but if you hate it, it will come off with a little bit more determination right away."

I laughed, and he grinned, and my heart melted a little more. I might not have loved him yet, but yes, I could honestly tell myself I was well on my way to falling in love with Zander. I sighed, a tranquil and contented sound, and tried not to fidget when his drawing on my skin started to tickle again.

"What are you drawing anyway?" I asked.

"You'll see," he said, smiling even bigger.

"Better not be something juvenile," I grumbled affably.

"I wouldn't do that to you, Sugar," he said, and I relaxed even more. He pulled the tip of the pen back and cocked his head to the side.

"Turn over on to your back for me?" he asked and I started to comply, pushing myself up. I froze when I caught sight of my left hand. A tracery of delicate ivy wound its way up the back of my hand and spiraled around my wrist and up my forearm. I blinked and pushed myself up the rest of the way. The vine was brown and the leaves a rich, dark green against my skin. Earthy and beautiful, some of the leaves were in a state of turning, not brown and withering, but to a deep crimson.

"Oh, my God... Zander it's beautiful," I murmured.

"Turn over for me? I want to finish," he said. I could hear the shine of pride in his voice as he said it. I lay on my back and he thanked me, but leaned in immediately, setting back to work.

The pen tickled over my shoulder to the front, and he spent a lot of time there. We were silent, and I simply watched him, his face set into deep lines of concentration that almost seemed grim if I hadn't known any better. From time to time he would pull back and tilt his head to the side and consider his work before leaning back in. The air had grown cool; likely the fire from the night before had gone out; but his close proximity warmed me and his breath, when it fogged across my skin, made me close my eyes. The sensation was so unique and arousing to me.

I let him do what he wanted and held very still. This was incredibly tranquil and relaxing. I felt connected with my lover in a very interesting, very different way. Zander would glance at my face and a warm light would suffuse his eyes before he would turn back to his drawing, which was quickly leaving my shoulder and spilling on to my chest.

I didn't care. I liked this, I liked it very much and as the serenity stretched into Lord-knew-how-long, I found I almost didn't want it to end. Zander started checking my expression with more frequency as time went on, and I soon felt why. He switched pens back to the brown and continued a sweeping curling line on to my breast and around my nipple. I giggled.

"Hold still! I'm almost done, I promise," he smiled. He worked for about ten minutes more, before sliding the pens back into a case of them lying open on the bed.

"Finished?" I asked.

"Oh, yeah. Come on!" He stood up and held his hands out to me. I placed mine in his and he led me across the hall to the home gym, where he switched on the overhead light. He led me to the bank of mirrors along the one wall and stood behind me, his hands on my shoulders as I stared, astonished, at my reflection.

"You were busier than I thought!" I blurted and he had been. Ivy vines circled my left arm from wrist to shoulder in a single spiraling vine. The vine split at my shoulder, running along the underside of my collarbone and curling delicately over my breast, following around the underside of my nipple. I turned to see the back and realized the vine actually split in three; another ran down my back and curved over my butt. I also had a vine running down the outside of my leg, the tendrils curling and ending in a few delicate leaves on the top of my foot. I looked just as he had described me, like the goddess of my name personified, like a goddess of autumn.

"Please, tell me you'll let me have some pictures of this," he said, and met my eyes in the silvered glass. I blinked.

"Oh, I don't know..." I bit my lower lip, apprehensive.

"Make you a deal, Red. Let me pose you, take some pictures and if you're uncomfortable with them, I'll let you delete them yourself."

I thought about it and realized that this was a moment in time that I could never take back. If I said no, then Zander would be hurt that I didn't trust him, but if I said yes, well, I would have to trust this man implicitly. I weighed my options carefully.

"Okay," I agreed, my heart in my throat. So many bad things could come of having nude photos taken of me, but the truth of the matter was, I trusted Zander. I trusted him not to hurt me, and showing those photos to anyone without my consent would be an incredibly painful betrayal.

As if he could read my thoughts, he said, "You can trust me, Red," and so I nodded and let him lead me back into the bedroom. He posed me artfully against his white sheets and brought out his phone. He took several photos and smiled from time to time.

"It's amazing what you can do with a few filters and some creative angles with a phone camera now," he said, as he worked. Finally he got into bed with me and cuddled in close to show me, and holy wow! Every photo was elegant and erotic and only one of them showed my face... and the one that did show my face? Well, it was simply a shot of my head and shoulders and stopped just above anything critical, enough to showcase his art and, even I had to admit, my simple natural beauty.

I had never in my life felt beautiful before, but the girl staring at me out of that picture... she was. She was absolutely breathtaking. I looked up at Zander, who was smiling down at me.

"You can keep them," I said quietly. "But only if I can have a copy, and you send them to Everett, right now."

Zander laughed, "Glad you like them, Sugar."

"I love them!" I pushed myself up and boldly threw a leg over him, straddling his lean hips. He groaned and pulled my mouth down to his. We kissed, a wild passion-filled thing. He pulled back and spoke against my lips.

"You going to fuck me?" he asked, and the question made me shiver.

"I'd like to," I murmured back.

"Condom's in the drawer," he said. I fished one out and he helped me put it on him, pushing the waistband of his black basketball shorts down enough to free his erection. I rose up on my knees, Zander watching me intently.

Awkwardly, at least for myself, this being my first time, I fitted him inside of me. And Oh. My. God. It was amazing.

The angle was much deeper and much sharper this way, somehow. It was different being the one in control, being the one doing the moving, doing the pleasuring, and I liked it very much. I let myself go, let myself enter into the persona Zander had inked onto my skin and I rode him, vaguely aware of the camera on his phone making its clicking sound one or two more times.

I didn't care. I felt so wild and free.

It. Was. Amazing.

15

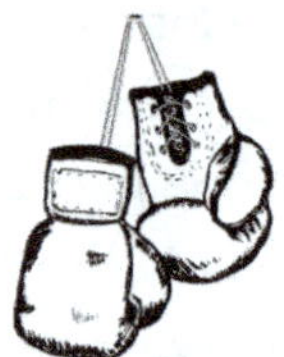

Revelator...

I was amazed as hell that she let me keep the two pictures I snapped of her as we were having sex. I thought for sure she'd nix them as soon as she saw them, seeing as they showed her, head thrown back, body arching so provocatively, from her face all the way to her navel. Her hands, where she had them planted on my chest, caused her arms to bracket those gorgeous tits of hers, bringing those lush globes front and center for the camera lens. Jesus Christ. She was one heart-stopping, beautiful, no, gorgeous, no, fine... *hell, all of the above!* woman.

We spent all damned day in my bed and I kept her nude for as much of it as I could. It had been forever since I spent that much of a day making love to a woman, and I showed her a few more positions that made her scream in pure bliss. I made sure to keep her hydrated but couldn't feel bad about leaving her sore. I'd brought her to the club with me when I had to be in church, and immediately, Everett had marched up to her and hauled her off to chat with the girls.

It wasn't lost on me that Red forwent some of the shit in her bag, opting for boots, jeans, a tank top camisole-thing with lace edging the top, and a cardigan, that she conveniently left off the shoulder I had drawn on. Man, if I had known how much she would love me drawing on her... I am so glad I didn't resist temptation on that one, and I was already planning for there to be a next time. I never imagined my preacher's daughter would be such a fucking wild child at heart. I fucking loved that shit. What's more, I loved seeing her happy. I settled in next to Trigger and he looked over at me, his eyebrow cocked.

"What'd you do? Spend all day gettin' laid?"

"Yup."

He looked surprised and then grinned. "Shit. Me too!" We pounded fists and Dragon called the meeting to order.

"Right, so we got a few things to go over. First, we paid our little buddies over the county line a visit last night. A little eye-for-an-eye. Took down one of their meth-lab operations. Now, nobody got themselves dead, because you know, that's just not how we roll anymore if we can avoid it. But I think we sent a pretty clear message, so I need you boys to be on your toes."

There was a sweep of murmured agreement and nods.

Dray followed up. "We have some intel that our antics last night have definitely pissed in their Cheerios, so you all need to be careful. No riding alone. Keep yourself armed, and if you got something preventing you from carrying legal... well, who fucking cares? It's gotten to that point. Neither side is backing down, which is what it is."

Dragon spoke again, "Got some other business to attend to. Gettin' on toward the beginning of the month, so if you got your dues, pay Reaver. If not, well, you got until next meet to get 'em in. Anybody need the floor?"

I shot a look over to Dray and he gave me the signal that he had this, so I settled back in my seat.

"A lot of nasty stuff been going down lately. Every man in here is pretty much here for the same reason. Lookin' to get out of the life, settle down some, and work towards something better. A lot of you guys know we didn't ask for this fight, and are standing your ground with us, and we appreciate that more 'n we can say... but a lot of us, me included, are feelin' like we're backsliding into the heavy shit."

There was a heavy silence and some uneasy looks. A few of the guys nodded at what Dray was saying, Trig being one of them.

"How many of you here have spent longer than five minutes with my girl's bestie, Mandy?" Dray asked. Guys looked at each other and hands cautiously went up. I smiled. Most, if not all, of the room had their hands up.

"I'm gonna give Revelator the floor to explain what's up."

Dray sat down and I stood.

"So, uh, how many of you guys actually like my girl enough to get up early tomorrow?" Most, if not all, of those hands went up again. I nodded, "Here's the deal…" I spelled it out for them, and by the time I finished there were a lot of grins, some feel-good, others downright feral.

"Now, I don't want to sound like a pussy, but I'd really like to do this for her, and for us, both to remind us that there are other ways of handling shit than fucking shit up and breaking faces, and because with all the shit that's been going down, we need to do something to at least try to balance the scales some. May not tip 'em far, but for some of us, we can at least feel like we're taking a break from digging our way straight to Hell."

There were murmurs of agreement and several nods. I took my seat. I think this had more to do with the guys liking my Red, than it had to do with me, but a win was a win in my opinion, no matter how down-and-dirty or how close you came, whatever you had to do to come out on top.

Dragon took back over. "Okay, so for those of you that are down for this, meet here at nine o'clock tomorrow morning. Data is our road captain so, you figure a route to take and shit, got it?" Data nodded at Dragon's words. "Good, I think that about covers it. Anything else?

The meeting devolved into a few questions about how Trig, Dis, and I were making progress on our business. We'd received an acceptable pay-out from the insurance and were just waiting on a check. Still having trouble finding a location to open up but had some promising ones lined up. As soon as we had the money we could look at getting a space and setting up shop.

Several of the guys stepped up to volunteer getting us up and running, by pitching in spare time on interior work in whatever space we got. Saving on labor for remodel work would be a huge boon, and some of it we could trade out in slinging ink. After about another hour, Dragon officially wrapped up the meeting and we sent Dis back to let the girls out of their cave.

None of us were surprised when none of them came out. It happened like that with the new setup sometimes. I hadn't seen Ghost at the meeting, but then again, I hadn't been at the last one. Trig said he was getting Shelly moved in to his house, so it didn't surprise me that Ghosty-boy played hookie. We all had lives outside the club, and sometimes those lives demanded we miss out on a church meeting so that we could keep a roof over our heads or food on our plates. It didn't mean we made a habit of not comin', though, because that shit just didn't fly.

If it was a more permanent situation, like work gettin' in the way with no way around it, then arrangements could be made.

Like in Lucky's case; blood came before anything, especially where his parents came in. They were good people. He came up and stuck out his hand. We clasped and pulled into each other for a hug.

"Good to see you back, man!" I declared.

"Shit, me? Look at you! 'Bout time you stopped fucking around and joined up!" he cried.

I grinned. "Yeah. Yeah, it was," I agreed.

"Y'know, Unkind would be real proud to see you wearin' that cut, and prouder still to see you keepin' out of trouble," he said. Lucky and Unkind, well, they had been best buddies. In fact, Lucky would have probably been right beside Unkind the day he died if he hadn't lived up to his namesake. He'd been pulled out of town for work that morning to a site outside of his usual area. Lucky, like a lot of us guys, was as blue-collar as they came. We caught up for a bit but I had to get going.

I had an afternoon/evening workout to put in and I needed to hit the grocery store and shit. The day was promising to be a long one with a super-early start to the next day, so I needed to get home and crash if I was going to make it all work.

I found my Red curled up on the floor in front of the media room's big black leather couch. The girls were all laughing and talking. I bent down and placed a kiss on her forehead.

"See you tomorrow, Sugar," I promised her. She smiled up at me.

"Services let out at eleven. Everett's going to church with me. Can you meet me at my parents at noon?" she asked me quietly.

I smiled, "Whatever you want, babe. What time do you guys eat dinner?"

"On Sundays? Between two and three. Sometimes later, just depends on what we're cooking." She said it as if eating dinner that early were a perfectly normal thing to do. I smiled wryly. For her, it probably was. I kissed her again.

"Okay, see you tomorrow."

"Bye." Her eyes lingered on me as I left the room, and damn, but I didn't want to do it. I wanted to take her home with me, sleep with her warm, soft body tucked in to my own, but I really didn't want to ruin the surprise I had in store for her. My girl was loved; loved by a lot more than just me and her best friend, and the next day she was just going to get an idea of how many people's lives she touched in a positive way.

At least, that was what I was hoping for.

Mandy...

Everett and I arrived at my father's church before anyone else. That was generally how it was for me. I'd get there about ten minutes before any of the parishioners arrived; that way my father, mother, and I could stand at the door and greet everyone as they got there, the perfect picture of what a family should be, as idyllic American as a Norman Rockwell painting.

It was the first time that I could ever remember doing it with such an angry resentment in my heart.

It was all lies. All of it. Every single bit of it was complete... complete... bullshit. There. I said it. Every bit of it was complete and total bullshit and I was incredibly angry, but you would never know it by the polite smile I held on my face as I shook hands with Mr. DelBene, or when I leaned forward to let old Mrs. Wainwright kiss me on my cheek.

The congregation was lined up out in the cold as we swiftly shook hands and smiled and said hello, ushering them into the warmth of the church. Everett stood beside me, smiling and saying hello with us, my mother, and then father bracketing me in on the other. I had talked for a long, long time with Everett the night before, and had made the decision for myself to make a determined effort to let the anger go, to tell my parents outright what I thought and how I felt, and to tell them I would be living my life my own way from now on, and would not be taking any more admonishing remarks from them. To tell them that if my father did, indeed, ever lay a hand on me or my mother again that they would never see me again.

I looked up, startled, at the roar of pipes.

"Oh, my!" my mother exclaimed. I looked over to Evy, who had a satisfied smile on her face, like the cat who had gotten the canary. The parishioners all turned, some open-mouthed in astonishment, some with wary expressions, and some with open hostility as the Sacred Hearts streamed into the church's parking lot, and I mean, almost all of them. I did a head count; only three were absent that I could see.

The men of the club got in line with the rest of the congregation and Everett slipped behind me and my parents, taking up her post beside my dad, making it so I was the first in line for the greetings. Dragon came up to me.

"How you doin', Red?" he asked with a wink and gave me a hug.

"Fine, um, it's good to see you!" I said weakly, at a complete loss.

Next was Dray. Then Doc, then Chandra; Trigger and Ashton next; followed by Reaver with Hayden; and Zeb, Data, Blue! One after another after another, each one of them with some of the sweetest things to say. 'We love you', 'We support you', 'You're beautiful'... an endless parade of positive things, but what's more, they told my parents those things, too.

More than once, I heard one of the men say to my mother, "You have a very special girl," and when they reached my father, they each looked him in the eye and said things like "You don't have anything to worry about, Sir. We like/love/have your daughter's back." It was all a little overwhelming.

And then Zander was in front of me, his eyes sliding over me in careful consideration, and I didn't care that half the church and my parents were watching. I hugged him and kissed him, a chaste press of lips compared to what we'd done yesterday. With a final look, his thumb caressing the side of my neck in a secret, loving touch, Zander let me go and went to my mother.

"Doing okay?" he asked her, softly. She smiled at him and nodded. I swallowed a bit apprehensively as he stepped up to my father.

"Good to see you, sir." Zander stuck out his hand, and my father shook it, all smiles that didn't even come close to reaching his eyes, but instead of hostility like I expected to see, my father's eyes were carefully considering. Zander's were flat and cold by comparison.

"And you," my father said shortly, following up with, "Please make yourself comfortable, and thank you for coming."

My dad smiled, and I was surprised to see that he meant every word that he was saying. Zander gave Everett a quick hug and followed his brothers into the church. My father didn't spare us a glance as he went inside, and Everett and I bracketed my mom as we headed up to our places in the very first pew.

My father settled behind the lectern at the front of our church and looked out over his flock. He spared a look for my mother and I almost gasped; it was a look of sadness, but at the same time, it held such warmth and commitment. I couldn't ever remember seeing him look at either of us in such a way.

"I have stood up here and spoken about judgment countless times over the years. Specifically, about how we should not fear being judged, except by one being and one being only... God." My daddy paused and bowed his head, collecting his thoughts, and I realized that he was completely off of his planned sermon, that this was new, that this was something unplanned and completely improvised. That was something that he never did.

"I am guilty of being a judgmental fool," he said plainly, as he stared out over the congregation.

Murmurs swept through the crowd.

"Many of you, I'm sure, have noticed our guests this morning."

There were slight nervous chuckles, and some good-natured ones from the Sacred Hearts.

"They are here at my daughter, Autumn's, invitation. Let us take a moment now to greet them."

Murmurs and handshakes, and even a hug or two from some of the older ladies, went around. I smiled as people retook their seats.

"Our Good Book has plenty to say about judgment, and the passing of judgment that we have on our fellow man. Most popularly, we remember the book of Matthew, chapter seven, verse one, which states: 'Judge not, that you be not judged'.

"But let us look beyond the first verse of that chapter and read the entire passage, which goes on to state 'For with the judgment you pronounce you will be judged, and with the measure you use it will be measured to you. Why do you see the speck that is in your brother's eye, but do not notice the log that is in your own eye? Or how can you say to your brother, 'Let me take the speck out of your eye,' when there is the log in your own eye? You hypocrite, first take the log out of your own eye, and then you will see clearly to take the speck out of your brother's eye.' Matthew, chapter seven, verses one –through five–.

"Brothers, sisters all, what do you think Matthew is trying to tell us?" he asked, which, of course, was a rhetorical question, but Duracell, pushy as ever, stood up and answered it anyway,

"He's sayin' don't judge someone because they sin differently than you!" His pronouncement was met by laughter and Blue pulled him back down into his seat beside him in the pew. "What? He asked!" Duracell cried, and this was met by yet more laughter. My father even cracked a smile.

"Well, yes, that is one way to look at it," my father agreed, "And you put it quite succinctly, brother..."

"Duracell!" Duracell called up, and there was more laughter. Duracell gave a cheeky grin and I couldn't remember a time that a service had been as informal and fun. It was quickly turning into almost a Sunday school for grownups with the addition of the MC. Well, some of them. Dragon reached forward and smacked Duracell in the back of the head and, with a grin, muttered something to the younger man. Probably about having some respect. Blue was smiling, which he almost never did, and I caught Zander's eye, who winked at me and puckered his lips in a kiss in my direction. The lot of them were incorrigible!

"Yes, well, you're correct, brother Duracell." My father seemed a bit flustered and my mother blushed faintly. I squeezed her hand.

"Let us now turn to Romans, chapter two, verses one through three, for a better understanding of what brother Duracell is saying. It states, 'Therefore you have no excuse, O man, every one of you who judges. For in passing judgment on another you condemn yourself, because you, the judge, practice the very same things. We know that the judgment of God rightly falls on those who practice such things. Do you suppose, O man—you who judge those who practice such things and yet do them yourself—that you will escape the judgment of God?'"

My father paused in his reading and took his glasses from his face, folding them neatly and setting them above his bible.

"Now, I didn't know that my daughter's friends were coming today, and no offense to our guests, but I have to ask, how many of you thought something negative upon their arrival? Be honest now..."

Hands went up in the air, tentatively.

"What if I told you that they were here in defense of my wife and daughter, that the man I have presented to you, that –I– am, in fact, a deeply flawed individual?"

The church was so quiet that you could hear a pin drop.

He confessed the whole thing, his jealousy, his hurt and his rage, his controlling nature, how he let his hand fly entirely too much and too often, and how he was not the man the church thought he was, just all of it. We all sat in stunned silence as he brought his sermon full-circle, back to the scriptures that he had initially quoted.

"And so, with a heavy heart, I confess to you my guilt. I have been a judgmental fool. I have spent years judging my wife, even after I spoke to her of forgiveness. I have spent years judging my little girl..." He sobbed, he actually sobbed. "For a mistake that she didn't even make, and I cannot apologize enough to her and to my beautiful wife. It took these men, my daughter's guests, to show me just how wrong

I've been. Specifically you, young man." He gestured to Zander. "And I don't even know your name."

Zander stood up, and with that smile, that endearing grin of his that made butterflies take off in my stomach every time I saw it, he said, "John Alexander. Most folks just call me Zander, but my brothers, here, call me Rev or Revelator. Out of all the names and titles I got though, really, I'm just the guy that loves your daughter." He looked at me when he said the last and I honestly think it was in that moment, right then and there, that I fell completely and endlessly in love with Zander.

My father brought the service to an end after requesting to speak with the deacons and other leadership of the church directly after. As always, there was a social in the church's basement which all were welcome to attend and my father asked 'his daughter's friends' to please stay for refreshments, and the congregation to welcome them.

I think nearly everyone stayed, as much from being rattled to the core by my father's pronouncements as out of just sheer curiosity when it came to the bikers in their midst. Everett, my mother, and I did our best to play gracious hostess to everyone, none of us having the faintest idea what was going on behind my father's closed office doors. My mother and I exchanged worried looks and remained silent. My father would do, and always did, whatever it was he did, and we were almost always along for the ride in some capacity or another, and this was much the same.

Zander found me in fairly short order and I stared at him for long moments and tried not to think the worst of things. Still, a small voice in the back of my head wondered: had they threatened my father into his confession? Zander grinned at me.

"It's written all over your face, Sugar, and no. I just asked my brothers who wanted to come with me today. I wanted to show my support for my best girl, my only girl, and wouldn't you know it? Just about all of them thought it would be a fine idea. Ghost wanted to be here, he just couldn't make it on a kind of movin' Shelly into his place."

I nodded dumbly.

"Thank you," I said, finally, and hugged myself to him. Zander's arms curved around my body and he held me tight.

"Anything for you, Red. You should probably know I did initially talk it over with Dray and he was going to send Duracell to kick your dad's ass, but then I thought about you. You're sweet and forgiving and all the things that are right and good in the damn world, and I got to thinkin' and well, this, showing up here... I thought it might be a better way of handling things this time, so I called Duracell off, and asked the club, and, here we are."

He drew back to look at me and I couldn't stop my smiling. I grinned and touched the side of his face reverently and said,

"Good call."

Zander barked a laugh and hauled me in to a tighter hug than before, smacking a kiss on my lips that made me blush, before letting me go enough for me to introduce my boyfriend to some curious parishioners.

It was a good day.

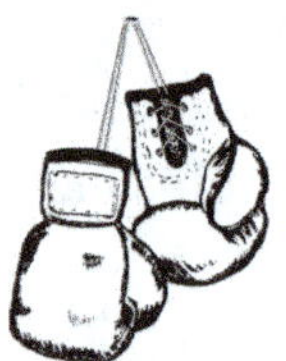

R evelator…

Taking the high road, doing the right thing, and using your words and actions that didn't involve letting fists fly was harder and way more time-consuming than just punching a dude in the face a few times and going out for a beer after. Still, I couldn't argue the result in this case. My Red had fuckin' glowed with happiness as she'd moved around first the church basement, then her parent's kitchen.

Her dad had pulled the church folks aside and asked if they wanted his resignation. They'd said no, but had put some decent stipulations on his staying. I guess one of their deacons was a retired cop. He had a good head on him and had suggested some anger management classes, said they'd helped him some years back when his temper had got him in hot water. Red's dad had agreed and when they all came downstairs, the deacon-cop had wandered on over to our Pres. and they'd started talking. There seemed to be some history there. Small world.

It was just me, Dray, Ev and my Red at dinner. The rest of the guys had split off at the church after all was said and done, and gone on to do their own things. I'd caught Zeb taking my girl aside, though. I'd shamelessly listened in while he'd told her that he was happy for her, but that he was sorry he'd missed the bus when it came to getting with her. He'd kissed my girl on her cheek and said they'd be friends forever, and when he'd caught me lookin' and listenin', said to take care of her. I could fuckin' respect that. He was a stand-up brother. At the same time, I found myself sending out a little something or other into the ether, thanking my lucky stars I'd pulled my head out of my ass when I did. Everett sure hadn't been lying about other guys taking interest.

"You ain't going to be expecting me to go with you every Sunday now, are you?" I asked.

We were laying on the couch at my place, a fire burning brightly in the hearth. The wind and rain were sweeping violently outside. It'd gotten downright stormy out there, but then again, it was the time of year for it. I'd ridden home in the rain and the wet, while she'd taken Everett home. It surprised me when she'd shown up at my place. I'd answered the door fresh out of a hot shower and she'd fallen on me, kissing me with a wild abandon that I was all fucking for. I'd made love to her right there on the entryway floor. Classy, I know, but when it was right, it was right, and it was right fucking then, so...

Red giggled and answered my question. "No. It was so amazing, what you guys did for me today." She snuggled against my chest and I tucked the comforter from the top of my bed closer down around us. I'd gotten it after we were through, pulling Mandy down on top of me as we lay in front of the fire on my couch. If only she realized how amazing she was.

"Anything for you, Sugar," I kissed the top of her head and felt her smile against my chest. She kissed me over my heart, and laid her head back down.

"What happens now?" she asked.

"Now, we get into some kind of new routine. Trig and I keep lookin' for a place to set up shop, I keep training, we figure out how to fit into each other's lives." I shrugged and she laughed.

"Listen to you! Deep thinker. I mean what happens, right now! Do you want me to stay tonight or...?" I laughed.

"You got tomorrow off?" She nodded. "Sweet. Then yeah, you stay here tonight. Tomorrow, well, shit, we'll figure that out when we get there, sound good?" She nodded again and settled against me, more relaxed, more at ease.

"Don't gotta plan everything down to the nth degree, Sugar," I murmured.

"I'm just so used to that being the way things are," she said.

"I know." I smoothed my hands up and down her body beneath the comforter.

"I wasn't sure before," she said suddenly, out of nowhere, after some time had gone by with nothing other than the wind and the rain in the eaves and the warm crackle and hiss of the fire in the fireplace to fill the comfortable silence.

"Before what?" I asked when she trailed off. I looked down my chest where she stared off into space, her autumn-colored eyes staring into the leaping flames. She blinked slowly as if hypnotized by the fire and propped her chin on her hand, which rested flat and warm against my skin. God, I couldn't get enough of her skin-on-skin!

"When you showed up with everyone today... what you said in front of the whole church... I think I love you."

I gave her a squeeze and smiled as I bolted forward and kissed her nose.

"You think?" I said, teasingly.

She smiled.

"I've never been in love with anyone before, but if this is what it's like, then I'm happy it's you."

I chuckled and felt suffused with warmth.

"I love you, Red. Never told any woman that. Not a one, so you're pretty fuckin' special."

She reared up and wiggled so she could kiss me on the mouth, which turned from a quick kiss to something much deeper and laced with some serious emotion. The kiss we shared had weight, and when I'd kissed her damn near breathless and let her go gently, she leaned back from me and searched my eyes with hers.

"I love you," she said, and I could see, plain as day, that it frightened her a little what she was feeling for me, and that made me hold her tight and tighter.

"Y'know, I used to know this dude, he was a part of the club a long time ago. They called him Unkind, because he was a surly bastard if ever there was one." Mandy tipped her head to the side, her look considering. "He said to me once, 'It doesn't matter who hurt you or broke you down. What does matter is who made you smile again.' Of course he was drunk as fuck when he said it, but it stuck with me." I could feel the smile on my face fade as I stared into Mandy's too-serious one.

"Why are you telling me this?" she asked, puzzled.

"Because in some ways you were that girl for me. I was working so damned much, busy as all get out..." I sighed, "You made me want to stop... and after Open Road Ink and a bunch of the other shit, you made me smile again and I just hope that in some way, big or small, that I'm that guy for you, too."

My Red climbed my body and straddled my hips, kissing me deeply. I sat up and she squealed, laughing, as I took her along for the ride.

"If we're gonna do this, I'm taking you to bed," I said and nipped her shoulder.

"Oh, we are most definitely going to do this," she murmured, and damned if it wasn't the most seductive thing I'd ever heard her say, her voice low and husky, and yeah. We were definitely going to do this.

I stood up and set her on her feet. I picked up the comforter and threw it over my shoulder and followed her down the hall to my room. God, she had the most gorgeous heart-shaped ass, and no matter how much I told myself I could get used to this, I knew I never would. And you know what? I was cool with that. Like, completely cool.

Mandy turned, her arms winding around my shoulders, and my

body met hers eagerly. I threw the comforter behind her onto the bed and pulled her silky warm flesh against mine. She giggled into my mouth as I gripped her ass with my palms and kneaded. I brought my head back and considered her a moment. God, I wanted to take her hard, just bend her the fuck over and pound her into next week!

She turned trusting eyes up to me and the wild, primal urge died down to something tolerable. I enjoyed some seriously rough sex from time to time, but I didn't think my virgin girl was ready for the rough stuff. Not yet. Maybe someday, but not today. I wasn't entirely sure how to even bring it up to her, so for now I simply walked her back into the bed and made hot, sweet, passionate love to her. We had plenty of time for all of the rest.

18

Mandy...

Finding a new sort of routine that included Zander wasn't difficult at all. What was difficult was adjusting to going out and being active, and just plain around more people, more often. I still enjoyed my solitude and my evenings in on any given Friday or Saturday night. For the most part I gave in and would go to the club with Zander, or go with Everett and meet Zander there, but every once in a while I needed a slow and quiet night spent in, either at my place or his, and I was surprised to find that Zander was okay with that. I was surprised even more when he showed up with a book or books of his own. It became one of my favorite things in the world, curling up with him, my head on his shoulder or chest as we each read our own book. The quiet nights spent in grew more frequent, the closer and closer we drew to the fight Zander was going to be in.

We'd talked about it and I'd told him truthfully that I worried about it. I was afraid he was going to be hurt, especially knowing that his opponent was from the rival motorcycle gang, the Suicide Kings.

The weekend after the club had come to my father's church, one of the men from the Suicide Kings had attacked Shelly in Ghost's house. She'd had to do something awful to save herself, but in some way, I think that it healed her a little bit from what had happened to her before. Still, I felt a keen sense of dread wherever I went, even when the men of the Sacred Hearts were near, watching over us, which was all the time now, even after both sides had met and agreed to a temporary cease-fire. Well, at least until the outcome of Zander's fight with their man in what he called 'the underground circuit'. I wasn't stupid. I knew that was a polite way of saying 'illegal fight', but I followed Everett's lead for the most part, and stayed quiet.

The questions I did have, I asked of Zander and only when we were alone. Some he answered and others he wouldn't... Well, that wasn't fair. Some he couldn't answer, as they fell under the ubiquitous umbrella of 'club business.' When it came to that, our relationship was wholly based on love and trust and a bit of blind faith, which I had in Zander, and so it was okay.

Now it was just after Christmas, but still before the New Year and I stood in front of the full-length mirror on the inside of my closet door with Everett behind me. I was wearing some of her clothes, and with the snow on the ground, I was pretty sure I was going to lose something to frostbite, but I had to admit, I looked like a whole different person. I wasn't wholesome Mandy, the preacher's daughter. No, I was Red, Zander's buxom girlfriend and someone who looked like they belonged on a fighter's arm. I tugged at the skin-tight top of the dress and shifted in my heels.

"I'm afraid I am going to pop out of this and flash the entire crowd," I complained.

Everett laughed. She looked just as tarted up as I did, except on her it looked good. She had this sexy confidence while me... I just looked freaked-out, and like I was wearing way too much eye makeup.

"Relax, Mandy. You look amazing." She rolled her steely blue eyes at me when I fidgeted one more time. "You aren't going to fall out, either. Welcome to looking like a modern woman and not a..." she trailed off.

"Preacher's daughter?" I asked, with a wry grin. She broke out into a sheepish one of her own.

"Well, yeah…"

"My father was right. You're a terrible influence!" Everett gave an indignant shriek and fell out laughing. I laughed with her, but quickly sobered.

"He's going to be okay, right Evy?" I asked meekly.

She sighed, "Mandy, you've never seen Zander throw a punch or get into a fight, but I have, at the last Lake Run. He's going to be fine. I promise you!" She hugged me. "You worry too much!"

A soft knock fell on the bedroom door.

"You girls ready?" Dray called through the wood. Everett opened the door for him. He took me in, deep dark eyes roaming over me from head to toe and back again. Everett grinned.

"You look good, Red," he said cautiously, eyeing Everett.

Everett rolled her eyes. "Just say it! I know I'm the only one for you," she teased.

"Fine. If Evy weren't in the picture, and you didn't belong to Rev, I'd be fucking you against the wall." He shrugged and I scoffed, mostly in surprise.

I took one last look in the mirror. I wore a skin-tight black dress of Everett's with long sleeves, but there were cut outs that left a ladder effect from shoulder to wrist along the outsides of my arms. The neckline plunged low and the short skirt rode high, barely covering the garter holding my stockings up. That was also borrowed from Everett. The only things I wore that were mine were the black high-heeled boots that came above the knee, and of course, my own bra and panties, a matching set that she and I had bought just for this occasion.

It was also weird to look into the mirror and not see curls. Everett had spent well over an hour, painstakingly straightening my fiery red hair with a flat iron. Her careful work would be completely undone as soon as it got wet, but for now it hung straight and beautiful, down past my waist. No one had ever seen me with my hair straight. I wondered vaguely what Zander would think, but I wouldn't see him until after the fight. I hadn't seen him since two day ago. We'd both hated that, but the guys seemed to think that it would help him focus. Well, it was what his trainer had always insisted upon, and Trigger and Reaver had just reminded him of it. He'd wanted to ignore them, but I'd been the one to insist upon it. I didn't want to be one to mess with a tried-and-true method.

Dray appeared behind me in the mirror and held up my coat for me to slip into, and I did, obediently. I didn't know what to expect when it came to this fight, but the men had assured us that the venue would be safe. As far as Sacred Heart women went, it would just be me and Everett. Ashton and Hayden had skipped on the notion of attending, preferring to spend girl time with one another. Chandra wanted to spend some time with her grandchildren, though Doc would be there to tend to the fighters. Shelly had said not only no, but Hell no. She didn't want to be anywhere near anyone even remotely related to the Suicide Kings, and who could blame her? She preferred to stay home and work on the numbers for both Soul Fuel and Pauley's Towing, her man's business. Ghost would be there though.

We left the house, Trigger waiting at the curb in his and Ashton's garnet-red Jeep. Dray opened the front door for me and stood to the side. I blinked in surprise; he was a gentleman to Everett –only–. I climbed up inside the vehicle and Trigger gave a low whistle, his eyes roaming over me appreciatively. He'd just proposed to Ashton the previous weekend, so I knew he was just being polite. The large man only had eyes for the petite auburn-haired beauty who was his woman. Still, he made me blush, which made him laugh.

Dray and Evy settled into the back seat, my best friend cuddling into her man's arms and I felt faintly jealous. I was surprised at how much I missed Zander – and it had only been a couple of days!

What surprised me even more was when Trigger pulled into a parking lot for a high school.

I frowned. Somehow I didn't picture a high school gymnasium as an illegal fight venue, but sure enough, that was where we were headed. When we got out of the Jeep, Trigger offered me his arm to steady me. High heels weren't usually a trick for me to walk in, but with the heavy layer of snow and ice on the ground, it was a different story.

It was hot in the gym and Trigger took my coat. I felt self-conscious when it came to my attire but decided that showing I was would be a really bad idea. There weren't many women in attendance, and the men who were... Well, let's just say, there were some rough characters streaming into the gym around us. Trigger mean-mugged a few of the more enterprising men who tried to approach me, and Dray did the same for Ev. They took us over to ringside seats, folding metal chairs close to the ring, which was encased in chain-link fence, almost like you would see at a construction site, but modified. I swallowed hard and jumped when a hand fell onto my shoulder.

"Easy, Mandy-girl! Just me." Zeb's familiar accent sounded from close by. I smiled up at him. Familiar was good.

"I have to go in back. Zeb, you look after her, man," Trig said. Zeb gave Trigger a little salute, and with a lingering kiss, Dray left Evy in the care of Duracell. We sat, bracketed by the men, who stood to the side and a little behind our seats, looking imposing.

The bleachers of the school's gym were filling, and Zander told me that the people in attendance had paid thirty to fifty dollars apiece to be here, which I thought was just plain amazing! It'd made me wonder, rather dubiously, why anyone would want to pay that amount of money just to watch two men beat each other senseless. It just didn't make sense to me, but to each their own, I suppose.

A young man, maybe my age, got up into the ring, wearing very baggy jeans and an oversized white tee shirt, a hat turned sideways on his head in the typical hip-hop fashion that made about as much sense to me as the whole fighting thing did. He raised a microphone to his mouth.

"Hey, yo! Yo! Check it!" he cried into the mic, and the crowd went a little wild. Everett laced her fingers with mine and smiled at me encouragingly.

"Usually, we save the best fight for last, and I'm here to tell you that the main event is gonna blow your mind, but," the man bucked

up straight and turned in place, "tonight is gonna play a little different, man, because we got an old friend with a new name coming back
to our ring and it's a special kind of grudge match tonight!" The
crowd cheered and stamped their feet in the bleachers.

"How many of you fools remember Zander?" the MC asked, and
the gymnasium erupted in cheers so loud my ears began to ring. I
almost didn't hear the music start; it sounded like an accordion and a
male guttural voice chanted 'Come with me now... come with
me now.'

The announcer put his mic back to his mouth and bellowed,

"Let me introduce you to a man who needs no introduction!
Please welcome, John 'The Revelator' Alexandeeeeeerrrr!!!" The
music swelled over the screaming, 'Come with me now, I'm gonna
take you down.'

Zander came out of one of the locker rooms at the end of the gym,
flanked by Trigger and Dragon, Doc trailing behind them with his big
black medical bag. All of them wore their leather Sacred Hearts vests,
Zander over his bare chest. He had on black satin shorts, like boxers
wear, with white on the sides and his hands were taped up past the
wrist, gleaming white under the overhead lights. When he leapt up
into the ring I could see his feet and ankles had been similarly taped.
They went to their corner of the ring– which seemed to have more
than just four– and the music stopped.

The announcer started up again, listing off statistics of the man
that Zander was about to face and the more he went on, height,
weight, and so on, the more nervous I became. He sounded a lot
bigger than Zander was.

I leaned towards Evy.

"I thought opponents were supposed to be of equal size and
weight!"

She looked about as nervous as I felt. "Me, too, but look at the
guys, Mandy, they don't seem fazed in the slightest and this fight isn't
exactly legal, maybe those rules don't matter so much."

I cast my eyes towards Zander; Trigger was shoving a mouth
guard between Zander's lips but Zander's eyes were all for the behe-

moth coming out of the locker rooms. He was easily head and shoulders taller than Zander and looked like a raging bull. He, too, was flanked on either side by men wearing Suicide Kings vests but no doctor followed in their wake.

The announcer introduced the man as Bjorn 'The Sweeper' Elmquist, and he was positively frightening. Long-limbed and broad-shouldered, he had a downright nasty look on his face. 'Scowl' didn't even begin to cover it; his features were twisted hard into a mask of pure hatred, and though I couldn't make out his eye color from where I was, there was no mistaking the intensity with which they burned. His long, light blonde hair was swept into a low ponytail which had been twisted into a knot at the nape of his neck, something that couldn't be grabbed on to. His shorts were yellow with red at the sides and before he even set foot into the octagonal ring, I found myself praying hard and harder for Zander.

"The fat guy in the denim vest, with the beard? That's Griz. He's their president. I don't know who the other guy is," Evy shouted over the screeching death metal that had accompanied Zander's opponent's arrival.

Dray sat down on the other side of Evy, and had evidently heard what she'd said. "Their fighter goes by the name Nord in their circle. The guy on his other side, that's their Sgt. at Arms, calls himself Gordy. You doing okay, Red?" he asked me. I nodded mutely.

"He's going to be okay, Mandy, I promise!" Everett squeezed my hand but I was glued to what was happening in the ring. Everyone but the two fighters and the referee had cleared out; the ref was giving the two men instructions. An electronic buzzer sounded and the ref backed out of the way as the two men circled each other.

I bit my lips together, squeezed Everett's hands, and prayed harder than I ever have in my life, as Zander's opponent made the first swing. Zander reared back and the punch went wide, and didn't even touch him.

Zander gave the man an icy-cold grin and lit into him with a singular fury that I simply didn't see coming. Zander punched out and unlike his opponent's, his punches landed. The man's head snapped to the side and came back, and then it was as if all bets were off, and the two of them went at each other with a brutality that I never in a million years imagined that Zander, with his loving touches and easy smiles, could ever be capable of.

Blood and saliva arched, both men bleeding freely, Zander from a cut on his cheekbone, and his mouth; the other man from a cut above his eye, and his nose, and maybe his mouth as well. The fight stretched on, two minutes, then five, until finally, with a savage grin, Zander punched the Suicide King in the face so hard the man toppled like a tree, his body hitting the mat and bouncing twice.

As I stared, Zander fell upon him.

He straddled the man's hips and rained blow after blow with his left fist while he held the man to the mat with his right. Punch after punch, his jaw clenched, his breath sawing in and out of his lungs, he beat the man who had given up all pretenses of trying to fight back, and instead was just trying to protect his head and neck with his arms. The taller, bigger man bucked his hips and scooted backwards across the mat and tried to get away from Zander.

The man in the center of that ring, who was beating the bigger man mercilessly, was not my Zander. He was some kind of demon, sent straight from Hell. His deep brown eyes darkened with his pure, white-hot rage as the crowd went wild around me.

I felt sick. I stared, open-mouthed, as Zander continued to beat on the man even after he'd fallen unconscious. The referee shouted and made a motion with his arms, the bell started ringing, and, with a final punch to the man's face, Zander bolted to his feet. His chest heaved up and down with his hard breathing and his eyes were fierce and wild and dark, his expression twisted into a mask of rage.

He stared dispassionately down at the man before he raised both his arms in victory. Turning, he locked eyes with me, and the look on his face was so stoic, so serene, it reminded me so completely of my father's look after he'd slap or smack my mother or myself. I felt equal parts horrified and suddenly very ill, which must have shown on my face because Zander's eyebrows collapsed into lines of confusion even as the referee gripped his wrist. I stood up abruptly and

Everett let me go. I think somehow she knew. I turned and crashed into Zeb, who gripped my elbows to steady me.

"Air! I need some air!" I blurted above the roar and stamping feet of the crowd.

"Zeb! Duracell! Stay with her, but take her out to catch her breath," Dray ordered and the guys nodded, and, one to either side, led me out into the cold. Everett stayed behind with Dray, worry for me creasing her brow. I swallowed hard and let Zeb and Duracell shelter me from the crowd until we burst out of the too-hot, too-close gymnasium and out into the sharp December night. I shivered and hugged myself. Zeb held up my coat for me; the cold air felt delicious but quickly became too much, and I shrugged into my jacket, all the while taking deep, cleansing breaths.

"You okay?" Duracell asked, and lit a cigarette, the red tip flaring in the dark as he sucked on it. I leaned back against the cinder-block wall and nodded.

"What's wrong, Mandy-girl?" Zeb asked me. I opened my mouth and closed it. What was wrong with me?

"I don't know, I... One minute I'm watching the fight and then Zander wins and he looks at me and... I really don't know!" My hands shook and I was grateful to have the wall at my back, with how unsteady I felt on my feet. Zeb sandwiched my hands between his and rubbed them to keep them warm. I sniffed, my nose beginning to run from the cold, and huffed out a breath which plumed the air between us.

"Easy, girl. Think you might be having a panic-attack."

I shivered and fixed my gaze out over the parking lot. I nodded and tried very hard to get my erratic heartbeat to slow down, and to swallow the offending organ back down into my throat.

"You're cool, Red. Not everybody handles violence the same way," Duracell said, and I looked at him. He looked uncomfortable, like he wasn't used to being supportive, but rather, just the opposite. He shifted on his feet and took another harsh drag off his cigarette.

Reaver rounded the corner and his cool blue eyes that reminded me of the sky above the mountains landed on me, his face set into lines of concern.

"Better come with me, Red. Rev is having a real epic freak-out over you bouncing like that. Won't let Doc look at him until he sees you."

I nodded and pushed off from the wall, a little unsteady. Reaver grasped my arm and with what now was a phalanx of leather-and-denim-clad, muscled guards, I was escorted back to the girl's locker room.

Everett, Dray, and Ghost were waiting outside. Everett hugged me and asked, "Better, Sis?" I nodded, and she whispered in my ear, "I saw it too, but they aren't the same, not by a long, wide mile."

I clutched Everett to me tight and felt so incredibly lucky and blessed to have her in my life. For so long, she had forged a path ahead for me, and for so long, she had towed me along when I was too afraid to step out on my own, and for the longest time she had been my rock, my center, my stationary piece of ground, while everything that was supposed to be stable in my life spun hopelessly out of control.

"Red, Doc needs to check him out," Ghost said gently, and his voice was tinged with enough worry that a worry of my own bloomed in my chest. I pulled back from Evy, squared my shoulders, and pushed through the door to the locker room on my own.

I found Zander on one of the hard, narrow benches in front of the open showers. He rocked back and forth, agitated beyond measure. Doc was standing nearby, trying to argue some sense into him. At the sound of my heels on the itty-bitty sandstone-colored and pink ceramic tiles, Zander's head snapped up and his chocolate-caramel eyes held such a raw fear, a raw pain, that a very new and different panic seized my heart in its grip. It was just a glimpse, a flash, and then it was replaced by a fine burning rage. Anger spilled through his warm brown eyes and turned them hard.

"Out!" He stood up, and gave Trigger and Doc each a scathing look. "Both of you!" Trigger put up his hands, Doc made to argue, and I shook my head.

"Just... just give us a minute," I said.

"Fine, but I gotta look at him, make sure he ain't concussed," Doc said darkly and I nodded.

"I'm not fucking concussed! Shit, I've had enough of 'em. Now, get out!" Zander growled.

"Be right outside," Trigger said to me and I nodded, maybe a bit too-rapidly. *Zander was Zander. Zander wasn't my dad.* I repeated it like a mantra in my head.

The locker room door swished closed behind them and the hollow thunk of it coming to a complete close was all it took. Zander rushed me, and instinctively, I backpedaled, fetching up hard against a set of metal lockers. Zander gave no quarter and pressed into me. I bit back a whimper, capturing my bottom lip between my teeth, and though I knew, in my heart and my mind, that I had nothing to fear, my body still braced for impact. Instead of a slap or a cuff, his hands gently but firmly cupped my face.

That raw, pained look from when I first entered was back on his face.

"Oh, God, Red. Promise you aren't gonna leave me. Just say you'll let me explain or fix it somehow. The look on your face, please, just please... don't do anything, don't make any decisions right now, tonight... just not yet."

Any fear I'd had simply drained from my body. I would give anything to take that look from his eyes, to strip the desperation from his voice. I shook my head, helpless to say anything; I mean, what could I say?

Zander relieved me of saying anything by crushing his mouth over mine. I put my arms around him and held him tightly to me, returning his kiss with an equal measure of urgency. Maybe if I showed him rather than told him? He kissed me savagely, with a near-bruising force and ground his body into mine. I welcomed it, holding him tightly against me. He shoved my coat back off my shoulders and down my arms and I let it fall, not even caring.

Any notion of being a proper preacher's daughter flew straight out the window in the face of Zander thinking I was going to leave him. Yes, I'd been frightened; yes, with my history, I apparently didn't do well around violence; but Zander had never, and I do mean ever, given me a hint, not one little iota of anything resembling violence aimed at me.

His large hands smoothed over Everett's short dress until they found the silk of the stockings at the too-short hemline. He smoothed his broad palms under the skirt and I moaned slightly into his mouth. He tore his lips from mine, his chest heaving, and with his savage yank my panties gave way, my hips jerking forward, my spine jolting at the insistency of it.

"I need you. God, after a kiss like that!"

I found myself nodding rapidly; I needed him too. I felt just as much urgency, just as much passion, and for once I didn't care about what was proper, or who was listening, or who might walk in and catch us. I just wanted Zander, needed him like I needed the very air we breathed. I needed for there to be no doubt, no lingering worry or fear that we were anything other than perfectly okay.

I felt him shove his shorts down in front, but I was too tall, especially with the heels. Zander's hands gripped my ass and the skirt rode up; he pressed me back into the lockers and kissed me again.

"Trust me, baby, I got you. Just let go," he said, and I did. I trusted that he had me and I let my legs go, let them give out from beneath me, and Zander indeed had me in hand. He pressed me back against the locker and simultaneously hauled me up his body by brute strength alone. I wound my arms around his shoulders and my legs around his lean hips and after a moment or two of awkwardly shifting his pelvis against mine, with a triumphant grunt he slid into me. Hard. While I was wet, I wasn't quite as ready as he usually made me, and so I cried out from the intensity of it.

That just seemed to urge him on. He shoved into me hard and harder, establishing a swift and punishing rhythm, and, oh God, the angle he had me at was perfect. He rode over that secret place inside me and his thrusting, with me against the bank of lockers, created just the right amount of friction between our bodies in just the right place. I felt my nails bite into his shoulders and his teeth set into one of mine.

The spike of pain combined with the pleasure sent me sailing out into the ether.

I cried out, a sharp, piercing sound of deep satisfaction. The locker room door burst open and someone swore as it swung shut again, but I didn't care. All I cared about was the man in my arms, who, trembling, carefully slid me down his body until I had my feet under me again. I let him help me stand, my legs shaking and unsteady, both of our chests heaving. Zander tugged my skirt back down into place for me, and I felt my face flame as he tugged up his shorts and the locker room door opened again.

"You two about done, so I can have a look at my patient?" Doc called in, hiding behind the door.

"Yeah! We're good," Zander called back and I tugged down on my dress one last time. I fixed my eyes on the bench behind Zander and he held my hand, refusing to let it go, his thumb swiping back and forth over the underside of my wrist in a soothing little touch.

"About fuckin' time, man!" someone said harshly, and a fighter in blue and green shorts barged past Trigger into the locker room. He eyed me side-long.

"Oh. What's your name, sweetheart?" he asked with a wry grin. I swallowed hard, my face flaming harder, now that the passion had cooled. In retrospect having sex in a high school locker room around this much testosterone seemed like a really bad idea. Though, heaven help me, I couldn't be sorry. Zander answered the man's question so I didn't have to.

"Property of Revelator. She's my Ol' Lady, so fuck off!" The man laughed and dropped onto a different bench toward the other end of the lockers.

"Easy boy, he's just being a dick. Save it for the ring if you go back, now let me have a look at'cha." Zander let Doc check him over while a new kind of warmth and glow took over me. Everett and the others had spoken of the importance of the title, of what it truly meant to be an Old Lady. I stood behind Zander and let him lean into my body, effectively using me as a backrest while he answered questions, letting Doc shine a light into his eyes, everything you might expect. Doc used a couple of butterfly bandages on Zander's cheek and pronounced him fit for travel.

Zander rolled his head back against my stomach and looked up my body at me. "You're staying with me," he declared, his voice heavily edged with some unnamed, but powerful, emotion. His eyes still held an edge of that same darkness that I'd seen in the ring, but it was much cooler, much more diminished now. His control was back, and it was absolute.

I nodded rapidly. I wanted to stay with him tonight, needed to stay with him. So his pronouncement was all right by me.

19

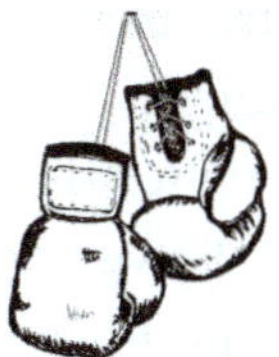

Revelator...

"What happened back there?" I asked her, softly, half-dreading the answer.

She turned in her seat to look at me.

"It was the look on your face, when you'd won... I just... it just... it looked like..."

I reached out a hand and covered hers where they were folded in her lap, as I carefully piloted my Chevelle through the snow-covered streets toward home. Red sucked in a deep breath and let out a gusty sigh.

"It looked like the one on my father's face every time he got done with me or mom." she rushed out, trailing off with, "It scared me."

I couldn't help it, I let out an incredulous laugh, "Shit, babydoll, the look on your face right before you bolted out of there liked to have given me a fuckin' heart attack!" I glanced sideways at her when she didn't say anything; her eyes were downcast and a look of incredible guilt stained her lovely face. I shook her hands and her eyes snapped up to mine as I rolled us to a stop.

"Stop. I get it; it's okay. I just never wanna do anything to put that look on your face again." Truthfully, I was just so fuckin' grateful that Mandy was as intellectual as she was at such a young fuckin' age; that she hadn't just gone on pure fucking emotion and high-tailed it out of there; that she'd actually stopped to think about why she was losing her shit so that I didn't lose her. She was just so fuckin' smart, and gutsy, and strong, and she didn't see a single damned one of those things in herself, I'd bet you dollars to doughnuts.

I pulled through the intersection when the light turned green and continued to hold her hands fast in mine. At least one of us had kept their cool tonight. I was kicking myself for fucking her in the locker room. She deserved so much better than that, and I'd not only done it, I hadn't been gentle about it. I owed her for that. I owed her for that –big–. I especially owed her something which I could never repay her for throwing caution to the wind and forgoing a condom. I knew she was on birth control, but still. I was a fucking douchebag. No way around that. I probably should, at the very least, buy her a new pair of panties.

"What are you thinking about so hard, all of a sudden?" Her quiet, lilting voice permeated the cabin of my car, strong but still soft beneath the muscle car's growl. I'd heard her though, and she deserved an answer.

"I was a dick back there. Tearing your panties off, and while I can't and don't regret what we did, I do regret not treating you better, not waiting to take you to a bed, and I really regret not protecting you better." She raised her eyebrows in question and I shifted in my seat. The adrenaline was gone, and I was starting to get sore.

"I should have put on a condom, I know you're on birth control but it still wasn't right of me... Red?"

She shifted in her seat, kneeling up on the black leather and leaning towards me. I pulled up to another stoplight and braked, and when we were solid at a stop, turned to look at her, just as her soft and gentle lips met mine.

"I love you, Zander," she whispered and sat back to look me in the eye. I stared back at this fucking fire-haired angel sitting in my car, and wondered for a minute how in the fuck I got so lucky.

"I love you too, Red. I love you, too." The light turned green and I put the car in gear and managed to get us the rest of the way home in one piece. Once in the driveway I shifted the Chevelle into park and turned my head to look at my girl, my gaze roaming her face, committing every freckle, every nuanced thing about her into memory.

"What?" she asked.

"You. You're just so fuckin' beautiful it breaks me," I admitted to her.

"Oh, Zander." She closed her eyes, a sad and somewhat pained look flitting across her features.

"I was fractured when you found me and the break in me was mending so badly. It took you a while, but I feel like you've finally set me. Like I'm on the right path, and I can heal the break now. You've made so many improvements in my life in such a short amount of time... I don't know how I could ever express my gratitude and just joy that you – "

She didn't get to finish her sentence. I'd reached out, lightning quick, and hooked a hand behind her head and pulled her mouth to mine. I kissed her fiercely, pouring every bit of love and pride I could muster into her mouth from mine as the interior of my car cooled, the engine ticking softly in the night. She pulled back, breathless, her lips slightly swollen and I felt my cock twitch in my shorts.

"Inside, baby. I need a hot shower and to bury myself in you all over again." She shivered at my words and I smirked, knowing it had shit to do with the cold creeping in. We got out of the car and I put my arm around her as we went for the front door, which opened before I could put the key in the lock.

"Hey, thought I heard your car," Disney said.

"Sup, Puddin'?" I asked.

"Did you win?" he countered. Mandy broke into a beautiful smile that held just the edge of sadness now.

"Yes," she murmured to Disney, and the lilt in her voice held such a weight, such a strain. I loved her, and while I couldn't or wouldn't stop fighting, I had to be okay with the fact that my girl wouldn't be at any more of my matches, because I wouldn't, I couldn't put her through it again.

"You gonna move, or are we gonna have to stand out here freezing our asses off all night?" I asked. Disney grinned and moved aside. Aaron looked up from a nest of blankets on the couch, the movie they were watching paused on a blur of blues and blacks.

"Congratulations, I think?" Aaron said, eyeing me dubiously.

"Yep! Another one bites the dust, knocked his ass out cold. Night, girls, I'm taking my woman to bed." I raised a fist and pumped it into the air, and Disney and Aaron laughed.

"Night."

"Good night!" they chorused, and I leaned on Mandy a bit as we went down the hall toward my room.

"Shower first, right?" she asked. I nodded. The tired was starting to set in, after all the adrenaline and emotions ran out. I generally slept after a fight like a fucking baby. But I wasn't ready for sleep, not yet.

"Shower with me," I said, and it wasn't a request. She smiled and nodded.

"Miss the curls?" she asked, and I nodded. I loved her curls; the straight look was okay but it had really thrown me for a loop. I'd said as much after our locker room throw down and after Doc had gotten done messing with me.

I probably should have phrased it better than "What the fuck did you do to your hair?" but I hadn't. I was a dick, and apparently I was batting a thousand tonight, with my actions as well as my fucking mouth.

Still, despite all my douchebaggery, she carefully helped me strip out of my jacket and cut and the hooded sweatshirt I wore underneath, undressing me before stripping herself in the bathroom. We got into a hot shower and pretty much kept it to all business. Well, she did. I stood there and let her look after me. I could tell it brought her a sense of pleasure by the gentle curve of her lips, and after taking a pummeling, damn if it didn't feel fucking fantastic. I was also about five grand the richer for the bottom-tier fight. Next one would be worth seventy-five hundred. Not bad for barely a nights work. Well, if you didn't count the almost-month of training in with it.

I'd stopped fighting for the year it took me to prospect for the club. I'd been totally committed to earning my patch, didn't half-ass a goddamned thing, and I was fucking proud as hell that I'd made the cut. I held Red's body close to mine and watched her wash her hair while I thought about things.

All in all I was fuckin' blessed. I had my brothers, I had my girl and pretty soon I would have a new shop, too. Trig and I had found a location in Old Town, down and across the street from The Spot and around six blocks over from Sugar's, the strip-joint we all went to from time to time but never told the girls about. Pretty fuckin' sure that they knew about it, though. I knew for a fact that Trig nailed Ashton's tight little ass to the fucking wall as soon as he got back to her. That fucker had never been shy about doing it in front of people.

"What are you smiling about?" Red asked and I think I actually blushed... fucking busted. She started laughing.

"I'm afraid to tell you, honestly," I told her.

"Oh, now you're telling me, mister!" She put her hands on her hips, and yep, no hiding it, my cock started to rise to the challenge. She lifted an eyebrow and gave me the 'you better tell me' look and I pulled her tight against me.

"I was thinking about how the guys sometimes secretly go to Sugar's," I said carefully.

"The strip-club? Oh, that's no secret," she said and I returned the 'you better tell me now' look. Red laughed.

"Look, all of the Old Ladies trust their men; none of them have ever been given a reason not to. The general consensus among the female population of the club is, and this is Chandra talking here, 'The boys know they can have their McDonalds anywhere, but they get their steak at home'. Ashton doesn't mind that Trigger looks, because he doesn't touch, and Hayden and Everett pretty much agree with Ashton, because as soon as their men get home, they reap the benefits of their little outing." She wound her arms around my shoulders as we stood sideways in the warm liquid spray from the showerhead so we both stayed warm.

"What does my preacher's daughter think?" I asked, my voice low and teasing.

"I think that I haven't had to deal with it yet, so I don't really know how I am going to feel until it happens. I think, that if I had to make up my own mind that I agree with the rest of the girls. I'm finding that the world isn't as black-and-white or set in stone as my father thinks it to be. I think that I love you, and I trust you, and I have faith that you feel the same, and that means you wouldn't cheat on me." Her hazel eyes were so wide and so sincere, and I thought half of what she was saying was a brave front. She didn't have a goddamned thing to worry about though, so I told her so.

"Sugar, you ain't got a damn thing to worry about. I love you, and I don't want anybody else but you. Sure it may be fun to look at, but the only body I want moving under mine is yours." Tension smoothed out of her posture and I reached down and shut off the shower.

"Sometimes I'm afraid I'm not quite... adequate. That my inexperience can be a turn off or..."

I laughed outright; I couldn't help it.

"Baby, I'm one seriously possessive prick underneath it all. You have no fucking idea just how hot I think it is that I'm your only one." I sniffed and handed her a towel, rubbing myself down as we talked, mostly because if I touched her now we'd never make it to the bedroom. The hot shower had limbered me up some. My hands weren't quite so stiff and my shoulders were a bit more relaxed. I had every intention of taking her one more time before bed, and figured since we were talking insecurities...

"Ask you something?" I considered her carefully.

"Anything." She replied, as she wrapped herself in the towel I'd given her and stepped out of the tub.

"I didn't scare you back there, in the locker room, taking you hard like that, did I?"

Her fall-colored eyes roamed my face and her voice when it came was soft.

A little bit," she murmured.

I hung my head and heaved a sigh.

"I just reminded myself that it was you, though, and that you weren't going to hurt me..."

I looked up sharply.

"Never," I vowed. She smiled and it was just like Trigger had explained Ashton's smile to me once, 'as if the sun had come out from behind the clouds'. The grace and beauty of the smile my Red turned on me warmed me all the way through.

"Sometimes when we're together, I feel like you're holding back," she admitted.

"Sometimes I do," I confessed.

"Don't next time, okay?"

"You sure you know what you're asking?" I searched her face and she smiled and it was a little sad this time.

"No, but I am sure that we can talk about it, and I'm sure that if I ask you to slow down or go easy, that you will."

"How did you get to be so pragmatic?" I asked. She laughed and gave this little endearing shrug that made me smile.

"Come on." She held out her hand to me and I took it.

"I meant it when I said we were doin' it one more time, tonight."

"You sure you didn't get knocked in the head too hard? I mean I know the fight was in a high school, but 'doin' it'? Really? Who says that any-" She shrieked and laughed as I picked her up over my shoulder, grinning. I swatted her on the ass and she yelped, indignant, as I flipped out the bathroom light and carried her across the hall in to my bedroom.

"Zander, put me down!" she cried and I laughed, tossing her gently into the center of the bed. She landed giggling, and I lost the towel. Her giggle ended on a gasp as she looked at me, fully engorged, and she got up on her knees. She handed me her towel and I dropped it to the floor. No need for that anymore.

I got up onto the bed and knelt across from her, kissing her, my hands cupping her face, and sucked in a hard breath when her fingers tentatively wrapped around me, stroking. Shit, that felt good!

"Lie back?" she asked and it was shy, but not, at the same time. Like she was working up the nerve to try something and damn, I wasn't about to deny my angel a damned thing, so I did what she asked.

In all the weeks we'd been together and with all the sex we'd had so far, there were still several things we hadn't gotten around to. Her mouth on my cock was one of them. Seemed that she was in the mood to rectify that now. God, it felt good. Her tongue gliding along the underside of my length, velvety soft, her mouth hot and slick and perfect. No, it felt amazing, but I was just one of those guys, you know? It felt good but it didn't really get me going, great foreplay, but not once had I ever come from a woman's mouth on my dick. Still, I lay back and let her do her thing, until I was so damned worked up I couldn't stand it anymore.

"God, Red, stop!" I cried, arching off the bed a little. "I need you up here! Now." I said before she could get any ideas that she'd screwed up or done something wrong. She crawled up my body and kissed all along the way, and that heated my blood almost more than her sucking my dick.

I groped at the bedside table for a condom but her warmth settling above me and her gentle voice saying "Stop," stilled my movements.

"Just stop, not tonight," she murmured and slipped me inside her, and holy motherfucking Jesus! That felt good. She rode me gently, her hands caressing my chest and stomach and it just came popping out of my mouth,

"God, Sugar! If this is what I get, I need to get into more fights!" Her laugh was high and sweet, musical to the ear. I let my hands hold her hips and smoothed them up and over her silky skin to cup her breasts. Soon, I was lifting my hips to meet her downward momentum, and our breaths were coming so ragged and uneven there was no more room for talking.

She was so fucking beautiful and she worked me so damned

good, so sweet and fucking innocent, and for such a long time, building me up slowly until I couldn't stand it anymore. I saw stars when I came, white flashbulbs going off at the edges of my vision, so bright, so white hot, and I was vaguely aware of her crying out in purest fucking pleasure, such a sweet clear sound. This was perfect.

She was my perfect, and God damn it, I loved her so.

20

Mandy...

About a week or so after the fight, just after the New Year celebration at the club, Everett stuck her head into Soul Fuel's kitchen and asked me, "Do you know who was supposed to be here today?"

"It's Tuesday, so Grinder, isn't it?"

Everett made a face.

"He's not here yet, and I'm wondering if I should call Dray." She looked thoughtful for a moment or two. I sighed and set down the piping bag full of French silk icing. I'd been decorating one of my mom's decadent chocolate cakes, a recipe I had unabashedly stolen from her recipe book for the shop; and it was no surprise that we sold the cakes, whole and by the slice, almost faster than I could keep them in the refrigerated display case.

I considered my childhood friend for a long minute and words didn't need to be spoken for each of us to understand the other's reluctance to call either of our men. Grinder might have made us uncomfortable with his overly flirtatious nature and close proximity, but he wasn't necessarily a bad guy. Involving Dray or Zander would make them upset with him, but not involving them might have made them upset with us...

"Give him like ten or fifteen more minutes?" I hazarded.

Everett gave me a pained look. "He's already an hour late. He was supposed to be here when we got here. Hell, before we got here."

I bit my lower lip. "What if something happened to him?" I asked, and Everett came more fully into the kitchen, Lexie had it handled out front, as far as I could tell.

"That was what I was thinking," my friend admitted and her phone appeared out of her apron pocket. She dialed and put it on speaker, sliding it onto the counter between us. It went without saying that if we were delivering bad or worrisome news, that we would do it together.

"Baby, what's wrong?" Dray answered his phone by way of greeting.

"We aren't sure," Everett hedged.

"Grinder isn't here, we're hoping he overslept, or that you'd heard from him?" I posed the last as a question and Everett and I looked at each other, each visibly holding our breath. Dray swore, low and vehement, away from the phone.

"No, haven't heard shit. Is there someone there causing you problems?" he demanded.

"No! No! Nothing like that," Everett assured him. "We were just worried about him is all; it's not like any of the guys to just not show up. At first we thought he was just running a bit late but, um, it's been like an hour, hour-and-a-half..." she trailed off.

"Dray, we really don't want him to be in trouble," I said.

He scoffed, "Grinder may be a pain in the ass sometimes, but he's a reliable stand-up dude. Look, call Rev, have him come in if he can, or find someone else who can. I need to touch base with Trig and Dragon. I'll talk to you later," and he hung up. No goodbye, just silence through the phone and the screen flashing, noting the call had been disconnected.

Everett and I looked at each other. She tapped across her phone's screen and Zander answered on the second ring, obviously winded, and his music blaring in the background.

"Just a sec," he huffed into the phone. The music stopped.

"Everett, what's up, my Red okay?" he asked and I smiled, blushing faintly.

"I'm fine, but Grinder didn't show this morning; Dray asked us to call you and see if you could come baby-sit, and if you couldn't, to see if you could find someone who could."

Zander blasted out a gusty sigh and was silent for a heartbeat, then two.

"Shop busy?"

"Very," Everett stated dryly, and she and I exchanged a look of pride.

"Good, if it's busy and one of those cockbites is around, they'll think twice before causing trouble in front of a bunch of witnesses. If it drops off and I'm not there, call me. I'm going to finish this set, grab a shower, and I'll be on my way."

Noises of agreement were exchanged, and, like Dray, he hung up without saying goodbye, which oddly, made me smile, mostly because I knew that meant he was driven, focused on getting through his weight-lifting and out of the shower, so that he could get down here. I looked a little forlornly at my cake. Everett rolled her eyes, but she was smiling.

"Better hurry up and finish getting that thing decorated. You're going to be all but useless when Rev shows up." I smacked her in the chest lightly with the dishtowel that was over my shoulder.

"Oh, like you can get anything accomplished with Dray here! Last time he was in the shop you were all but dry-humping in the office." I stuck my tongue out at her.

Evy scoffed and with a wicked gleam in her eye, deposited her phone in the pocket of her apron.

"Had a skirt on, and I can tell you, there wasn't anything dry about it."

"Everett Mary Moran!" I screeched and she pushed out of the kitchen door, laughing her head off at me. I stood there red as a beet and prayed that she was just trying to get my goat and she hadn't really had sex in our office, which was at least, thankfully, well away from any foodstuffs.

I finished placing the line of frilly decorating around the top and bottom of the cake and with a sly smile, brought out the thin solid-chocolate ivy leaves, arranging them artfully on the top. I picked up the piping bag, with its liner tip, and piped out vines in a dark chocolate fudge icing, adding thin curls of chocolate as the vine's little curling offshoots near the leaves. A fine dusting of some silver leaf on the leaves to give them the appearance of frost, and the cake was perfection. I brought it out front and was sliding it into the refrigerated case when movement on the opposite side of the glass caught my attention.

I looked up, smiling at whatever potential customer was standing there, but the smile softened and turned to something much more intimate when I met Zander's devilish grin, warmth and love radiating from his chocolate-caramel eyes.

"Hey, Sugar," he murmured, and I could see that he was touched by the decorating job on the cake, which had most definitely been inspired by him.

"Hi, come on back if you'd like," I invited.

"Sounds good."

He followed me back in to my kitchen and no sooner had the door shut behind us, closing out the front of the shop, than he was pulling me back into his arms. He tucked his nose behind my ear, standing on his toes to do it, and breathed in deeply.

"God, you smell so fucking good," he growled.

"I missed you, too," I said, with an edge of laughter. We'd just been together the night before, although I had left his house in favor of going back to Evy and Dray's, so that I could be up, showered, and have all of my things at my disposal to get ready for my workweek on Tuesday.

"I should let you work, huh?" He pressed a reverent kiss to the skin behind my ear in that way that always made me shiver. I felt his lips curve into a smile before he pulled away, going flat on his feet, his arms reluctantly sliding from my waist as he let me go.

"Might be a good idea," I conceded. "Still have to make a living." I turned and smiled at him.

"So, what'cha making today?" he asked, slipping up onto the vacant stool.

"Just finished a cake; the baked goods case is looking a little barren so I was about to start in on some cupcakes; then I'll get to work finishing up some truffles." We chatted amicably about chocolate, and I loved that Zander not only listened to me but was genuinely interested. He sat at the counter and asked questions as I moved about the kitchen and plied my craft, a smile cementing itself to my lips. I felt warm and safe and happy, and I really liked that Zander expressed interest; that he cared about not just me, but what I did, what made me happy.

Eventually there was a comfortable lull in the conversation, and he picked up a mostly-empty backpack that he had stowed near his feet. I didn't even know he'd had it with him. I worked diligently, folding the vanilla batter in my industrial mixing bowl as I prepared to transfer it into my batter dispenser for nice, neat, even pours into my cupcake liners, all the while paying attention to what he was doing, curious.

"Thought if things got quiet, I would draw a little while you worked. Get some work done of my own," he commented, withdrawing a box of paper and a kit of art pencils from the bag. He laid out a clean sheet of white paper onto the countertop and opened up the pencil kit which held an array of drawing, shading, and colored pencils of very high quality.

"I love to watch you draw," I confessed, and he grinned at me.

"Yeah?" he asked, then his voice pitched lower, "Need to draw on you again?" I blushed and he laughed.

"I'll take that as a yes."

I moved about my kitchen and poured about five baker's dozen cupcakes, sliding them neatly into the industrial ovens and setting the timer for them. I sighed and washed up my bowls, measuring cups and spoons, and the batter dispenser in the industrial sink before setting to work on the chocolate icing.

I was just pulling the cakes out of the oven and Zander was just starting to add detail to his drawing, when Trigger poked his big blonde head into the kitchen.

"Figured you were in here," he grunted and pushed his way in. Dray followed and was scowling, his look as dark as the rest of him, eyes snapping with impatience.

"The fuck, Rev? You're supposed to be looking out for my girls," Dray griped.

"He is, Dray." Everett said from behind him, "The kitchen is the best place for the guys on watch, out of sight of the strait-laced customers, out of mind... Just because we love you and understand, doesn't mean the rest of the world doesn't judge, and it's the best you're going to get. Mandy and I need to make this shop work."

My best friend crossed her arms and I sighed, taking the last of the cakes out of the oven to cool. She and Dray didn't disagree often, but when they did... oh, boy. I wiped my hands on my apron; they were slightly damp from sweating inside the oven mitts.

"Our business, our rules," I said firmly, and Dray and Evy both looked at me, surprised. I didn't put my foot down often, but when I did, Dray generally backed off and respected my wish on the matter. Likely it was because I asked for so very little. Trigger and Zander watched the entire exchange with amused smiles and glints in their eyes.

"Whatever. We'll talk about it later, back at the house," Dray grumbled and Everett and I smiled, because generally that meant we'd won our way. Not always, but generally.

"What's up, VP? Partner?" Zander asked leaning back on his stool, his pencil forgotten on the counter besides his drawing and in danger of falling onto the floor.

"Got someplace private we can talk?" Trigger looked from me to Ev apologetically. "Club business."

Everett snorted and I gave her a sharp look. She was irritated easily by secrets, which after Jerry, didn't surprise me. Still, I was well aware there were certain things we simply should not know for our own safety and wellbeing.

I gestured to the office. "A bit cramped, but Shelly's not in today, she does most of her work from home now. Feel free. Can't hear a thing out here when the door is shut."

"Thanks, Red," Trigger said softly, and the three leather-and-denim-clad men ducked into the back office, shutting the door behind them. Everett gave me a dirty look.

"Go wash your face!" I exclaimed and made a shooing motion with my hands, which made her smile and shake her head.

"It's not like I would ever say anything." She rolled her eyes.

"I know, but did you ever stop to think that Dray isn't so much worried about that, as he is about you going through the stress of potentially being grilled? Sometimes it really is best if you don't know, then when you're asked, you won't be lying."

Everett sighed. "Scares me too, sometimes," she confessed. "The idea of him possibly going to jail, to prison, all because he was trying to protect one of us, stop us from getting hurt before it happened." She scrubbed her face with her hands and gave me a look, one that I shared, bleak and frightened.

The police couldn't do anything until an actual crime was committed, so there wasn't really any help there. I nodded solemnly and Everett and I shared a quick hug before she went back out front to rescue Lexie from having to wash windows. It was the slow time of day.

The three men didn't stay in the office for very long, fifteen minutes to a half-an-hour. When they emerged, their faces were carefully schooled into lines of neutrality, which told me that, whatever it was, it wasn't good.

"Hey, Red," Dray said quietly.

"Yes?"

"Think you could get Em to agree to stay at the clubhouse tonight? The both of you." His dark eyes were pleading, and my heart sank.

"It's bad, isn't it? Grinder, I mean."

"We don't know, Sugar. That's the God's honest truth," Zander stated.

I nodded. "I'll get her to come."

Trigger smiled. "Thank you. Sunshine, Hayden, and the girls will be there too, if that'll help you convince her."

"I'll do my best." I promised. Dray stalked out front and Trig went over to look at what Zander was doing. He gave a low whistle.

"Art Deco, nice, man." They talked for a while about their business and I listened, intrigued, asking a few questions here and there. They had a location almost completed and ready to open just down the block and across from their favorite bar, The Spot, on old Main Street.

Eventually Trigger left, and Zander and I settled back into the tranquility that was just being around one another while we respectively worked. Everett poked her head in close to closing.

"Wrap it up, girl, apparently we're staying at the club tonight. You don't need to talk me into anything." She gave a gusty sigh and I smiled and nodded.

"They can't find him, can they?" I asked. Everett's expression said everything it needed to, while Zander's did too, for very different reasons. His simply shut down. I nodded.

"We'll go by the house first," I murmured. Everett nodded and ducked back out front.

"Pack some shit so you have some standbys in my room," Zander said and I fixed him with a look. He grinned, "I like the thought of you having some things there to use in case impromptu shit like this comes up, but mostly," his voice softened, "I just like having you in my life and I want some things in my room to remind me that you're real and want to be there."

I went to him. How could I not? He opened his arms and pulled me in close, between his knees where he sat on the high stool. I put my hands on his chest and kissed him and he kissed me back, oh, so sweetly.

"Go on, finish up," he urged quietly, and I nodded, slipping from his grasp. I finished cleaning up and put the chocolates aside to harden in their molds overnight. We shut down the shop, set the alarm and departed into the freezing cold winter air. I looked into the leaden dark sky.

"More snow is coming," I observed.

"Yeah. Let's move. If it's cool with you I'll leave my car in your driveway and we'll take yours." Zander said. I nodded. All it had taken was us fishtailing once on a tiny patch of black ice the first time it snowed for me to want to use my little, more-reliable car the rest of the winter. You know, the one with the added modern safety features of ABS, shoulder belts, and airbags.

We made it to Ev and Dray's before the flakes started to fall and Everett and I made quick work of packing some things into a couple of bags. Hers was one of her ever-present gym bags, while I packed neatly in my little carry-on suitcase that had never actually seen a flight. Zander had stayed out with my car, keeping it warm.

We dashed into the cold and down to the car, locking everything up tightly behind us. I didn't mind that Zander had slid behind the wheel of my car. Everett got in back without a word. We rode in silence, at half our typical speed, through the snow-covered streets, and when we arrived at the club, we were surprised to find that we had to wait to pull up into the lot.

"Has everyone been called in?" Everett demanded.

Zander gave a terse one word reply, "Yeah," and looked uncomfortable. I studied his profile.

"It's bad, isn't it?" I whispered, but he didn't answer, the muscle in his jaw clenching. I could tell he wanted to tell me, to be truthful with me, but he had a code to live by and the decision had been made by his club, and I understood that. I rested a hand on his leather-clad arm, a reassuring touch, and looked at his cut, neatly folded in my lap.

"Sometimes your silence is all you need to say," I reassured him and with a glance in my direction, he marginally relaxed.

We moved it inside, fast, out of the cold and wet and into the warmth of the common room, which had just about every man, woman and child of the Sacred Hearts MC in it. Zander gave me a quick kiss and shoved me a little in the direction of the club rooms with a meaningful look. Everett captured Dray's eyes and something was telegraphed between them. She gripped my hand and we both hurried out of the common area and into the back, just as Dragon's voice boomed over the low chatter, "Okay, listen up!"

Everett and I both stole into Dray's room and shut the door firmly. She sighed, her shoulders drooping.

"I think they got him," she said, dejectedly.

"What?" I didn't want to think about it, but she was right.

Evy pitched her voice into a low murmur. "Dray and I talk. All of the men talk to their Ol' Ladies behind closed doors; we always know things we aren't necessarily supposed to, it's just the way things are. Grinder left here in a huff over something or other, two nights ago when it was dry. He hasn't been seen or heard from since. Him not showing up at the shop today? I think cinched it." She gave me a sorrowful but meaningful look.

"They think the Suicide Kings got him?" I swallowed hard.

Evy nodded.

"I think they're organizing a search out there. I wouldn't expect to see much of Zander tonight." She huffed out a breath and flopped onto her back in the middle of her man's bed. I sank down to sit on the foot of it.

"I wish we could get along with them," I murmured, and Evy let out a short barking laugh full of derision.

"We tried that," she said, bitterly.

"I know." I looked my friend over and didn't miss when her hand unconsciously drifted to the spot on her thigh where she'd been hurt. She rubbed it with her fingers through the denim of her jeans.

"Does it hurt?" I asked.

She nodded. "Doc said it might, when it got cold. He was right. I guess it's kind of like when you break a bone."

I nodded. "My wrist aches sometimes, too."

"I remember when you broke it. I knew your da' did it, there was no way you'd be caught dead on a skateboard." She snorted at the absurdity and I laughed.

"That purple cast clashed with my hair something awful, but I was just in love with the color at the time." I made a face.

Evy laughed.

"Yeah, you were seven, you weren't quite the fashionista then as you are now." She shook her head and got up. "Pretty sure if you make a quiet break for it, you can make it to Rev's room unnoticed. Meet you in the inner sanctum after that." I nodded.

"Sounds good." I slipped out the door with my little suitcase and walked to Zander's room and let myself inside, shutting the door softly and tightly behind me. I set about putting things neatly away in his little closet and tucking a few essentials in the corner of the drawers where he kept such things. I was startled when I looked up and he was leaning against the door frame, smiling.

"Meeting over?" I asked.

"Yeah, it was a short one."

"Going out?" I inquired, but I already knew the answer.

"Yeah, have to."

"The weather is bad." I remarked, my hands trembling.

Zander pushed off the doorframe and tugged me gently into the circle of his arms. "Not going out by myself, Sugar. I'm headed out with Trig; we're taking his Jeep. We don't even know where to start lookin', but he's our brother and we gotta try."

I nodded and hugged his hard body to mine. "Just be careful. Promise me."

"I promise, baby. I'll be back when I can. Try and get some sleep, no need to throw off your schedule." He kissed me gently and with a final appraising look, smiled and let me go, disappearing out the door.

I finished up and slipped down the open hallway to the media room where the old ladies and a few club bunnies were lounging around. I dropped onto one of the beanbag chairs and Ashton smiled at me.

"Where's Hayden?" I asked.

"Out of town." She made a face. "One of her clients is opening a hotel in Chicago and brought Hayden in to do the decorating. Poor

Hayden is going nuts, the woman keeps changing things in the middle of them being installed; Hayden says she's a complete psycho but this project is a big deal. It's what might fix everything that the scandal Andy caused, wrecked." Ashton looked sad for her friend. "She misses Reaver."

Shelly snorted, "He misses her, too. He's been over just about every day this week, bugging the Hell out of me."

Ashton laughed. "He's been staying in our guest room, says the townhouse is weird without her in it."

I listened to the women gossip and chat, closed my eyes, and just relaxed, until Moira, one of the clubs' regular bunny girls spoke up, a couple of hours in.

"Do you think they'll find him?" she asked quietly. Usually Chandra would snipe at a girl, but she surprised me this time.

"I don't know, honey, why? You and him have something going on?"

Moira shook her head.

"Nah, Moira is all about Lucky, and he's crazy about her, too. Surprised he hasn't made you his Ol' Lady." Shelly said.

Moira chewed her bottom lip and looked uncomfortable.

The room fell silent, the television mindlessly playing in the background for a while, though no one was watching it.

Data called out, from his little closet full of computers, "We got incoming! Cops."

Everett rose from her place on the couch with a frown, and we just about all followed her out to the common room. Ashton and I held hands, and Chandra and Everett took the lead as the clubroom front door opened and two county deputies stepped in, shaking the snow off their boots, trying to keep the outside from coming inside with them.

Disney and Data went up to flank Evy and Chandra. Chandra spoke while Data texted next to her.

"Help you fellas?" she asked.

"Yes, do you know a," one of the deputies checked his notebook, "Jose Trujillo?" he asked.

"That's my father-in-law." Everett lied boldly.

"He filed a missing person's report on behalf of a," he checked his notebook again, "David Chandler AKA 'Grinder'." The deputy looked grim.

"That's right," Chandra said and lit a cigarette. The second deputy, who had been silent up to this point, frowned.

"You do know there's an ordinance against smoking in public places don't you?" he asked Chandra. He was definitely the younger of the two deputies, and the older one closed his eyes for a moment – it looked as if he was praying for patience.

Chandra gave the younger deputy a smug look and blew a plume of smoke into the air. "Private club," she uttered shamelessly, and raised her eyebrows, daring him to say anything.

The older deputy cleared his throat.

"Do you know where Mr. Trujillo is?" he asked Evy.

Evy hugged herself and gave him a steely look.

"Did you find Grinder?" she asked quietly. We all waited with bated breath, all of us suddenly focused on the older deputy, who sighed, defeated.

"Do you know if Mr. Chandler had any next of kin in the area?" he asked gently.

Chandra's back straightened.

"We're his family. I'm sure you get that," she stated, "What's happened to him?"

"I'm sorry to have to inform you that there seems to have been some kind of accident..." I fumbled with my phone, the deputy's voice turning to a senseless drone buzzing in my ears as he said words like 'accident', 'highway' and 'skid marks'. The phone rang in my ear over and over before Zander finally picked up.

"You need to come back," I said automatically, my voice cracking. Sure, I hadn't known Grinder terribly well, only a matter of a few months, but he was a part of this club; for better or worse a part of Zander's family.

"Red, what's wrong? What's happened?" Zander demanded, his voice strained with an urgent need to know.

"The police are here," I said numbly. "They found Grinder; can you just come back please?"

"Shhhhit!" Zander swore, then spoke to Trig, holding the phone away from his ear, his voice fainter but still clear as he told the other man, "Back to the club, cops are there saying they found Grinder. Mandy's freaked out, I can hear it in her voice." He came back on the line stronger, "Hang on, Sugar, we're on our way back."

"Okay," I nodded. The other girls were on their phones too, likely with their men, as the deputies stood by patiently.

Evy looked at them, her phone pressed to her ear and said, "Both Dragon – Jose," she corrected, "And Dray are on their way back."

I realized I was missing what Zander was saying.

"Mandy, sweetheart, baby, are you there?" he asked, anxious.

"Yes, yes, I'm here," I murmured.

Zander asked me the one question I had been begging silently he would leave alone, but I suppose it was only natural and I had to expect it. "Sugar, is Grinder all right?"

I didn't want to answer, I didn't want to be the one to tell him that his brother was dead. I closed my eyes and swallowed hard. "Are you driving?" I asked him, and I was met by a cold silence on the other end of the line.

"Zander?" I asked, when the silence had stretched for too long.

"He's not okay, is he?" he asked quietly.

"Just, how soon until you can get here?" I asked.

"Just tell me, Mandy." His voice was so hard, I could hear the barely-suppressed rage in it.

I swallowed again.

"He's gone, Zander, I'm so sorry – " I didn't get to finish because I heard Zander scream 'Fuck' at the top of his lungs and then there was a loud thump and crunching sound and the line went dead. I stared into the wide golden eyes of Ashton, and she put a hand on my own.

"They're fine, Zander threw his phone, they're okay, Ethan is driving and they're on their way back," she quickly reassured me when I stopped drawing breath. I felt tears well up hot and immediate and I dashed at them with my fingers. I tamped down the emotions rising uncontrolled and furious, choking me up, sorrow and anger paramount among them; sorrow that Zander was hurting so keenly, and anger that there wasn't anything I could do except sit there and wait for him to come back, half-afraid of what would walk through the door wearing my man's skin.

I'd never seen Zander in a fine burning rage except that one time in the ring, but that was exactly what I had heard on the phone. I walked a little way away from the rest of the girls, away from Data and Disney, and sank into a chair. Evy was speaking into her phone in a low voice and was dashing at some stray tears of her own.

Disney came over and pulled out a chair, straddling it, and linked his long, brightly-colored fingers through mine on the hand that wasn't taken up by the phone. He sighed. Likely because if I looked as ashen as I felt I was frightfully pale. I looked at him and his sympathetic brown eyes almost had my fear level rising rather than easing.

"I've seen Zander pissed off plenty of times, Red. He'll scream and yell and hit things and generally fly off the handle, and it's scary as fuck when he does it, but I've only ever twice seen him put his hands on somebody outside the ring. Both times the motherfuckers deserved it, and both times they were dudes. Zander would never hit a woman. Not after watching his dad tune his mom up as a kid. You ain't got nothing to worry about," he soothed.

I nodded, but strangely, his words didn't make me feel any better. I sniffed, and fought to beat back the despair taking root in the center of my chest.

"What do I do?" I asked hollowly. "How do I help him when he's hurting this badly?"

"Just don't get scared if he gets a little rough with you in the bedroom," he said starkly and I blinked, startled.

Disney shrugged inelegantly.

"I've known Rev a long time," he said quietly and had the grace to look embarrassed.

I stared at the young man, open-mouthed. He gave my hand a squeeze and got up, moving off to comfort one of the club bunnies, who was really taking the news hard.

I sat patiently and waited, turning things over in my head. Finally, needing something to do, I asked the deputies if they would like some coffee while they waited. The older one smiled wanly and nodded.

"That would be much appreciated, miss," he told me, and even the younger deputy nodded, grateful.

"I'll be right back," I said, and went in to the club's kitchen, moving around the stainless steel, industrially-kitted room automatically, measuring and grinding beans, pouring water and just generally going through the parade of motions, all the while my mind trying to grasp on to what the police had told us.

Grinder was dead. What's more, his death was labeled as 'under suspicious circumstances'; they were almost certain that his accident was no accident. Someone had run Grinder off the road. Someone had run one of the Sacred Hearts' brothers off the road and left him to die.

21

———————

R evelator...

I sat in the passenger seat of Trig and Sunshine's Jeep and seethed. I wasn't pissed at Red for not wanting to tell me, I was more pissed that she'd been put in the position to have to deliver the bad news in the first place. Trig drove carefully; the snow was dumping in buckets from the sky and it was hard to see anything. The feeling of futility just added more fuel to an already raging pyre of pissed-off.

"You good to talk yet, brother?" he asked me. He was fuming, himself, but I think that had a little bit more to do with the dent in his dash, from where I'd thrown my phone in a fit. I felt like a jackass for it now, even if it had felt really good at the time. I felt like an even bigger asshole when he'd turned and told me that it was okay, Ashton had let Red know we weren't in some kind of accident, that it was just me throwing a temper tantrum.

Not that he faulted me for it much. I could see Trig was in his own head over the news. He was that creepy and distant silent, in the place he went to when he was behind the scope. Fire and ice, that's what we were. While I was burning up from the inside out, he was one big, deep well of chill in the driver's seat, in control, focused.

"No, I'm not fucking good to talk," I growled.

Trig grunted in return, but didn't press it. Rather, he fielded several calls from other Sacred Hearts men as we piloted our way through the snow dump outside. I wouldn't be surprised if the power started going out; there was a reason I had a woodstove at my place.

He pulled up into the drive at the club carefully, sliding a couple of times before making it up into the lot and parked near the Sheriff Department's cruiser. It looked like Ghost and Reave made it back. Dragon had stuck them together to see if they could work out their differences over Shelly. Reave still hadn't completely forgiven Ghost for fucking up there, and it hadn't exactly been a gas keeping those two from tearing each other apart a few weeks back.

First thing I did when I got inside the clubhouse door was scan for Red's copper curls. Ashton was immediately in Trig's arms, and with a solemn search of my face with her golden gaze, she whispered timidly, "In the kitchen with the deputies," before she shied into the shelter of my big partner's frame. I shook myself like a dog coming out of the water and tried to lose the scowl. I didn't like scaring the shit out of the diminutive woman.

"Sorry, Sunshine."

"I understand," she murmured, "but be careful with her."

I nodded and went into the kitchen, and there was my girl, fixing coffee for the two Sheriff's deputies that belonged to the cruiser out front. She looked up, startled, and bit her lower lip, like she was waiting to see if she was in some kind of trouble, and immediately my anger fucking cooled. It was like she was some kind of soothing salve for my soul or something. I'd never felt anything like it, but I wasn't about to question it. You didn't question things like that, you just went with them and remained grateful for them.

"C'mere, Red," I said gently, and she obediently came around the counter and reached for me. I held her to me and breathed in her pristine floral scent, and leveled my stare at the older of the two deputies.

"Are you Jose or Draven Trujillo?" he asked.

"Naw, man, they're on their way. Can you fill me in, though?" I asked. Mandy pulled back a bit and searched my face.

"Perhaps it's best we wait until everyone is here," she said. "That way, they don't have to keep giving the bad news over and over."

I eased my hold on her into a gentler thing and smiled at her, even if it was tinged with the hurt and anger surrounding what was what with my club brother.

"Yeah, sure. Okay, babe, makes sense." I nodded and she slipped from my grasp to bring the coffee, with its tray of cream and sugar, along with mugs, out for everyone.

I gave her a hand and we happened to come out the kitchen door just as Dragon, Dray, Reave, and Ghost came through the front door. I turned and called back over my shoulder to the deputies that our Pres. was here and they both pushed off their stools.

Dragon shook hands with the older deputy and then with the younger one before he motioned for them to step into the chapel with Dray, Trig, Reave and Doc. Mandy made sure they were set up with coffee and murmured that she would make hot chocolate for everyone, to get them warmed up. Dragon pulled her into a one-armed hug and pulled her down to kiss her temple.

"Thanks, Red, the club owes you," he said. She blushed faintly, and I accompanied her back to the kitchen to help her out.

"Are you mad at me?" she asked, bringing out some bricks of Mexican chocolate from the pantry.

"No, baby! No, not at all, Sugar. I'm pissed that you had to tell me, I wanna know what happened, I want to fuck somebody up, but you? No, I'm not mad at you, not at all." I pulled her into my arms and she pressed her mouth to the side of my neck and trembled in my grasp. I felt her lips waver against my skin and with a deep breath she let out a sob that just broke my heart.

"I didn't even know him that well." Her voice was watered down by her tears and she sobbed against me. "Still, it's awful!" she cried, and the whole truth came spilling out of her, what the deputies had told those assembled back here at the club.

Grinder had been run off the road in the cold, in the dark, and no one had found him. How my brother had lain, trapped beneath his bike, in the cold, in the snow and had taken a day, maybe two, to die.

How no one knew how to get in touch with his family. How the only reason the police had come knocking here was the club dues receipt in his wallet.

I frowned and pulled back. "Wasn't he wearing his colors?"

She shook her head violently back and forth.

"I don't know, they didn't say."

I nodded and pulled her back into my arms, and rocked her until she quieted.

"I need to do something, anything," she murmured and went to splash some cold water onto her face. I slipped up on the stool to be near her, in case she needed me, while she shaved chocolate with her knife and set milk on to heat.

She moved about the kitchen with a single-minded determination to just not think and I had to admire her silent strength to do for others when she was hurting, too. The fact that she spared a thought for the cops and their feelings, on how it must be for them to deliver bad news to people over and over? Shit, her grace and generosity never ceased to amaze me.

"Can you get me the Fireball from behind the bar?" she asked.

"Yeah, babe. Be right back." I slipped off the stool and out the kitchen door and picked up the bottle of cinnamon whiskey. Everyone was sitting somber and stoic, waiting for Dragon and the rest of the Sacred Hearts officers to come back out. We couldn't see shit because of the heavy black curtains, but there really wasn't much doing until they came out and brought the rest of us up to speed. I brought Red the bottle like she asked, and she considered it thoughtfully, before liberally dosing the pot of drinking-chocolate she'd concocted.

"Trying to get us all drunk, Sugar?" I crooked a smile, but it was met with one of the most heartbreaking looks from my girl.

"I think we're all going to need the edge taken off tonight," she said, and took the pot off the stove before the alcohol could cook off.

I nodded. "I'm thinking you might be right."

She directed me to bring a cushy silicone mat-thing out to the bar so she could set the pot on it and prevent the wood beneath from burning. Soon, Sunshine had pitched in, taking paper cups of the steaming liquid and passing them around, almost as fast as Red could ladle them out.

Those who had been out in the cold searching were served up first, and it was as she passed out the last few cups that the door opened to the chapel and the men all filed out. The deputies shook hands with Dragon at the door and with a final subdued thanks to my girl for fixing them coffee, they slipped out into the snow. Just about everyone held their breath, waiting to hear what Dragon would say. He turned back to the lot of us, and with a heavy sigh filled us in.

"Grinder's been murdered," he said.

He told us everything, sparing no detail. Grinder had been run off the road maybe two, three nights ago. It was obviously intentional, a car-versus-bike scenario. Last time he'd been seen, he was wearing his cut, but he hadn't been wearing it when he was found. He'd been pinned under his bike, a leg broken, and some ribs too. He'd suffered. There was evidence that whoever had run him off didn't like him much; on that Dragon wouldn't elaborate, but whatever details he was holding back, likely on account of the women of the club being present, well... it didn't take a genius to see how much it stoked his fires and pissed him the fuck off.

"Tonight, we get our heads around this, around him being gone. Tomorrow, I need the Ol' Ladies to do what they do best in times like these." He gave a nod to Chandra and Shelly, who would know.

They nodded back their understanding.

"We'll take care of it," Chandra assured him, while the rest of the women looked on mystified. Not my Red, though, she was a preacher's daughter, and likely knew her way around a funeral.

"I'll speak to my father about a service," she murmured.

"Graveside? That would be nice, sweetie but we don't do no church service, and the wake will be here." Chandra's tone was gentle and Red nodded.

"I need to call the chapter he come from," Dragon's tone was heavy. "He's got three guys he come up with, I imagine they'll be wanting to stick around and see this through. Church tomorrow in the AM. Doc, I need numbers for his family."

Dragon held out a hand and our VP put a bottle of tequila in it, then he disappeared back into the chapel, Doc on his heels. Dray pulled Everett into the circle of his arms and kissed her, holding her close, foreheads pressed together as he spoke with her softly.

Red looked on with a watery smile, happy for her friend, yet still attempting to process the news that someone she knew, had interacted with weekly, if not daily, was gone in a seriously insidious and horribly painful way. I could see it in the pinched lines of her face, in her tight and rigid posture; she wasn't handling it well, but she was carefully holding herself together, giving an appearance of calm to benefit the rest of us who knew Grinder better. I pulled her into my arms and she startled. I was seated on one of the stools at the bar and it gave me added height, so for once, when I pulled her back to my front, my knees carefully bracketing her hips, I could rest my chin on her shoulder from up here. I tightened my arms around her and held her to me.

"It's okay, Red. You ain't gotta pretend for me or no one else. You're hurting. You don't have to put on a good show here. No one expects it." Her breathing all but stopped. Her fingers dug into the sleeve of the thick leather of my jacket and the hooded sweatshirt beneath that.

"I don't want to fall apart out here," she breathed, barely loud enough for me to hear it. I kissed the side of her neck and slipped off the stool, shoving her forward gently. I propelled her towards the back, towards my room, and caught a glance from Everett, who nodded gracefully in my direction.

It was awkward walking, her back pressed to my front but I didn't care, as soon as I had us through my clubroom door, I kicked it shut behind me and she trembled. She turned in my arms and we held each other while she cried silently.

"I shouldn't be this upset, I mean, should I? I didn't even know him that well." Her voice was mournful and I sighed and smoothed my hands up and down her back, which felt like an exercise in futility, encased as it was in her thick forest green sweater. I leaned back and chucked her under her chin.

"Baby, you were just told that a man you knew died in a horrible way and that some living, breathing, human piece-of-shit out there did it to him. You're allowed to feel any way you feel. Ain't nobody, least of all me, going to tell you otherwise; if anybody does, well, fuck 'em."

She blinked rapidly, twin tears slicking down her face, magnifying her freckles.

"I feel like I should be doing something, like I should be helping," she murmured. I smiled sadly at her.

"You are, baby. Just by letting me hold you, you are. I promise. Not much else can be done tonight, so let's go to bed, huh?" I didn't think she'd go for it but she nodded mutely, miserably, and we helped each other out of our street clothes and into some sleepwear.

I got into bed and held the blankets for her and she snugged herself perfectly into the curve of my body, her head resting on my shoulder.

"I love you, baby," I whispered into her hair. It suddenly seemed triply important that she know that, that I speak the words out loud.

"I love you too, Zander," she murmured back and I felt complete; the last of my anger cooled to a manageable level, some of the tension eased out of my muscles.

I held her for a long time, and simply stared at the ceiling above our heads while sleep eluded me.

The Suicide Kings had gotten one of us and if the game had been high stakes before... well, this was a game-changer, for sure. I listened to Mandy's soft breathing in the close dark of my room and wondered what the hell I was going to do, because now, more than ever, I had so much more to lose. To say that sleep, when it came, was as uneasy as it could get, was an understatement.

22

Mandy...

    When I had woken the morning after we'd all received the news about Grinder, it was to an empty room. Zander had already risen and was cloistered in the MC's little fishbowl of a room they reverently referred to as the 'chapel'. I rose and, with a shiver, dressed quickly. It was a white and pristine winter outside, beautiful and serene. To add to our heartbreak it was just past the New Year, a time that was supposed to be all about new beginnings. That just made this seem all the more awful, to greet the New Year in such a way.

I found Ashton and Everett in the kitchen, the three of us being the early risers among the Ol' Ladies, a title I was still coming to terms with.

Zander had presented me with a leather vest on New Year's Eve, beautifully embroidered with the somewhat distasteful moniker of 'Property of Revelator' on the back, the little name patch on the front boldly spelling out 'Red'. But when he explained to me what it meant to belong to him, the commitment he was offering me, suddenly the choice of words on the back, *Property of*, didn't seem at all distasteful, but rather a very special honorific.

Evy and the rest of the girls had a laugh over my initial reaction and all agreed that Everett's first reaction had been along the same lines as mine. Evy had nearly torn Dray a new one and they'd had quite the argument, until Shelly had stepped in and explained it to my sister from another mister. Apparently, Reaver and Trigger had been much better at explaining it to Hayden and Ashton. Shelly and Chandra had just been around the MC long enough to know what such a thing meant. Chandra had put it best when she said for a lot of the men, an engagement or wedding ring meant far less than bestowing a woman with their 'rag', as she called it.

"You look thoughtful," Evy remarked, lifting a steaming mug of coffee to her lips. She blew before taking a tentative sip.

"Just wondering what happens now. I mean, what do we do?" I stretched, and Ashton poured me a cup of coffee. I took it gratefully and added the requisite amount of cream and sugar from the tray of offerings to make it palatable.

"I talked with Chandra and Shelly until late last night. They said it's up to us to do what it is women do during funerals: make the arrangements, buy a casket, and have the funeral home bring him here once he's released. Cook for the club, clean up after, and be there for our men, for whatever they may need." Ashton shrugged.

"Best be expecting a lot of company in the coming days," Chandra said from the kitchen door, her sentence punctuated by the flick of her Bic lighter. She took a deep drag off her cigarette and released a large plume into the air with a harsh exhale.

"Shit gets crazy at a biker funeral," Shelly agreed, shoving past the older woman.

"How does it work?" Evy asked, thoughtfully.

"Well, just about every chapter across the states sends out at least one representative, unless the entire chapter shows up. Not sure how many brothers Grinder was good with; that makes a bit of difference. We could be packed to the gills and then some. Two, three hundred strong, maybe more. Given the weather here, though? My guess would be more like fifty or sixty. Again, depending on who he was good with," Shelly explained, fixing herself some coffee.

Chandra smoked some more and sighed, running her long nails

through her short platinum-blonde-dyed hair, the dark roots coming in.

"We have a wake here, things get crazy. A lot of eating, a lot of drinking, and a whole lot of fucking, with no mind to where they do it. You girls better wear your man's rag or it's just assumed you're fair game, you get me?" She pinned us all with a hard look and we three nodded mutely.

"Everybody gets up the next mornin', hung the fuck over, and the ride happens, a grand ol' procession to the cemetery. I don't know if Grinder's brothers are takin' him back to his home state or if he's being laid to rest here. The Sacred Hearts were in such a bad way some years back, gettin' killed, that Dragon bought a hell of a plot over at the ol' Brundle Hills cemetery. Bought half the damned place out. There's still a lot of ground out there left for anyone in the club has no place else to go. Sacred Hearts take care of their own, no matter where they're from." She took another thoughtful drag and pushed off the doorway where she'd been leaning.

She was dressed in jeans and knee-high boots, a white lace-edged camisole peeking out from the front of her fitted snap-button flannel shirt in reds, whites, and blues, the club colors. She tucked her cigarette between her lips and set about fixing herself a cup of coffee. Chandra never went without her makeup and this morning was no exception, the kohl lining her eyes making their light color stand out vividly, her cigarette stained with her light pink lipstick.

"I can handle food, but could use some help," Ashton remarked, looking at me. I nodded.

"I'll talk to my father today about conducting a graveside service," I said.

"I can keep the coffee flowing," Evy shrugged, "and pitch in with whatever else."

"I've got the funeral home's number that we use, Shelly can help me with figuring the cost. Everett, you need to make sure the bar is stocked, because these boys are going to go through it." Chandra looked my friend up and down, but Everett was already nodding.

"Aye, I can do that."

"I wonder if Reaver has called Hayden," Ashton remarked, and speak of the devil, there he was, just appeared out of thin air in the doorway.

"Yeah, she'll be here for the funeral but then she's got to fly back out," he said, and didn't look too happy about it.

Ashton immediately went to him and hugged herself to him. Reaver smiled down at her and kissed the top of her head, rubbing up and down one of the small woman's arms.

"Thanks, Sunshine," he murmured, and she beamed up at him.

"Well, okay. Everyone knows what to do. You boys got a count and a time frame for me?" Chandra asked.

"Looks like around fifty to eighty, and about a week, Chandra. Body won't be released until the final autopsy is done. Dragon's gone down there, but from what the po-po was telling us last night, best we just do a closed casket." His words dropped like a stone into the well of silence the kitchen had become. None of us wanted to think too hard about the implications behind his words. The whole thing was already bad enough.

Zander found me a short time later and we took a time-out to hold each other before the flurry of activity set in. Before long, Everett and I had to head in to work, and Chandra commandeered Shelly and Ashton into giving the clubhouse a good going-over.

Dray drove me and Evy in to work in my car; his Trans-Am was not exactly built for the snow. He stayed with us until Reaver could come in and then left. I let him take my car, with the promise that he or Zander would be back to take us to the club later.

Reaver played on his phone in my kitchen and from the odd smile or chuckle I gathered that he was texting back and forth with his wife, Hayden.

I snuck him an odd sample or two of chocolate when he grew too solemn. It was hard to see Reaver, who was always laughing, or smiling, or telling a joke, look so terribly unhappy. The light in his eyes was decidedly dimmer than usual.

The rest of the week went much the same. I spent my days keeping the shop stocked with confections, and made enough to set aside for Grinder's wake, too. My evenings were spent with Ashton in the club's kitchen making enough food to feed an army. The first night was spent preparing lasagnas in foil throw-away pans. We made so many, and then froze them, so all we would have to do was pull them from the freezer and reheat them.

We spent the remainder of the week doing similar things. The night we did the cinnamon rolls for breakfast, we could barely keep the men out of the kitchen and ended up having to make quite a few more than we initially anticipated because of it, but it brought with it a margin of levity to the club as men and women from other clubs began to trickle in.

The evening before the wake itself, Zander slipped into the kitchen and held out my *Property of* vest out to me with a sad little smile. I slipped into the proffered bit of clothing with a quizzical look and retied my apron over it to protect it.

"Bunch more brothers just showed up," he explained. "The three brothers that came up with Grinder are out there. They might come back and talk to you and Irish. He did spend a bunch of time in your shop." I nodded and Zander sighed.

"Not how I pictured you wearin' my rag for the first time, Sugar." His voice was tinged with such a deep regret my heart gave a fractured ache for him. I nodded again and he left the kitchen. Ashton turned from the sink full of dishes as Trigger brought her the vest he'd given her, giving her a lingering kiss after she'd donned it.

The women of the club were kept feverishly busy all the way through the wake and I have to honestly say, I have never seen anything like it! The drinking and partying and carousing was just phenomenal and I was almost grateful when Zander pulled me into his arms and walked us to his club room, even with as drunk as he'd gotten.

Still, something was different about him tonight than ever before and Disney's words of advice tumbled through my mind, *Just don't get scared if he gets rough with you in the bedroom...* I didn't fully understand the implications of what Disney had said until the door swung shut behind us and Zander fell on me.

He shoved me back, hard, against the closed door, his thigh riding up between mine, pinning me, my sex pressed to the top of his leg, as his mouth crashed up into mine and his hands delved beneath my black sweater to find skin. The ferocity of his kiss stole my breath and my heart very nearly stopped in my chest, doing a flip and plummeting into the pit of my stomach. Fear fizzed through my veins like sour champagne and I dragged a deep breath through my nose and fought my urge to squirm, to try and get away. Instead I cupped his face with my hands and kissed him back and kept reminding myself over and over *This is Zander, this is Zander, this is Zander.*

He broke the kiss only long enough to rip my sweater over my head. I yelped as one of my earrings caught and pulled painfully before slipping free of my earlobe. It stung for a moment; there was no real harm done, but it was as if Zander hadn't even noticed. He pulled me back tight and tighter against his body until I cried out into his mouth, which just seemed to excite him further. He pulled me away from the door, turning me and giving me a shove onto the bed.

"Zander, you're scaring me!" I cried under my breath.

"Sorry, Sugar," he said with a crooked grin, but he honestly didn't look or sound sorry at all, which only served to scare me more. I'd never seen him so drunk before, either, and so I kept telling myself that he would be sorry when he sobered up. Still, it wasn't exactly a good feeling.

"Ohhh, hey, don't look like that, Red," he said, his voice deep and unsteady. He came to me where I sat on the edge of the bed and cupped my face in his hands, pressing his forehead to mine. His eyes were closed and he seemed to be sobering a bit.

He asked me, "Remember the locker room?"

I covered his hands with mine, firmly, as his thumbs stroked back and forth over my cheeks.

"How could I forget?" and I tried a tremulous smile.

"Can I have that, Red? Do you trust me enough to give me that?" he asked, and he shook lightly with his restraint.

I closed my eyes, not entirely sure what it was I was getting myself into but the short answer? Yes. Yes, I trusted him, yes, I loved him, and so I would see. I would see if I could take what he needed to give. My heart in my throat, I let the answer he was looking for fall from my lips. "Yes."

He hauled my lips up to his and feeling a bit less left of center, a bit more like I was in control, him having asked and me having given him permission, I let him kiss me and returned his kiss with an equally-savage intensity. We clawed at each other's clothes, and Zander ripped his shirt completely in two to be rid of it. I pulled myself further back onto the bed and with a snarl, he came after me. He got between my thighs and shoved his way inside, brutally fast, brutally hard, wringing a cry from my lips that was half-fear, half-desire. It felt good, surprisingly so, with just that little bit of added edge of pain from my not being quite ready, not being quite worked up enough to take him easily.

It was okay though, my body would catch up soon enough and it wasn't like Zander was going to give me any quarter. He slammed his body against mine and set a punishing cadence of hard fast thrusts, the report of our bodies coming together filling the room with rhythmic pounding to match the pulse of blood through my veins.

There was nothing kind, nothing gentle or loving about this, but it felt so good, so freeing and intense, and so, just, unlike anything I had ever experienced before, just ever. I was vaguely aware of my nails biting into the flesh of his back, of scoring down his skin in such a way that it left him arching into me harder, his thrusting stilling.

"Oh, aw fuck, baby! Yes!" he cried above me, and adjusted his angle. He grabbed me behind the knees and folded them up to my chest, his hands pressing the backs of my thighs as he drove into me harder. I bit back a scream at the intensity of it and tried to relax, but it was almost too intense, too extreme. I cried out, a feral sound, and squirmed, and he eased up just enough to make things comfortable again.

"Shit, sorry," he gasped, and the love in his voice turned me on that much more.

"It's okay, don't stop!" I cried, breathy, and he smiled and brought the intensity back up to a slow rolling boil between us, his hand straying from the back of my leg, his thumb finding and sweetly torturing the top of my sex until my womb grew heavy, weighted with the promise of orgasm.

"Yeah, Sugar, come on for me, baby, come for me, sweetheart," he urged, and when I did, it eclipsed my whole world, though instead of being cast in the dark it was just the opposite, I was lit up from the inside out until every nerve, every filament, and every fiber of my being glowed with purest, shining, bright pleasure at the hands of the man who rode my body, plunging deeply and drinking sweetly of the pool that was me, until he met his own end. Zander came, crying out above me, thrusting deeply and unevenly a few more times, touching off aftershocks in me nearly as intense as the original cataclysm.

We came back to ourselves slowly, our breaths sawing in and out of our lungs in a ragged race to supply oxygen to our overworked bodies, lightly slicked with a dew of sweat and further down below, heavier, wetter things denoting our very good time. Zander unset his teeth from my shoulder and I hadn't even realized he'd bitten me, though the impressions left behind from his teeth were a stinging arch in my skin that would surely bruise.

"Ow," I uttered, and he pressed the pad of his thumb into the marks and massaged them. I couldn't tell if that made it better or worse, but to have him touch me so tenderly, I wasn't about to complain.

"You okay, Sugar?" he asked, between breaths.

"Yeah, I think so."

Zander pushed himself off of the top of me and stared down into my eyes.

"You're fucking incredible, you know that?" he asked me softly, caressing my bottom lip with his thumb. He covered my mouth with his in a slow sultry kiss and I felt a surge of pride in myself for having not been afraid, and truthfully I was so glad I had kept it at bay. I was pretty sure I was going to learn to enjoy rough sex with my man, if it was like that all of the time.

"Mm." Zander pulled back at the sound. "I liked that," I told him.

"It's not going to be a problem, then?" he asked.

"Mm-mm." I shook my head no.

"Good, because I was going easy on yah." He winked and I a laugh bubbled out of me. He gave me a cheeky, if satisfied, grin and slipped from me, then cursed.

"Fuck, hope you're keeping up with the pill, baby."

I looked down between us; we'd forgotten a condom again. I sighed, nodding. I'd had my period a couple of weeks before but still, we needed to stop tempting fate.

He kissed me and grabbed his robe.

"Don't go anywhere," he murmured and slipped out of the room. I laughed to myself; I didn't think I could get up and walk if I tried! My legs felt like they weren't up to the job of standing.

Zander returned and cleaned me up before pulling me into the curve of his arms. We talked quietly about what the next day was going to hold before falling into a fitful sleep, one that was all too short.

23

R evelator...
    The ride to the cemetery was colder than shit. I had on two pair of long-johns under my long denim shorts and it still wasn't really enough. I had on gloves, a hooded sweatshirt, and a tee with actual sleeves hugging the shit out of my biceps on, under my leather jacket and cut, and I was —still– freezing my balls off. Wraparound sunglasses kept the wind out of my eyes, and a bandana wrapped around my face tried to keep out the cold. It only worked marginally well. The ride was a slow one and it felt like forever before we were standing beside a gaping pit in the ground, a mound of astro-turf-covered earth at the yawning darkness' side.

My girl's father, and I do use that term loosely, presided at the top of the grave. When he said some nice shit about Grinder, a man he didn't even know, my fury towards him loosened its chokehold some. My Red looked somber and washed-out by all the black she was wearing and I longed to see her back in the autumn colors that complimented her so well.

I hated it. Hated standing beside that open grave, hated commit-ting my brother to the cold hard earth, when it could have been prevented.

A bunch of us guys felt guilty as hell. Grinder'd been striking out with a bunch of the girls around here. They just weren't his speed and we'd all been giving him some hell about it. He was trying hard to get out of the life of gun- and drug-running over the border back where he'd come from, and was looking for a new start with the mother chapter out here.

None of us bargained that he had a temper or realized that we'd been fucking with him on the wrong topic.

He'd told us all to fuck right off and had gone off on his own. None of us had really thought anything of it. We'd figured he'd gone down to The Spot, found himself a willing pussy, and had gone balls-deep in it back at the apartment he had gotten; he was one of the ones that didn't live at the club. Surprisingly few guys did, anymore.

That had been a Friday night.

We really hadn't thought much of it; Grinder was a big dude, and from what we could tell, a smart dude. We'd fucking let him slip through the goddamned cracks, and didn't even really notice 'til Ev and Red mentioned it on Tuesday morning that he was still MIA, and that, well, that made us all a bunch of fucking douchebags.

We'd failed our brother and you could tell by the stony expressions of the brothers from the mother chapter that it wasn't a mistake we would ever make again. The Suicide Kings had gotten lucky catching Grinder out alone, but it wasn't ever going to happen that way again.

There would be no solo riding until every last one of those motherfuckers was taking a dirt nap in an unmarked grave in Cicada Woods.

We filed back to the club the way we'd come, in a proud procession, our heads held high, but that didn't stop the Suicide Kings from parking along the funeral route, smiles of glee pasted to their faces, tryin' to look all badass. It took everything we had to keep Grinder's three brothers on their fucking bikes and away from scrapping with those dimwitted fucks.

The police escort was even pissed-off. One, because they couldn't prove shit. There was no probable cause to go after anybody without a motive and we couldn't exactly supply the cops with one without incriminating ourselves. Two, the Suicide Kings weren't exactly doing anything illegal. They were just legally parked along a section of the road we happened to be driving on, giving us the one-fingered-salute as we rode by. It was bullshit, but it was also bullshit we couldn't do a goddamned thing about... Yet.

Back at the club, Mandy had the coffee and hot chocolate flowing and was doing her level best to warm everyone's soul as much as their bodies with words of comfort. I'd been fucking afraid she wouldn't be okay with the rough stuff we'd done the night before come the cold light of morning, but she'd kissed me silently until I'd quit asking, and had slipped off to a hot shower, looking as thoughtful as I'd ever seen her.

She came up to me and pressed a steaming ceramic mug into my hands. The warmth was unbelievably welcome to my frozen-ass fingers, even with the gloves on.

"I was cold just watching you," she said, with a slight smile.

"Yeah, brutal out there, but as far as riding in frozen conditions go, couldn't ask for a better day for it," and that was true. The sky was blue, the sun shone brightly, and even though it was still predominantly a winter wonderland out there, the streets had been mostly dry as a bone and the few, small icy patches had been stark and apparent. It'd been easy riding despite the frozen conditions.

"Women," Dragon's voice interrupted the low murmurs, and everyone turned to the original P. of the Sacred Hearts.

"Appreciate all you done for us these last few days, but if you could kindly give your men the floor it'd be much appreciated." His voice held all the respect we felt for the girls and everything they'd done in getting this together. The women of the Sacred Hearts, both from here at home and abroad, beamed with pride under the praise and graciously melted into the back, towards the media room.

Dragon cleared his throat. "I wanna thank all you brothers for coming out during such a difficult time. Grinder was still relatively new to us, but overall was a likeable guy. For him being here such a short time, we're sure gonna miss him." Dragon raised his glass and we all did the same and put down some of whatever we were drinking.

"So, the mother chapter and Grinder's home chapter out in Phoenix have some business. Namely, Archer, Nox, and Rush from the Phoenix chapter would like to patch over into the home chapter. I would like to put it to a quick vote, since we're all here." Dragon's gaze captured the gaze of the Phoenix president, a guy called Dom; if it was short for 'Dominic' or calling him out on his personality was anyone's guess.

"Dom, is having these three guys up and leave your chapter going to cause you any undue hardship?" Dragon asked him.

Dom was a tall motherfucker with tan leathery skin and long brown hair graying at the temples and braided tight to his skull. . He eyed Dragon speculatively.

"I appreciate that you'd ask," he grated, his voice deep and gravelly. "Losing all three would put me one man short of the bare minimum of keeping my chapter aboveboard on a headcount. But. I got four prospects, and two of them are on the verge of patching in next month. The other two ain't too far behind. If the other chapters can give me a couple of months grace on being a man down, I could make it work. I ain't going to stand in the way of these boys and their revenge, but neither am I gonna let my chapter fold from it."

"Fair enough. We got reps from at least every chapter out there nationwide. Those of you who are here can act as proxy for your people. You wouldn't be here otherwise. So first up, a vote on grace for a period of three months for the Phoenix chapter being one man down. All in favor of granting that grace?" Every hand in the room shot up. Dragon nodded, his expression clearly communicating that he wasn't surprised.

"So ordered. You reach out to other chapters, see if someone is willing to prop you up, see if a nomad is willing to stick around and help you out in the meantime, but you got your grace period."

Dom nodded.

"As fer us, all in favor – " he didn't even get to finish before every hand in the home chapter shot up. We'd heard Archer talk about growing up in foster-care with Grinder, Rush, and Nox, heard their stories about coming up in the same house, the four of them. Rush and Nox were twins, even though they didn't look a thing alike, and Archer and Grinder, being older, had pretty much lain their asses on the line to keep the younger boys safe from a fucked-up set of foster parents more interested in the state money than actually looking after their charges.

Archer seemed a little hot-headed, but that wasn't anything that these guys hadn't already dealt with when it came to me. That had mostly been Unkind's doing, though Trig had carried my original mentor's torch just fine. I was pretty confident that the three new guys would fall into our line of thinking after the dust had settled and the Suicide Kings were just that, dust.

From what I had been able to tell so far, Rush and Nox were pretty quiet. Not nearly as quiet as our boy Blue, who damned near never spoke, but Rush and Nox usually fell in line behind Archer, and according to everyone who was close to the dudes back in Arizona, Archer had almost always fallen in line with Grinder. Grinder had been the glue holding the four brothers together for the longest time... and now he was gone.

Archer, Nox, and Rush all nodded in Dragon's direction, and the party welcoming them into the fold got started. Reaver and Trig went off to talk to them, but my mind was on one thing and one thing only: being near my Red.

Disney appeared in the archway leading back towards the club rooms in the main building and the girls started trickling back into the common room around him. There would be no discussion of the Suicide Kings and what to do about them tonight. We'd just laid our brother to rest. Tonight would be devoted to memory and to welcoming our three newest members, and for the Phoenix chapter to say goodbye to three of their guys.

I found Red in the media room, curled up on one end of the couch, her nose in her e-reader thing as she read to herself. I asked Evy silently with my eyes if I could take her place on the couch and she smiled and rose gracefully to her feet, heading off in search of

Dray. I dropped onto the couch cushion vacated by my girl's best girl and she looked up and smiled, her face lighting up.

She rose, indicating I should get comfortable against the arm of the couch, which I did, and she got back down, nestled between my thighs, resting against me before resuming her reading. Times like these, life was good. Perfect and serene, this time was no exception, even if it was laced with guilt and sadness. I held my woman and turned to the screen. Several other brothers filtered in and some action-comedy flick was put on and we all just sort of chilled. I decided we needed more nights like this.

I lazed with Mandy in my arms as people drifted in and out of the media room before finally heading for their home towns or to a room for the night. About midnight I looked down to see she was fast asleep against me, her e-reader resting on her chest. I smiled and gently shook her. She startled awake and yawned, stretching.

"C'mon, babe, let's go to bed," I murmured and she turned the most beatific smile on me and nodded. I think that's the moment that it really became clear to me. Mandy was mine, not because I wanted her to be, not because she was my Ol' Lady, but because she wanted to be.

Trig had once told me that Ashton had said as much to him once, the first lake run they'd ever been on together, and I'd nodded and thought it was really cool, and thought I'd understood but this very moment, right here, with her smiling at me like that, I realized that it was one of those things that you couldn't really know until it happened to you.

I followed her into my room and shut the door, pulling her into my arms. She startled and caught the expression on my face and everything about her softened.

"What's wrong?" she asked.

"Nothing, Sugar. Nothing at all." I kissed her gently and held her close for long moments until she pushed back to look me in the eye.

"Are you sure you're okay?" She looked concerned and I felt a smile of my own tease the corners of my mouth.

"Never better, baby..." and I meant it.

24

Mandy...

Life resumed some semblance of normalcy in the days and weeks following Grinder's funeral. Still, a seed had been planted by the Suicide Kings and the plant that grew from it was an ugly, spikey thing, full of fear and loathing, dripping a poisonous rage. It swept through the club, spawning more secret meetings for the guys behind closed doors, and took Zander from my side and Dray from Evy's more, and for much longer than either of us were comfortable with. We were afraid for our men as much as, if not more than we were for our own safety.

She and I were at the club, along with Chandra and Ashton, in the media room quietly watching television. Most of the men were out; just Reaver, Trigger and a couple more were there. Dragon and Dray had gone to settle a dispute in another chapter. Archer, Rush and Nox were finalizing their permanent move from Arizona. Ghost was out working, Shelly preferring to ride with him and cement and explore their relationship further. As dysfunctional as their relationship sometimes appeared on the outside, those two were devoted to one another. Despite their near constant disagreeing on this or that, there was something about Ghost that was visibly healing Shelly. It was good to see.

I missed Zander. He was on his way from his house and his evening round of training; he preferred his home gym to the piece-meal equipment here at the club. Evy, Ashton, Chandra, and I were all watching a romance story on the big television screen. It involved time travel and a beautiful story crossing time between 18th century Scotland and the 1940's post-WWII. Chandra, with her glasses on, was crocheting in one of the recliners and I was sitting with my Kindle forgotten in my hands absorbed in the tale on the screen.

It was tranquil, as peaceful as it'd been for a while at the club, but still with an edge of worry, of concern... all of us were living with a fractured ache in our chests, in the back of our minds a *What if?* It had been so very quiet, the animosity between the Sacred Hearts and the Suicide Kings, since the discovery of Grinder's body. It felt as if the pressure were building, mounting, and we had no notion as to when it was going to explode.

I didn't realize anything was wrong at first; there was an exchange of musket fire on the TV and the surround sound in the media room was really good. It was loud, very loud, but then Chandra was bounding out of her recliner and there was shouting that was most definitely not a part of what was happening on the screen.

Everett pulled me to the floor and Ashton snugged herself in a crouch beside the behemoth entertainment center. I blinked rather stupidly at Evy, who was rooting through her purse, until the distinctive sound of a shotgun being cocked dragged my attention away from my best friend's peculiar behavior.

Chandra, a grim expression on her face, was going around the recliner and couch towards the big thick double doors. She paused in the doorway and leveled the shotgun and pulled the trigger. A riot of noise and gun smoke exploded from the end of the gun and a shout emanated from the other side of the door. Everett stood up abruptly, a handgun very black against the palm of her hand.

I forgot to breathe, so fixated was I on the determined and fierce look on Everett's face, and so I had no breath to scream with when Chandra's body jerked horribly and she began to fall backwards. Ashton cried out and shoved her small hands tight over her mouth and I made a grab for Everett, but it was too late. She was out around the couch and up against the wall by the door, then turning, and, her arms straight, she fired three shots into the hall before ducking back against the wall.

"Stay here!" I whispered harshly at Ashton and she nodded, her golden eyes wide with fright. I stayed low and crawled across the black carpet to where Chandra lay. I put my hands over the blossom of blood on the camisole beneath her form-fitting plaid shirt and pressed down. Blood welled warm and immediate beneath my hands and I checked her face, but she was gone. Her light blue eyes stared sightless at the ceiling, the spark of her essence, her life, her energy – just dark... gone.

A shadow loomed over me and I looked up into the eyes of a grinning man wearing Suicide Kings colors.

"She's dead," I proclaimed hollowly and the man grinned wider, leveling his gun in my face.

"So are you, bitch!"

I stared at the man beyond the gaping barrel of the gun pointed at my face and tasted regret. I had no control over what happened next, no say on if I would live or die, and so I blurted the first thing that came to my mind.

"I know, and it's all right, I suppose. I forgive you."

I closed my eyes and thought of Zander, of Everett and Dray... Everett, where was Everett?

Boom!

Boom! Boom! Boom! Click, click, click, click, click...

I looked up and the man blinked at me, his eyes much too wide. I looked down. Blood began to soak into the front of his shirt and he dropped to his knees. Everett stood behind him, hands outstretched, the gun shaking between them as she pulled the trigger over and over again... *Click, click, click...*

She looked at me, agape, and finally screamed at me, "What the fuck was that? You forgive him? Seriously, Mandy?"

I looked down to where my hands pressed against Chandra's still chest, wet and slick with her blood, and felt my tears run down my face, hot and salty damp, tightening my skin in their wake. I looked up at Everett, my sister, my best friend since the second grade.

"I don't know what made me say that," I said.

"You're a good person, that's what made you say it," she grated, and reached down to haul me to my feet by my wrist. I stood and we hugged each other, shaking, in the midst of the wreckage of splintered doorframe and wall plaster littering the carpet. Ashton came around the couch and bit down on a low and broken moan; I pulled her in tight with me and Evy.

It was silent... eerily quiet after so much violence and ruckus.

"Ethan..." Ashton moaned, her expression plagued by fear. It was a fear all three of us shared.

Everett picked up the man's forgotten gun and discarded her own.

"Stay behind me," she urged, and we carefully edged our way out into the hallway. I held Ashton to me as we followed my best friend out into the open area, skirting around another man's body in Suicide Kings colors, and past doors, towards the common room.

We reached the corner, the turn through the archway bracketed by the bar on our right and the fishbowl-chapel on our left. The shattered glass from the windows and door to the small room crunched under our shoes, the curtains worrisome with no indication as to if anyone hid behind them. But any thoughts about the fluttering black cloth were immediately dashed when we heard him.

He coughed, his breath sawing in and out of his chest in rapid-fire pants, his head and neck were propped against the top of an overturned table, and his legs were splayed out in front of him.

Ashton stiffened in my arms and Everett's gun lowered.

There was a cell phone, the screen cracked but lit, beside his hip as he choked out to whoever was on the other end, "Promise me, man... You have to promise me you'll take her, you'll get her out of here and protect her."

Trigger leaned over Reaver's prone form and pressed a wad of cloth, which appeared to be his tee shirt, to the younger man's side.

Reaver wore a white tee with stark black body armor over his chest, but that hadn't stopped the bullet from entering his side.

"You're gonna be fine, man! Listen, we're on our way up, don't you worry 'bout a thing!" The voice over the phone was optimistic but strained.

"You gotta promise me, Trigger has Sunshine, you gotta look after my Doll. She trusts you, she likes you and you..." he coughed.

Zander, who I belatedly realized was by the door, turned around. He was speaking low and steady into his cellphone which was pressed to his ear, and his warm chocolate-brown eyes rose from Reaver's prone form and met mine. Ashton's knees buckled and she emitted a low wail. I held her up; it wasn't hard, the tiny woman was so slight. I murmured to her that it was going to be okay. I mean, it had to be, didn't it?

A siren sounded in the distance, growing nearer while Reaver continued to urge the voice on the other end of the line to take care of his wife.

Trigger cursed and shouted at the phone, "Will you just fucking promise him?" The silence after his outburst hung thin and brittle until the voice on the end of the line sighed out.

"I promise, man, but I still maintain you're going to be fine."

I tore my eyes from the phone, from my broken and bleeding friend on the floor, and searched Zander for any injury, but there was none. Ashton was sobbing, big, noisy, wracking, broken sobs and it was taking both Evy and I to hold her up. Hayden was out-of-state again, back in Chicago putting the finishing touches on the hotel she'd been contracted to do the interior design work on. She didn't know, she wasn't here...

The door slammed open and we three women jumped, a short startled scream escaped my lips and Zander took six long strides across the wreckage and reached us. He folded us all in his arms as best he could as the EMT's rushed to Reaver's side with a stretcher. They began to work on him, and Trigger reluctantly relinquished his best friend to the professionals' care.

"Is anyone else hurt?" a medic demanded, and Trigger looked at us.

"The girls, check the girls. Take them with you, they might be in shock," he mumbled, and stumbled a step back. We couldn't have held Ashton back if we wanted to then; she flung herself out of our grip and at the love of her life, and the big man caught her up in his arms.

"Are they all gone?" I asked, my voice high and breathy, shaky now that the adrenaline was wearing thin.

"Yeah." Zander nodded and held me tight, and I held on to him right back. The door blew back on its hinges and Dray and Dragon burst into the room, the police right on their heels. Everett disengaged from Zander and me, and Dray caught her and squeezed her tight as she finally gave over and burst into tears.

That was Evy. As strong as you needed her to be, until she just didn't have to be anymore. Now that Dray was here, she most definitely didn't have to be. He held her tightly, a string of Spanish escaping his lips, half-cursing, half-soothing.

Dragon surveyed the scene dispassionately.

He made a query in Spanish and Zander answered him, their eyes darting over the medics and police in the room. They were taking Reaver away and people were jostling out of the doorway to let them pass. When no comprehension shone in the Sheriff Deputies' or medics' eyes at the Spanish exchange, Dragon and Zander continued their conversation cautiously, until one of the deputies intervened.

"Hey! Enough of that!" he said gruffly. "There's a whole lotta blood on the floor and more than a few dead bodies, so you fuckers speak English until we get a handle on what the fuck is going on!"

I found my voice. "Excuse me, but we were attacked, and I would appreciate not being spoken to in that tone of voice." I said, and trembling, drew myself up to my full height. Zander stepped aside, his arms remaining tight around my waist and I was grateful for that, extremely grateful, because I was terribly afraid that if he let me go, I would crumble into all that broken glass and I wouldn't know how to get up again.

The deputy grumbled out an apology and a female medic came and took me away from Zander, more fire department and medical people took Everett and Ashton, too and led us outside. I kept staring over my shoulder at Zander, who looked as resigned and as closed-down as I had ever seen him, his brown eyes darker, not in color, but with his rage. It scared me, seeing him standing in the wreckage of his club, all that raw hatred and deep emotion playing out over his face and I saw it plain as day, really, for the first time: *Through me you go into a city of weeping; through me you go into eternal pain; through me you go amongst the lost people.*

I shuddered and closed my eyes, turning towards the frigid outdoors, the waiting aid car, and the scratchy blanket the paramedics were wrapping around my shoulders. A numbness started to fill me from the center of my being out, a comforting lack of feeling, lack of emotion, a lack of despair, and I welcomed it, because what had happened in there was just too awful to ever want to think about again.

"What?" I asked, and looked into the woman's eyes.

"Oh, honey, I've been asking if you're hurt. Can you tell me if any of this is yours?" the female medic asked again. I looked at my hands where they clutched the blanket around my shoulders, detached, nothing.

"Oh, no... it's not mine. It's not my blood." It was Chandra's... poor Chandra... I sobbed and my world fractured. I broke down and sobbed and keened, and longed for it to be just an hour ago, or days from now. Anything, so I didn't have to feel what I was feeling inside, this awfulness, this loss, this violation.

I don't really remember what happened next. I don't remember going to the hospital, I don't remember being checked over or changing clothes into a set of scrubs given to me by the doctors and nurses since my clothes were too bloody to continue wearing. I do remember Zander finding me, my love, my rock in this storm-swept landscape of emotions no one should ever have to feel. He found me in the curtained area, and with a fierce growl at the nurses, climbed up into the bed with me and held me close while I cried, waiting for them to discharge me.

I was treated for shock, whatever that really entailed. I don't know. Everything that happened I just seemed to gloss over, or blow through, everything was hazy and disjointed and not really real. I can't remember so well, or rather, I didn't want to remember, and I was okay with not remembering.

Minutes crept by, the small hour hand made its slow, lazy crawl around the face of the clock. Detectives asked questions, and when I woke up from the nightmare, it was to find I had slept, but it wasn't really a dream. Not at all. I lay curled in the fetal position, my head in Zander's lap, covered by a jacket and a Sacred Hearts cut. The club filled the small waiting room to overflowing. Evy sat beside Dray, her head on his shoulder; Ashton curled up in Trigger's lap, a ball of sightlessly staring nerves, clinging to her man, who held her like she was a treasure that he'd nearly lost.

I looked up at Zander, whose fingers were tangled in my curls. He had a peculiar look in his eyes, on his face, and after trading a look with Evy, I suspected they had spoken. I blinked slowly and sat up, stretching.

"How yah doing, Red?" he asked me softly. His hands rested on his thighs and I grabbed for one, twining my fingers with his.

"I think I'm okay," I murmured, but my voice was somber and tentative at best. I drew in a deep breath and looked over at Shelly, who was pacing nervously, her thumbnail, which was in her mouth, nearly chewed to the quick.

Ghost sat on the floor, his back to the wall, his legs outstretched in front of him and crossed at the ankle as he followed his woman's pacing with his gaze. My heart broke for Shelly all over again.

I hugged Zander's arm and he swept my face with his gaze, opening his mouth to speak, but just then the doors to the waiting room burst open and Hayden appeared. Dragon, who was by the door, caught her by the elbows, and she raised her face, her expression stricken.

"Is he..?" she asked and held her breath.

Dragon sighed, "Still in surgery, Doll. We just don't know."

And the waiting went on, another hour, then two, and then three, until they all just blurred together into an agonizing length of time. Cutter and several other men of the Kraken arrived; was that who had been on the line? Was that who Reaver had called? It must have been, else why would they be here?

Dragon and the President of the other motorcycle club stepped out into the hall while Ashton and Hayden clung to each other and cried, Trig doing his best to comfort them. When the two men returned, it was with Doc, looking worn and tired in his scrubs and white coat, a funny little matching blue surgeon's cap on his head.

Hayden pulled away from Trigger and Ashton and swallowed hard. Cutter went to the other small woman's side, and put a hand on her shoulder.

"Just, tell me!" she pleaded of the older man, and his face, which was pinched, collapsed into sorrowful lines.

"I'm sorry..."

Hayden's face was stricken. She hugged herself around the middle and bent at the waist, her mouth open in a scream, except there was no sound, just an eerie hissing silence that came from her throat. She sucked in a great breath and the sound came this time, low and broken and defeated. She wailed her agony to the room and were it not for Cutter, doing his best to hold her up, she would have gone to her knees.

It was the most painful, heart-breaking, gut-wrenching thing I had ever seen or heard in my life and it was the thing that made me want to crawl into a bed somewhere and simply never come out again. I had never, not once in my life, ever questioned if there was a God, but right then, right there, I questioned everything. I questioned everything there ever was and then some, while Zander held me, my gaze locked with my soul sister's. Everett and I cried to the sound of everything Hayden loved and held dear burning down to ashes all around her.

25

Zander...

Sober, somber, stoic... those were the best words I could come up to describe my Red as she held it together in that goddamned waiting room.

The firefight had already started when I'd pulled up. I'd left my car in the turn lane of the highway and streaked low and fast up the drive, taking out the motherfucker that'd gotten Reave. Trig was topside, on the roof, and had downed two fuckers in the driveway.

My adrenaline pounding through my veins and the rabid fear that they'd got my girl had to take a back fucking seat to me calling an ambulance for Reaver. Once that was done, I'd immediately dialed my P and my VP, who should be back any minute from their run. What a fucking thing.

Disney had texted from the back of our club compound to say that he, Blue, and Duracell had one of them. There had been six of the little cock bites. I called him from the burner in my pocket and told them to get the fuck out to my car, which was running out front, on the highway, and to get the son of a bitch out to Point Nowhere and keep him locked down. They'd made it away before emergency people started showing up.

Then there we were, hours and hours later, one of our brothers, one of our council dead, and one of our women gone with him. Were it not for Red, trembling in my arms, I would be out burning the whole fucking world down.

Hayden was a near-catatonic ball in Cutter's arms. He knelt on the floor holding her to him. Shelly had disappeared, Ghost hot on her trail as she'd run from the room and hit the stairs with a crash. He'd texted the club saying that he'd meet us there with her later. Zeb and Disney had been cleaning up busted glass and boarding up the club's front windows as soon as the cops had cleared out.

As soon as Doc delivered the bad news to Hayden, Dragon and Trig had led the older man into the hallway and delivered the news about his woman. He'd shouted and crumpled to the floor himself, back sliding against the wall, his chest blown open, his heart ripped out... plain as day for all to see.

It'd taken some logistics, and Zeb to come with the van, to get us all back to the club. Ashton, Red, and Ev were all in with Hayden. Shelly was locked in Ghost's room and refused to deal with anyone or anything. Now here we all were, Doc included, standing in the boarded-up shell of our clubhouse with five of the Kraken, trying like hell to come up with a plan on what to do.

"I can't do it anymore," Doc said plaintively. "I'm sorry. I will always be a part of this club, I will always be a Sacred Hearts man but I can't be this club's Secretary anymore. Not with a clear head, not with a clear conscience. Not and do what I have to do." He crumbled, folding in on himself and no one said a damned thing when he sobbed. His pain was the paramount thing; we all waited somberly for the storm to pass. Not a single damned one of us was about to tell him to suck it up. He and Chandra had been together over twenty years.

"Right, so we got Treasurer and Secretary up for a vote. Nominations?" Dragon intoned.

"Do we really gotta do this right now, Pops?" Dray asked. Dray's Old Man searched his son's solemn face.

"No. No, I don't suppose we do. I don't suppose we should until

Archer, Rush and Nox get back. Just... just be thinking about it. All of you." He dropped heavily into his seat to a round of grunted agreements.

"When they back?" I asked.

Trig answered me, "'morrow, maybe the next day."

I nodded, "What about the girls?"

"I think maybe we can help with that. Y'all're gonna have to get real down and dirty over this. The last thing you need is to worry about your women. You got a bit of time, what with the cops sniffing around and the like. Me and mine can stay up through the funeral, have your girls make arrangements; they could use an extended stay down in my town. We got a comfortable safe house. They'll be looked after, and you can do what needs doing with a clear conscience, at least where they're concerned." Cutter crossed his arms, his expression unreadable, but it was a hell of a thing he was offering.

We all exchanged looks. Ghost spoke first, "Think they'll go for that?"

"We don't give them a choice." Dray said with about as much conviction as I'd ever heard come out of him. I nodded my agreement.

Trigger sighed, "While I agree it needs to happen, I've never been away from Sunshine for longer than a day or two."

He pulled a cigarette out of Dragon's pack sitting on the table, the real deal, and put it between his lips. Dragon handed my partner and our Sergeant-at-Arms his Zippo lighter without a word and Trig lit it with a clear and concise snap. He cupped the flame, an old habit from being used to lighting up outside and drew in a great breath laced with tobacco and nicotine.

He held it for a real long time, the expression on his face somber, one of greeting a long-lost love that he'd never really have a chance with again, lines of regret, sorrow, and grief etching their way into his face, his posture, before he let a cloud of the rich smoke out towards the ceiling.

"How long are we talking?" he asked.

"To do this right? To move careful so none of us get arrested, to make sure we've eradicated every last one of those fuckwits..? I'd say six months. Maybe more," Doc said, and downed a shot that one of the Kraken poured for him.

Cutter nodded, and Dragon spoke, "Sounds about right."

"Jesus fucking Christ. How are we going to keep them occupied for six fucking months?" Ghost said what we were all thinking.

It was Dray who had the idea; he was a smart fucker for being so damned young.

"Soul Fuel is doing good; Everett showed me the books. Her and Mandy been planning on hiring on more help."

"What's Soul Fuel?" Cutter asked, puzzled. Dray laid it out for him.

"You thinking new location?" he asked, and color him impressed.

"I'll convince them." Several of us startled and whirled, I chuckled. Only one of our girls was that quiet.

"Baby, this is club business, you shouldn't be here," Trigger was saying, but his voice was gentle and he was taking the few short steps to where Ashton huddled miserably in one of his oversized hooded sweatshirts. Her golden eyes were already welling and she was the picture of heartbreak, so small as to be childlike.

She surprised us all when she dodged Trigger's outstretched arms to come around him and more completely into the room.

"That's precisely why I'm here."

She sniffed, swallowed hard, and looked at Dragon, "You're all I have, all of you, my family. I need you all to be okay and I know..." she swallowed again, "I know what you have to do and that it will be dangerous, but I want us all safe. So, take this," and she held out a piece of paper that looked suspiciously like a check.

"Fix the clubhouse and pay for..." She sobbed. "Pay for Reaver's funeral and I will convince them to come with me, come with Hayden, and open a new store in your town."

Dragon, as solemn as I had ever seen him, plucked the piece of paper from Ashton's fingers and pulled her into a hug. He looked at it over her shoulder and frowned.

"Baby, while I'm willing to do what you say, I'm not going to take all your money," he said gently, and held her back so he could look at her.

Ashton scoffed. "That's not all of it... Shelly is good at what she does. That's only a quarter." She sniffed and wiped her eyes with the sleeve of Trigger's sweatshirt and the big man, standing just behind her, looked as soft as I had ever seen him, which did my heart glad. Dragon nodded and dare I say, looked a touch emotional himself.

"It's only money. Reaver... I don't want to lose anyone else. Ethan, Andy, you, the people of this club. None of them can be replaced. So take it. Fix this place, fortify it, do whatever you have to. I just want us all to be safe. Once and for all." She stepped back from our President and hugged her man once before untangling herself from his grasp and drifting back to wherever she'd come from.

"You got some damned fine women," one of the Kraken remarked.

"You don't know the half of it," I muttered, and shortly after that plans were laid and meeting fucking adjourned.

"Trig, Rev, go make some peace with your women then get on out to Point Nowhere. The boy 'n' me, we'll meet you there." Dragon heaved himself to his feet.

"I'm going with you." Doc's voice was full of steely determination.

"Not sure that's a good idea, old friend." Dragon eyed the man speculatively.

"Yeah, probably not, but I'm a doctor." Doc's voice dropped low. If I had to guess, his mind was on any eavesdropping women in the back. "I'm the only one that can keep the bastard breathin' long enough to get all our questions answered." He clenched his teeth as devastation flickered across his face like heat lightning.

"You just said it yourself; you're a fucking doctor, man! Don't you got some kind of an oath or something?" All eyes turned to the Kraken man who'd spoken.

"If it were your woman?" Cutter asked quietly, and he was very still, eyes fixed on a distant point while he waited for his man to answer. It was quiet and tense for several long moments. The man, who was young, very young, and wearing just a prospect's cut, looked queasy and then resigned.

"I don't know, Captain... I just... I really don't know," he said truthfully.

Cutter nodded. "That's a good lad. You might want to get to thinking real hard on that. This is what this life is about, not always, maybe not even in your time... but sometimes this is how it is." Cutter straightened and gave a hard sigh.

"You can trust me and mine to look out for things here. I'm goin' on in with Li'l Bit in a minute. You do what you boys gotta do." Cutter held out his hand to Dragon who, with a nod, clasped hands back.

"'preciate it, man. More 'n you could know." Dragon turned to the rest of us.

"No sense standing around here, let's do this. Send the boys out at Point Nowhere back..." He bowed his head and shook it. "Let's get going."

I slipped back towards Reaver's room where I'd left my Red and the girls with Hayden, but when I poked my head in, it was just Sunshine with her best friend.

"Your room," she murmured, and I nodded and let Trig brush past me and go to his girl.

Just as Ashton had said, Red was in my room. Dray was drawing Ev out into the hall and she nodded somberly to me as I slipped in and shut the door. Red was curled on her side and fully in the throes of her grief, the day having finally caught up with her. Her pale face was even paler, her freckles standing out stark beneath the slick mois-ture of the tears that coated her face. She lay curled on her side, sniff-ing, her hands tucked beneath her cheek, and I lowered myself to the edge of the mattress by her stomach.

"You're going out, aren't you?" she asked, miserably.

"Yeah, Sugar, I'm needed by the club."

This touched off some fresh weeping that she tried valiantly to stifle. I smoothed some of her stray copper curls from her face and she closed her eyes, turning her face into my touch.

"Just... come back to me. Please? I need you to come back to me."

She sat up abruptly and fell into my arms, hers twining around my neck as I curved mine around her back and held her close to me.

"I'm coming back, baby. I promise, I promise you." I clutched her to my chest and rocked her, planting the odd kiss to her hair.

"I love you so much," she sobbed and it tore at me, having to leave her when she was like this, but a gentle rap at the door let me know it was time. I looked up into the sympathetic eyes of my VP and nodded, my brave girl withdrawing from my embrace of her own accord.

"Just be safe." She looked at Dray, "You watch him. You take care of each other! You promise me, Dray."

"I promise. It'll be okay," he said solemnly and I gave another nod in his direction, this time one of appreciation. Everett came back and took my place with Mandy.

"We'll be here," she told us, and with how everything was going down, spiraling out of control, wreckage raining down around our club, it was all any of us guys could ask for. That our women would stick it out, see us through, and be there for us at the end of the day. You never really appreciate what a fine and true gift it was until you were either in danger of losing it, or had lost it. I bent and kissed my Red one last time before heading out the door.

26

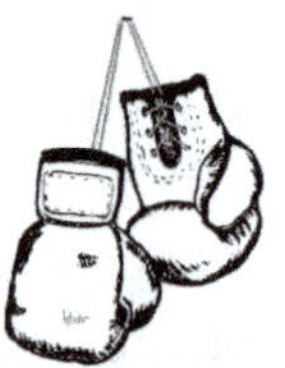

Revelator...

Trig was quiet, like sniper-quiet, in the seat beside me. I didn't particularly feel the need to fill the silence as we drove, but at the same time I could tell something was eating my partner, and that was just something I couldn't leave alone.

"What's eating you, man?"

"What, aside from my club getting shot to hell, my best friend dying, and the fact my Sunshine girl is wrecked?" He made a sound somewhere between derisive and disgusted and his hands tightened on the wheel of his Jeep, the steering apparatus giving a groan of protest.

"It's not real yet. Reaver being gone," I said, and it wasn't, at least for me. I was still running on a mixed fuel of anger and fading adrenaline. It was mostly rage at this point, and if it was one thing that could fuel me for days at a time, it was my rage. I cracked the knuckles of my left hand.

"It's as real as it gets, buddy... It's as real as it fucking gets," Trig observed dispassionately and I turned my attention to the dark rushing past the outside of the windows.

"Yeah," I agreed quietly.

By the time Trigger pulled us past the gate and up the long drive of Point Nowhere and, finally, up to the corrugated steel building, I was ready to work out some of this aggression. More than ready.

We climbed out of the Jeep beside my Chevelle, our doors clipping shut in unison. Dray pulled up beside the Jeep, with Dragon in the passenger seat of his Trans-Am. We waited as Doc climbed out of the back and we went into the building pretty much in order. Dragon, Dray, Trig, Doc then me. Disney stood up from where he'd propped himself on the edge of a low table against one of the opposite walls. He clasped hands with Trigger and then me, and looked just about tore up from the floor up. Emotion shone in his brown eyes, silently pleading with us to tell him it wasn't true.

"Sunshine is back at the club with Hayden in Reave's room. Cutter, the Kraken's President is in with Hayden but I really need you to go and look out for our girl," Trig held out the keys to their Jeep and Dis nodded, taking them and held out my keys to me.

"Thanks, man," I gave him a watered-down half-smile.

"He's really gone then?" he asked us quietly. Trig couldn't look at him, his gaze pinned to the floor, and so I did the talking.

"Yeah, man. Doesn't feel like it, but we need to be strong for each other as much as for our girls."

I hugged him. Dis was a sensitive guy and had had a bad run of it. Reaver had been his mentor as he'd been coming up in the club. Dis choked, and cracked a little on the surface and a low rumbling laugh filtered towards us from across the room.

I stiffened and looked over, our guest was none other than the dumb son of a bitch I'd beaten the motherfucking brakes off of in the ring a little over a month ago, the illustrious Nord. I sniffed.

"Dis, Blue, Cell, get you gone back to the house," Dragon ordered and his voice rang, cold steel.

"If you don't mind, Pres., I'd like to stay. This is the best part." Duracell's expression was cold and he was sporting a hell of a bruise along his cheekbone.

"Surprised you got this big bastard to cooperate," Dray remarked. Blue smiled, showing a whole lot of teeth and Dis cleared his throat.

"He didn't. He was aiming for Blue and I jumped him from behind. I choked him out, the way you showed me." Disney gave me a look and I let my pride shine right on through.

"Scrapper to the last, ain't you, Puddin'?" I asked, looking up at him.

He nodded. "It was just him and one other dude that broke in to the outbuilding with our rooms in it. Duracell shot the other guy; he was going to shoot me in the back while I was choking the shit out of this one." He was looking the man hanging from the ceiling up and down before eventually tearing his eyes from him and meeting Trig's.

"I wish I'd been in the main building, maybe if..." Trigger was already shaking his head.

"Don't even think it. Just do me a solid, and go look after our girl. You did good, Dis. You did real good." Trigger pounded the equally-tall, but way lankier younger dude on the back. Dis made for the door, Blue keeping pace, and silent as ever.

"See you back at the house, bro!" Duracell called and Blue waved over his shoulder. Those two had the weirdest fucking dynamic, none of us had quite figured it out yet. Truthfully, it was none of our damn business.

As the gravel outside crunched beneath the departing Jeep's tires, I turned my attention back to our guest. His hands were cuffed in front of him, the hook from an engine hoist mounted to the center beam that was the spine of the outbuilding's ceiling held the links between the manacles fast. His arms were stretched high above his head and he'd been hoisted so his feet hung a good four to six inches off the ground.

He had a blue bandana between his teeth and his hair hung in a long-ass fucking braid down his back, wisps escaping and flying around his face. Someone had relieved him of his jacket and cut, which lay in a heap on the floor beside him. The moniker of the suicide king made bile rise hot and furious along with my rage, scalding the back of my throat. I racked my neck from side to side and found the Nord's gaze fixed on me; I met it with a hard stare of my own.

Dragon pulled a metal chair from against a wall and walked out to where he was in front of, but a decent distance away from, the man. He set the chair down and sighed.

"Got some questions for you boy," he said, as he pulled out his cigarettes and shook one from the pack. He pressed it between his lips. When he spoke again, it set the cancer stick bobbing as he fished for his lighter.

"'N how you answer is gonna have a direct bearing on how you're treated from here on out." He punctuated his proclamation by lighting his cig.

"You get me?" He snapped his lighter closed, and rolled his dark eyes up to meet the bastard's. The bastard hanging from our ceiling like a side of beef.

The Nord snorted and turned his head. Dray went up and pulled the gag out of his mouth. He spit and kicked out at Dray, barely glancing his shoulder as the younger, more agile man ditched off to the side. I growled, but The Nord was speaking.

"Man, fuck you!"

Dragon cocked his head to the side and dropped into the seat, slouching, leaning way back. He hooked a thumb into one of his front belt loops, and, cigarette grasped between index and middle fingers, took a thoughtful drag.

His dark eyes raking the other man over in contemplation, he exhaled, the smoke curling up towards the ceiling before he said dryly, "Now you see, so far we've treated you with as much hospitality as we could muster. I mean sure, you been hanging there a while, but you ain't been beat on and you sure ain't dead. So you might be a bit uncomfortable, but I'm just trying to have a friendly chat here is all. Think we can do that?"

The Nord's expression was stark, as blank as a slate that'd yet to be written on.

"So, what made you boys decide to pay us a house call?" Dragon asked.

The Nord turned his head to the side and stared off into space, pointedly refusing to answer. Dragon's mouth turned down at the corner and an eyebrow went up, he didn't look at all surprised or amused.

Trig's hands fell on my shoulders, his fingers wrapping around my collar, and I let him take my coat. I rolled my shoulders and stripped my shirt over my head, and then I cracked my knuckles on both hands, squeezing them into fists, getting a feel, making myself ready.

"Like I said, how this is gonna go is going to be completely up to you. We ain't gotta do this." Dragon contemplated the stubbornly silent man and, finally, after several moments of silence, sighed out.

"Go to it, Rev, don't hurt him too bad or too quick," Dragon ordered. I nodded.

Doc's voice filtered out from the corner just at the edge of The Nord's vision.

"Oh, there ain't nothin' Rev can do, that I can't fix. I can put him back together enough to take plenty of what we dish out and have him comin' 'round for a round two." The Nord's eyes widened a bit as Doc ejected some liquid from the tip of a hypodermic needle.

I went to the bigger man and Dray caught him around the legs, holding him fast like a heavy bag for me. It wasn't fair sport, but then again, I had no problem letting the deepest darkest part of me take the reins here. There was no guilt for what I was about to do. None at all. The image of my girl's tearstained face, Everett's low and strained voice telling me that one of those fucks had a gun pointed to my Red's head, in her face, and that she fucking told the SOB she forgave him! Knowing he was going to pull the trigger, knowing he was going to snuff her out and take her from me for-fucking-ever...

No, there wasn't one iota of guilt as I let my first punch fly. If anything, there was a surge of utter satisfaction. The Nord gave an oomph of surprise as my kidney shot landed and he writhed, flopping like a landed fish for several moments. I knew how much that shit hurt, but there was no sympathy to be had. Not from me, not from my brothers. He was going to die tonight; we just didn't need him to know that. We needed him to believe he had a chance at survival. We needed to give him a glimmer of hope to hold on to, that if he told us what we wanted to know, what we needed to know, that the pain would stop, that he would be tended to, that we might even let him go.

I worked him over methodically, but he was one tough son of a bitch. Doc finally stepped up, a scalpel in his hand and cocked his head to the side, considering, after about an hour of us getting nowhere.

"Think we should be thinking more like Reave."

We all went very still and I swallowed hard. Doc was one of the milder-mannered brothers. For him to go there, to even be standing here, was a testament to how far and how deeply losing his woman affected him. The Nord tried feebly to raise his head, he was bleeding pretty freely from his nose and a cut on his cheek, another above his eye.

"Doc..." I said, but the older man wasn't listening to me.

"You killed my woman," he said softly. "She had kids, grandkids... What am I supposed to tell her grandbabies? Huh? What do I say to her daughter, to her granddaughter, her grandson?" he asked.

"You tell them she was a whore," The Nord sneered.

Duracell snorted, "That was really original. Hey, Doc, step off, man, I'm tired of playing with this fool. I got a better idea."

Doc was staring daggers up at the Nord, who was staring right back and smiling pretty fucking evilly. Doc stepped back and let Duracell, who was holding a handheld little Taser, step up. Duracell smiled, and it was that smile he usually reserved for the girls back at the club when he was tryin' to get some. He fired up the little Taser with a loud crackle, and for the first time The Nord looked uneasy.

Duracell started with the soles of the dude's feet. He started talking, then screaming, when the pain, mixed with the smell of his own flesh cooking, got up to his nose. Took everything I had not to gag. None of us let a damned thing show. Truthfully, I didn't think Duracell had it in him to get that evil. At any rate, we got what we fucking wanted, but it wasn't pretty.

When Dragon was sure he'd told us everything, he put the fucker out of his misery by blowing half his face off, and half his fucking brain with it, with his fucking hand cannon. We all stood lost in our own thoughts for a minute.

"A fuckin' rat. Huh. Didn't see that one comin'," Dragon uttered and we all exchanged looks.

Dray swore, low and fierce.

"Fuck!"

"Think he was lyin'?" Doc asked, and he half-sounded hopeful.

"No," I said dispassionately.

"Who the fuck you think it could be?" he asked.

"No one at the club," Trigger was scowling. "Not a brother or one of the Ol' Ladies, but someone near the club..." My partner was scowling one of the deepest and fiercest scowls I'd ever seen on record from him, and I'd seen some real doozys in my time.

THE NORD HAD TOLD us that there weren't supposed to be that many men at the club; that it was just supposed to be a few of us guys and the women. That the Cunt's VP had given the order, but they all knew the orders came from Griz. They were told to go in and take all of the girls out. No one had bet on any advanced warning coming through, that a sniper would get two of them before they even breeched the front door. He'd said they'd been assured that six guys would be enough.

"Seriously, who the fuck you think it could be?" Doc said, and he looked like he was past his fucking limit for tonight.

"We never would have had any warning at all if Data hadn't hooked up those fucking cameras down the drive and off the back fence," Trig grunted. "That's what makes me say none of our boys or women are the rat, they all knew about the cameras, but the Suicide Cunts didn't or they would have avoided them. I mean, shit, they would have been easy as fuck to avoid if they knew they were there but they walked right on by. Data called immediately, blathering on about motion sensors texting him, which let me and Reave get into position before they hit. Let us warn Dis. and the guys out back."

"They had way more information than they ever should've had in the first place. We need to find that leak." Dray stared dispassionately down at the body on the floor.

"Cops have wind of a war going on. We're going to have to lay low for a while, and if those cocksuckers have any sense at all, they will too. We know if any of 'em got away?" Dragon glanced from one face to the next.

"I got two out front."

"Chandra took out one, Everett got another, Reaver hurt the one that got him bad but I finished him off." I ticked them off on my fingers as I listed them off.

"Then this piece of shit makes six." Duracell put his foot against The Nord's cooling body and gave it a shove.

"Right. Let's get this place cleaned up, this big bastard buried and go the fuck home." Dragon's tone brooked no argument and none of us were going to give him one anyway. I helped Trigger move the damned body; it was going to be an exceptionally long fucking night for all of us. We dug a hole out in Cicada Woods and made quick work of burying the brute.

It was kind of a shame; he'd been a decent opponent in the ring and had had some promise. Not anymore.

27

Mandy...

I lay in Zander's bed in his club room facing Everett, our hands clasped between us as we spoke in the dark, like when we were children, sleeping over at one another's houses. It was comforting in that way that all childhood things were, but instead of discussing which Disney princess we wanted to be or what we wanted our Prince Charming to be like, the things that passed between us tonight carried much more weight.

We had all been with Hayden while the boys held their club meeting with the Kraken out front. The woman had always been small in a physical way, but her presence, which had always been vibrant and bold, was simply less. It scared me. It made me face the reality that one day, it could be me lying there staring off into space, despondent, lost... which made me realize just how much Zander and I connected, how much we went together, because the mere thought of him being gone, just there one moment and gone the next, like Reaver, like Chandra... Well, not only did it have my heart squeezing down tight in my chest, it had bile rising in my throat and had sent me running for the nearest bathroom.

Everett had supported me and held back my hair, and when we

returned to Reaver's room, Ashton had gone and Hayden was alone for the moment. Evy and I had resumed our places, curled on the floor, against the wall, huddled together in our misery while we waited.

Then Ashton had come back and said decisively and in a tone brooking no argument that we were all going to Florida.

Evy, being Evy, had balked, and it was the first time I had ever seen Ashton not only stand up to anyone and do it fiercely. She hadn't minced words. At all. In fact, she'd even sworn a few times. I'd never seen anything like it out of the fragile, small woman, and by the time she'd finished and collapsed onto her hind end in the middle of the carpet, gasping and bursting into tears, I think both Everett and I would have been willing to agree to anything to give Ashton even one small measure of comfort.

Everett sighed out, her breath rushing across the small distance between us carrying with it the faint smell of mint. We'd brushed our teeth before coming to Zander's room. It was late, so late as to be early and we'd left Ashton with Hayden, hugging her friend from behind while the woman broke and fell into more weeping against Cutter, who'd come into the room some time back.

"I'm no motorcycle club queen, Mandy," Everett said quietly. "That was Chandra."

She sniffed and her blue eyes filled up with tears. We'd all been crying off and on and I suspected it would continue for days to come.

"Out of all of us, you're the strongest right now. You've always been." I told her.

"I don't want to be the strong one this time."

"I know, but one thing, one day at a time. You and Shelly paid closest attention when it came to arranging Grinder's funeral, and Shelly..." I sighed this time. "I think it's you and me this time, Sis. Hayden needs Ashton, Shelly isn't in any shape, so that leaves just you and me."

"How are we supposed to do all of this and keep the shop going?"

I chewed my bottom lip.

"Shop isn't going to fall apart without us. We'll just need to hire some more help to run the counter and the coffee part of things. I can do the chocolates from any kitchen. We might be a bit light on cakes and pastries for a while, but those were never really our big sellers... Well, except the Chocolate Croissants, but those should ship just fine." I went on and on, figuring this and mapping out that, and Everett relaxed marginally after a while and began planning and thinking with me.

I think all of us were more than a little overwhelmed and who could blame us? We'd lost three people close to us in the span of a month, two of them in less than twenty-four hours, and one of those right in front of our eyes under threat of having our lives taken. I was willing to think about just about anything other than that.

Eventually, as the sky began to lighten outside, Everett and I both fell asleep out of just sheer exhaustion.

I jolted awake, the blinds and curtains drawn over the high window turning the room to cool twilight. I frowned, unsure of what had awoken me, but then I felt it again, the press of lips to the back of my shoulder where my nightgown didn't cover with its thin spaghetti straps. I turned my head; Zander placed his hand on the same shoulder and smoothed it down my arm.

"Shh, just me," he said softly. He had stripped down to just his boxer shorts and lay on his side, his front to my back, head propped on his right arm.

"How long have you been back?" I asked quietly. The club had that stillness to it, the kind that any building got when most, if not all, of its inhabitants were still fast asleep.

"About a half hour ago. Dray's back, too; Evy's with him."

He leaned over me gently and captured my mouth with his, the warmth and strength of his body enveloping me. I sank gratefully into the kiss but couldn't help the tears that welled in my eyes as once again my mind drifted, carried on a wave of fear and 'what if', borne to that dark place in the far reaches of my mind that whispered *It could happen to you.*

"Hey, hey, hey..." He cupped my cheek with his hand and smoothed his thumb through the wet track left behind by my tears.

"I apologize," I said, but it came out warbled and piteous. Zander groaned and kissed me deeply, as if he were bent on kissing away my pain, bent on reassuring me with his body rather than his words. I couldn't deny that being close to him right now, as improper as my upbringing would have it, appealed so strongly to me that I simply didn't care. I needed him, I needed to be close to him, to have him hold me, kiss me and caress me. To reassure me that it was okay, even if things were so terribly uncertain in so many areas of our lives right now.

Our kiss heated, hands smoothing over skin, gathering material, him pulling and me pushing, all in a bid to get more skin-on-skin contact. We were rushed but not feverish, the intensity somewhere along the lines of a gentle but still rolling boil.

Zander pressed me back into the mattress and kissed every bit of me he could reach before gliding inside me. He looked down into my eyes from inches away and we met in the middle, my neck craning so that we could kiss again. He rolled his hips, withdrawing gently to surge forward again, deliberately, with strength, but without being rough.

He made love to me. Both of us took our time, kissing, touching, intertwined and intimate for far longer than I could have imagined possible. He murmured between kisses how much he loved me and I felt a surge of joy despite the heavy burden of sorrow on both of our souls. When I came, it was different than all the other times I'd been with Zander. Rather than a wild passionate explosion, this time, it was a sweeping, gentle thing that was so much more profound than any other time before. He kissed me as I shuddered beneath him and cried out into my mouth with his own release.

I held him to me, and we lay together like that for a long time, breaths coming at an uneven cadence as we slowly came down. I felt muzzy, incredibly satisfied, fluid, and as relaxed as I'd ever been. I was positively drugged on his love and it was the most incredible and exquisite feeling I had ever known, made even more so by what he blurted out.

"Marry me. I know, it's shitty of me to ask like this, but I mean it, I love you and I need you, and I just..." He let out a harsh breath. "Just say you'll marry me, agree and I promise I will ask you with a ring and on bended knee with everyone around to give you that experience, but I just need you to know how much I love you. How in love with you I am." He pushed up, bracing himself on his arms to look down into my eyes.

I was speechless but I wanted so desperately to say yes to him that I found myself nodding emphatically, pulling him down over the top of me. My body jerked with silent sobs but I welcomed the tears this time. I didn't want to contain them. I was simply just so happy, my tears of sorrow turned to ones of purest joy.

28

R evelator...

    Despite everything going on, life went on, and so I found myself standing inside our new tattoo shop which was pretty much ready to go, ready to open. I put the finishing touches on a piercing tray and went back out front, meeting Trig, Dis, and Sunshine in the lobby. We were supposed to have our grand opening today, but instead we were having a wake. Tomorrow we would be laying Reaver to rest for good.

It had been Chandra's daughter's wish that they have a closed, family-only funeral. She was hurt, bad, and wouldn't let Doc attend, blaming him and the MC for her mother's death. It was BS and hurt like a son of a bitch, but none of us could argue. We were chosen family, not biological, but still, no matter how much I kept telling myself that, it didn't take the burn out of what Misty was doing to Doc and the club.

"Next week?" Trig asked. Disney and I nodded. We would be opening next week, but it still wasn't the same, because after tomorrow, Sunshine and the girls would be in the Sunshine State. Ashton looked grim. She wound her arms around Trigger's hips and tucked herself tightly to his side.

"I feel so badly that I'm going to miss it. That things have to be this way," she murmured.

"Us too, baby, believe me."

He drew her in tighter to his side and we all stood in the brightly-colored lobby to our new shop. It was so new it still smelled like paint, and wallboard, and construction, over the smell of antiseptic, which was just beginning to seep in before it overpowered.

The lay-out was much different than the old shop had been, but some things we'd tried to keep the same. The linoleum on the lobby floor was still black-and-white checkered tile. Disney's area was a riot of new-school art and color. The walls of the front of the shop were decorated in neatly framed, freshly-drawn flash, though the walls beneath the black frames were a deep eggplant purple this time.

The front counter was mostly glass cases now instead of particle board. Body jewelry of every type was proudly and professionally displayed. From earrings to gauges, to nipple rings, to belly button piercings... hell, you name it, I had it at my disposal, which was nice and would hopefully help the piercing side of business pick up. Before, we'd had the stock in the back and a binder full of pictures, due to a lack of space.

The new shop was big enough that we could probably hire one or two more piercers or artists if business was good, and we were kind of counting on it to be. Open Road Ink had a damned fine reputation from before. Dis, Trig, and I all had a pretty solid client base, but where we were located now? We had bars, and with lowered inhibitions came customers, and we weren't about to turn that down. In fact, we were probably the best guys to be in place to have them walking through the door because we were professionals at our craft. That meant we wouldn't be sending anyone home with a shitty-looking or stupid tattoo. If we thought they were too piss-drunk we'd send them away. Being near the bars could prove to be a double-edged sword but between me, Trig and Dis we knew we could handle it. Ashton had grown over these last couple of years, she knew we would come to her aid if anyone freaked her out or disrespected her and she wouldn't hesitate to call out.

We were a family. A good team... and for the next few months we were going to be missing our heart. Disney went to her first, and crushed the little woman between his lanky frame and Trig's as the first tears stood out in her golden eyes, making them shine just so damned bright.

"C'mon, man, suck it up, and bring it in," Disney grinned at me over the top of her head and I grinned right back.

"I knew you loved me, Puddin'," I said and went to them and we all group hugged, for Ashton's benefit, for a long minute in our lobby. The bell above our door chimed.

"Thought this was a shop run by bikers not a bunch of hippies with their freaky love-fest bullshit," Duracell commented dryly.

"You sure do know how to ruin a moment, asshole," Trig said, but he was grinning. We broke apart and Duracell looked surprised.

"Shit, Sunshine! Didn't even see you there!" he exclaimed. Ashton laughed and wiped her eyes with a Kleenex, which she tucked back into the sleeve of the cardigan she was wearing over one of her 40's style dresses.

"Sorry, just a little emotional."

Duracell's expression softened marginally. "No, hey, I get it. I liked Reave, too, but I didn't know him even half as long as you guys did."

"Whatcha here for, man?" Trig asked and held Ashton against him, her back to his front, an arm across her chest. She brought both her small hands up and hung them off his forearm, leaning back and cuddling into his embrace. He smiled down at her and she smiled up at him and you could just see that they were each other's entire fucking world. I felt something in my chest loosen in gratitude because, fuck, I'd finally found that too with my Red and I wouldn't trade it for the fucking world.

"Club meeting, Dragon says it's time to get the whole officers' thing straight, before tonight... you know? Archer, Rush and Nox got back night before last and we're all here so there's nothing doing, man." He looked apologetic and the five of us traded some grim looks.

"Yeah, man, we get you." Trig said.

"Sunshine, you good to drive over to Dray's place? Everett, Mandy, and Shelly are there dealing with food and stuff for tonight. Dragon wants just the guys at the club for the time being."

Ashton nodded silently and craned her head back. "I love you," she told my partner simply and he smiled, bent and kissed her on the mouth.

"I love you too, Baby." He gave her a little shove forward and she gathered her purse and keys. We locked up and got Ashton settled in the Jeep. I drove myself and Dis, while Trig opted to ride with Duracell in the ginger's beat-up old black Jeep Wrangler. We would escort Ashton to Dray's.

I was unsettled, not liking the idea of leaving the girls on their own at our VP's place, but I didn't have a damned thing to worry about. Dray's driveway was crammed full of bikes when we got there and one of the Kraken was in his driveway smoking a cigarette and talking on his phone. Ashton carefully pulled her and Trig's Jeep Cherokee up to the curb and parked before getting out. Cutter appeared on the front stoop, shutting the door behind him.

I rolled down my window to ask Ashton to tell Red I loved her, so I heard Cutter call out, "Hey, hey, Li'l'er Bit," which made me smile. He'd been calling Reaver's Doll 'Li'l Bit' since the day he'd seen her. When he'd finally met Ashton in person, and seen that she was even smaller than Hayden, he'd started calling her 'Li'ler Bit'. It was cute as hell, but you'd never hear me admit it out loud.

"Sunshine!" I called, before her attention was grabbed completely by the Kraken's president and, no doubt, by her best friend, who was probably inside. Where Cutter was, so too Hayden would be found. Ashton startled hard and turned around, wide-eyed.

"Sorry, just, tell Red I'll see her tonight!" I was suddenly and stupidly embarrassed to tell her in front of these other dudes to tell my woman I loved her. Stupid but true. Ashton broke into one of her beautiful smiles and she winked her understanding, and I couldn't help but grin. She mounted the steps and gave Cutter a hug, then slipped past him into the house. Once she'd disappeared from sight, Duracell's Jeep pulled forward and I followed in my Chevelle.

The club was immaculate, and as somber as I'd ever seen it when I arrived. It held only the brotherhood from our chapter, those who had come from out of town likely making themselves scarce for our benefit and the benefit of this meeting. No one was about to ignore the elephant in the room, Reaver's casket on the small stage, the black lacquered top and the silver handles and edging gleaming softly under the overhead lighting, even with as dim as it was in here.

In the last week, this place had gone through a major overhaul, and it had gone through it fast. The fishbowl was a fishbowl still, but the wall between it and Data's closet had been knocked out to make it bigger. Not for meeting purposes, but for a space to monitor the state-of-the-art surveillance system that'd gone in. Between the computer set-up and the banks of monitors, Data was happier than a pig in shit, and it was nice to see the reserved brother happy and a little less introverted than he'd been, locked away in his little command center closet like he'd been.

The curtains were still up and could be closed during parties and the like, to hide the new setup, but right now they were drawn back, putting the whole spectacle on display. The black cloth hung straight at the corners of the little room where the glass panels met up in their frames. Data pushed up from the office chair in front of the monitors and stretched, and then he joined the rest of us in the common room.

Next week or the week after, the new fencing surrounding the entire property would be going in. So would the new gate across the front drive, a heavy, no-nonsense, big black wrought-iron monstrosity to replace the chain link fencing we'd had before. The black metal bars, square and stout and strong, reminded me of prison bars to a certain extent, but they weren't meant to keep us in, just any bad guys out. Truthfully, despite the prison connotations, I liked the new fence, it was burly and badass and made the property surrounding the club look more like an MC resided here and that the outside world should fuck with us at their own risk.

"Right, looks like we're all here so let's get to it." Dragon's voice boomed over all of us assembled and those of us left standing, we took seats, everyone turning their chairs toward the front where Dragon stood. It wasn't lost on any of us that Reaver's casket was providing the backdrop to this little discussion.

"We got two leadership positions in the cabinet to secure, two out of the five council seats are vacant. One was Reave's as our Treasurer, and while Doc, our Secretary, has no intention of leaving this club, he just don't feel he can hold office no more, and I don't blame him."

Silence; no one so much as coughed as we waited for our Pres. to go on.

"We'll deal with Reave's spot first. Nominations?" Dragon's dark eyes swept the room slowly but surely, waiting for someone, anyone to speak up.

"Ghost," Disney said at last. Everyone turned.

"Reasoning?" Dray asked and his eyes were both calculating and tempestuous. Disney blushed, but the ballsy kid held his ground.

"Seriously? It really ain't no secret, Reaver couldn't do math to save his life; it was pretty much always Shelly crunching the numbers. Shelly is Ghost's Old Lady. I think if she lost the ability to keep doing for this club, that it would finish her." Disney swallowed and waited, along with the rest of us.

It was Archer who spoke up. "That ain't no reason to make him a Cabinet member."

"You're right, it's not," Ghost agreed. "Do you want to do it?"

Archer shut his trap. Ghost looked from Trig to Dragon to Dray.

"I'm all in. This club gave me the structure I needed to go on after the Marines. I run my own business, I know how to keep the books. It ain't my favorite thing, but I'm qualified and I'll do my best to serve this club or die trying. Count me committed if you all decide that's what you want."

"Any other nominations?" Dragon asked and swept the room. No one stepped up or came up with a name.

"You know the rules, it's in our by-laws. In order for a cabinet member to be elected into office for any charter or club of the Sacred Hearts, he must hold at least eighty percent of the vote. So put 'em up. All in favor of Ghost for Treasurer?"

I put up my fist, and the vast majority of the room followed suit, including Archer who was the only reluctant hold-out, and he only did it when Rush scowled at him and Nox gave him a look that clearly communicated to anyone with half a brain, *Really dude? This is how you want to start our stay with these guys?*

"So entered, so ordered." Dragon went to Reaver's cut, which lay atop his casket, and sighed heavily. He plucked a knife out of his jeans pocket and hit the switch, the blade leaping free on one of Reave's stilettos. Hayden had said Reaver had so many of them that every one of us should have one. We'd each taken what she'd given us and she still had a shoe box full of them, and those were just his stilettos.

"I'm sorry, buddy," Dragon murmured as he cut the Treasurer's flash from Reaver's cut. He stepped down off the stage and crossed the room. Ghost rose out of his seat and took the scrap of felt material embroidered with the position, and I think that's when it really crashed into a few of us. Some of the guys sniffed, me included, as our eyes watered. A few heads bowed and the room became deathly quiet.

Dragon returned to the raised stage and cleared his throat. "I nominate Data for the position of Secretary."

"Wait, what?" The lanky man tossed his slightly greasy hair out of his eyes.

"You heard me."

"I can't be Road Captain and Secretary, too," he protested.

"We'll get to that if you get the spot, one problem at a time," Dray grunted.

"Any opposition?" Dragon asked. No one spoke up.

"Any other nominations?" Dray asked. Again, no one said a thing.

"Vote it, all in favor?" Every hand went up.

"Congratulations, son," Doc grunted. Data just looked stunned. Doc swung off his cut and laid it on a table. He flicked out his own blade and cut the flash off his cut. Data did the same for his Road Captain flash. He took the Secretary flash from Doc and they hugged, pounding each other on the back.

"Thank you, man. I mean, thank all of you." Data was hoarse, beyond moved, and if anyone had any misgivings on if he were the right man for the job, they fucking evaporated.

"Anybody been a Road Captain before?" Dray asked and he sounded weary. I think all of us knew how he felt. None of us wanted to be here, doing this, restructuring just about everything under these circumstances. It was bullshit, but there wasn't any other choice, nothing else we could do. We had to wait. Get the girls safe, lose the cops, before that we couldn't do anything else or even begin to right the wrongs done to us.

"Archer," Rush and Nox said at the same time.

They grinned at each other and Rush said, "Jinx, you owe me a beer."

Nox laughed, "What are you, twelve?"

"I am, then you are too, genius," Rush punched Nox in the shoulder and Nox laughed.

"Both of you shut the fuck up," Archer grated. Both of them automatically fell silent but it was Rush who rolled his eyes behind his brother's back; Nox fought not to grin. Weird dynamic, those three.

"Anybody else want to try for it or got anyone else in mind?" Dragon asked.

"Lucky." Trigger was the one who had spoken. Lucky looked across to the big man and nodded.

"You ever done it before?" Duracell asked.

Lucky shook his head. "First time for everything I reckon."

"All in favor of Archer?" Dragon called.

Hands went up. I knew Lucky, but if Archer had experience, I was willing to give the dude a try. Lucky just seemed a little too nonchalant about it. I don't think I was the only one erring on the side of experience. The majority voted the new guy, Archer, into the spot without so much as a second thought. I knew the right decision had been made when Lucky looked secretly relieved. I knew as well as anyone else that he would do anything for this club, anything at all that was asked of him, even if he didn't particularly want to. Data handed the Road Captain flash to Archer.

"Right, any other business?" Dragon asked, looking over his shoulder to Dray. Dray sighed, leaned in and muttered to his Pops, and Dragon nodded.

"Right, Reave was our Enforcer too..." Dragon sighed and looked up, hopeful that someone would step up for the grim job.

"Oh, gladly!" Duracell put up his hand and bounced on the balls of his feet. A bunch of the guys traded uneasy looks. No one should be that excited about taking a job that was about hurting people in most clubs. There were a couple of misplaced chuckles, one even escaping me at just how Reaver-like Duracell's reaction was to the spot needing filled.

"It's yours." Dragon shook his head and laughed low and all of us turned, mute and introspective, to look at the damned black box behind him. There wasn't a thing on God's green earth that would ever replace Reave.

Dragon stepped off the short drop from the stage, his boots clacking hard against the polished cement of the club room floor. He sighed and walked purposefully to the bar and went behind it. We all stood and followed our Pres, lining up along the bar's front as he lined up shot glasses along its scarred wood surface. He cracked open a bottle of tequila, his go-to drink and poured them out in one long line, not even caring about spilling. Everyone grabbed one, handing them back to the guys not bellied up directly against the bar top.

Dragon waited until everyone had one in hand before he raised his glass. We all raised ours in unison.

"To Chandra." He hiked up his glass a little higher and we followed suit. No one spoke, the sounds of creaking and sighing leather and the rattle of an odd buckle were the only sounds to accompany the toast. We drank it down and there was an odd cough or two, the rush of breath as some sighed out at the bite and burn of the alcohol.

"Line 'em up," he ordered, and we did, and he poured another round.

"Trig," Dragon leveled his dark gaze at the big man. We all looked to the big SAA, our friend, our brother, and Reaver's best friend. His eyes were particularly shiny as he raised his shot.

"To Reaver. My brother; my best friend. Ain't no one like him, God could never have made two of a man like that."

We drank, and truthfully, I don't think any of us really stopped drinking. Half of us were already half-gone by the time the girls arrived with the food and the Kraken and other-chapter Sacred Hearts returned and I don't think any of us could wrestle up one bit of sorry for the state we were in by the time the night was through. It fucking hurt, and every damned one of us that were any kind of close to Reaver would have done anything to drown the pain.

29

Mandy...

The wake for Reaver and Chandra wasn't anything like the wake for Grinder. It was as if the men of the Sacred Hearts mother chapter, Zander included, were determined to drown their sorrows, to numb the pain any way they knew how. They drank, they threw knives in honor of the fallen brother, and when night well and truly fell and the bar had essentially run dry, they tried to drown their pain in the women that hung around the club.

Zander came to me, and while I hadn't drunk anything, I still felt vaguely nauseous, though it wasn't at anything going on around me. Not at all. I understood that everyone dealt with the pain in their own way, and this was the way the MC chose to grieve, in celebration of the fallen man's life, drowning their heartache in wine, women and song. The 'song' was provided courtesy of some hidden sound system, blaring 70's rock so loud you could barely hear yourself think.

Throughout the night, Hayden remained numb. She was seated in a folding chair beside her husband's closed casket, her hand laying on the gleaming lacquered wood. Her shoulders hunched, her green eyes vacant, she stared off into space, barely blinking. She wouldn't eat, she wouldn't drink, and she wouldn't respond to anyone. Not

Ashton, not Trigger, and not Cutter, either. It was heartbreaking and sometime, late into the night she'd started sobbing and trying to work the latches holding the lid to Reaver's coffin closed.

Dragon stepped in at that point, with Dray not far behind him. I drifted over to see if I could be of use, some sort of help, standing on the periphery, bearing witness to the disaster unfolding. Dragon knelt on the floor of the stage in front of Hayden, grasping her hands between his own, much larger ones.

"I want to see him," Hayden keened.

"No, chica you don't. You don't wanna remember him that way, Baby. He wouldn't want you to remember him this way. You gotta hold on to what's in your heart," he told her and drew her in. Hayden collapsed, sobbing and wailing into the shoulder of Dragon's cut and it was so awful and no one could do anything for her except stand in silent support around her. Doc finally came and sedated her. Cutter lifted her in his arms and carried her back to Reaver's club room. Everyone stood mute and sober and the drinks began to flow afresh and it was almost like people were doubly as determined to party after that.

It wasn't long after the heart-wrenching display that Zander found me in his room, brushing out my curls, braiding my hair tightly, just finding things to do with my shaking hands as I readied for bed. He came up behind me and kissed my shoulder.

"'S not gonna happen to me, Red. I promise. I'm gonna be here, I'm gonna stay here." He swayed on his feet; it was the most drunk I had ever seen him. I closed my eyes. It was as if he had pulled the thoughts from my head, plucked my deepest fears out of the back of my brain, and I was scared and hurt and so many things that I grew angry.

It was our first fight, but it wasn't really a fight. I lashed out at him, he was taken aback and he lashed out at me, and the things we said... good lord. I accused him of lying to me, of making promises he couldn't keep. He yelled back at me that he was going to keep them, that he didn't know what was going to happen, but that he had things in hand, and the argument, which wasn't really an argument at all, culminated in his screaming at me that the last thing he would ever do would be to leave me alone in this world.

We'd ended up holding each other, me crying, him begging me not to cry, before he laid down with me and holding me close, passed out cold from all he'd drunk. He reeked of alcohol and smoke from his time out in the common room and I felt overly-sensitive to it, my gorge rising that much further as my nausea of earlier increased.

I fell into an uneasy sleep, tying myself in knots with worry about if I were coming down with something before the long drive ahead of us the next day. We were set to depart for Florida directly after the burial. All our things had been packed. Everett had been masterful at delegating responsibilities and keeping everyone on task over the last two weeks. Tomorrow we would leave our home, our men, and that which we loved most behind, and it was killing me inside.

I woke early, felt horrible, and so I showered and dressed before anyone else. I shouldn't have been surprised that Ashton and Evy were up too. I went in to the kitchen to find both of them up and ready for the misery the day would bring as well. Everett was brewing coffee, Ashton was heating aluminum pans full of cinnamon rolls to feed the masses, and it was supposed to be my job to pick up around the common room.

I went for the giant black trash bags in the pantry but stopped when I caught them both looking at me, their brows furrowed with concern.

"What?" I asked.

"You feeling okay?" Evy asked. I grimaced and shook my head.

"Terrible time for it, but I think I may be coming down with something. I'll be fine." I did my part and was grateful when they let it go, though truthfully, if people hadn't started waking up and coming out, they probably would have pressed me further.

I made quick work of cleaning up and washed my hands so I could help Ashton serve. Everett gave me a cup of coffee and I went to drink, the rich aroma wafting up to me. My stomach flipped, and not in a good way, and I barely made it to the trashcan in the back of the kitchen in time. Everett was right there beside me and I moaned. Ashton passed her some wet paper towels and I wiped my mouth.

"You need to stop stressing," Everett observed dryly and I nodded. She was right. I was a master at literally worrying myself sick. I'd done it just after the shooting and I was probably doing it now. I straightened, waited for a wave of dizziness to pass and felt much better.

"Move." Zander shouldered his way into the kitchen, looking a little the worse for wear from his night before.

"Red, what happened? You all right?" he demanded.

I nodded.

"I'm sure it's just stress."

He pulled my forehead to his lips and after several more moments of my reassuring him I was fine, went back out. Everett, Ashton and I made quick work of clean-up along with the ladies from other clubs before we went to don our funeral attire. We'd kept Shelly and Hayden as busy as we could over the last two weeks, but when it came to the actual activities of the night before and the day of the funeral, well, we asked them to do nothing. We had it handled. Ghost was outside his club room door when I passed in the hall. He had his forearm leaned against the doorframe, his forehead resting against his arm.

"Come on, Princess. I know, baby, I know it's hard, but you gotta come out here and face the day." The door cracked open and Ghost looked visibly relieved, shoulders dropping from where they'd been tensed.

I darted into Zander's room and put on the black slacks and blouse I'd chosen for the day. I didn't want to do this, either, and I hadn't been nearly as close with Reaver as any of the rest, including Everett. I paused and stared in the mirror at my pale reflection. Deep dark circles had taken up permanent residence under my eyes from sleepless nights filled with nightmares of watching that man shoot Chandra, of staring down the barrel of the same gun with my own eyes, only in my dreams Everett hadn't shot him in time. In my dreams, I always woke screaming as fire and smoke poured from the barrel of that gun, and I watched, helpless as that bullet spun towards me in slow motion like something out of a movie.

I swallowed hard, the nausea making a return trip, and sighed, forcing myself to go out and stand silently aside out front. We watched as Reaver was loaded in to the back of a sleek black hearse by Zander, Disney, Trigger, Ghost, Dray and Dragon. Shelly stood pale and miserable beside Hayden, her arm around the smaller woman as she fell apart. Cutter stood with them, reverent and grim, and did what he could for his fallen friend's wife, who was beyond anything any of us knew how to cure.

Trigger closed the back door to the hearse and the men of the chapter moved around the vehicle to their bikes parked in front. The police were already here, blocking the traffic on the highway and to serve as an escort for the funeral procession to the cemetery. We moved to our vehicles. I let Everett drive and it was just me and her in my car. Cutter helped Hayden into the back seat of Ashton's Jeep, Shelly got in beside her. Ashton drove their car and as we watched them ahead of my little Focus, Everett and I held each other's hand over the center console. We didn't feel that all of us cramming into Ashton's Jeep was appropriate, given that the vehicles were all already packed for our trip.

The order of the procession was all the Sacred Hearts from the mother chapter, followed by the hearse, followed by all from the Sacred Hearts chapters from abroad, followed by us in the cars, with the Kraken bringing up the rear.

As with Grinder's funeral only weeks before, the roar of the bikes starting was both startling and deafening. I swallowed my leaping heart and closed my eyes as we pulled into the flow of things behind Ashton's Jeep. The drive was agonizingly slow, as all funeral processions tended to be. At the cemetery, the men all lined the pathway from the cars and bikes to the gravesite. The pallbearers carried the casket on their shoulders between the two lines of people. Everyone's hand was pressed to their heart.

It was poignant and as we walked behind Reaver, behind Shelly and Ashton supporting Hayden between them to the sitting area beside the open grave, I was surprised I felt a little lighter, a little less burdened by sadness, because how could I be, with so many others here with me to share the load?

Behind the women of our club's chapter, the men of our chapter walked until all the seats were filled. As the men of our club passed the beginning of the line, the people we had walked between fell in behind them, the column folding in and drawing up to the grave as everyone found their place around it.

My father stood by to officiate and my mother smiled sadly and encouraging off behind him. He said words that really didn't mean anything to this club and its people, but were nice none the less, before he turned the floor over to Dragon to speak... but he couldn't. He bowed his head and choked up and our president cried. Trigger stepped up and grimly told a story or two about how fiercely loyal Reaver was and how he loved Hayden, and it was all very beautiful and stirring.

And I couldn't pay attention to any of it.

I was fighting too hard not to throw up. I closed my eyes and breathed in through my nose and out through my mouth, and eventually the nausea subsided, but by then, the ceremony was over and I felt heartily guilty that I hadn't been able to pay attention. Zander caught my eye as we walked back to the cars and pursed his lips in a kiss. I hugged my parents, who were worried about me and Everett, incredibly so, but who couldn't argue with our logic for leaving until the violence was sorted.

"You all right, sis?" Everett asked me, concerned, once we were shut into the car. I looked up the little hill, to the plot held by the MC, watching the sleek and shiny casket lower into the cold, frozen ground, and frowned.

"I don't know," I said honestly, swallowing hard.

We fell in behind the Kraken, who took the lead for the ride and drive to Florida. Zander and Ghost fell in behind us. They would ride down with us and make the return trip without us after we were settled... Dray and Trigger couldn't come because of their positions within the club. It just wasn't viable.

The drive was sheer hell. The nausea quickly redoubled its efforts once the pavement began to rush beneath the car, and about an hour into the drive I was frantically begging Everett to pull over. She blasted the signal on the horn, two long bleats, and dove for the shoulder. Ashton repeated the signal for the Kraken ahead and pulled off up ahead. Zander and Ghost pulled up behind my car as I threw myself into the tall, dry grass at the side of the road and everything I'd managed to put down after my incident in the kitchen came back up.

Zander's hand fell on my lower back and rubbed while I held back my hair. Everett handed me a bottle of water and so it went... all the way to Florida. We had to stop six more times and I could tell that some of the men of the Kraken were getting irritated with me. Cutter, though, Cutter was not among them.

The fourth, or was it the fifth? At any rate, one of the times he came back, he gently led me away from the mess I made. Zander and Everett were by the car, talking low and vehemently, concern etched in every line of their faces.

"You get carsick like this on every big trip?" he asked.

"I don't get carsick like this at all." I rinsed out my mouth and tried to catch my breath.

"I see. You feverish?" He put his hand to my forehead. As soon as he removed it, I shook my head.

"No, I don't feel hot."

"No, you don't," he agreed. "Ask you something personal?"

I nodded wearily and waved my hand vaguely in a gesture for him to go ahead, not trusting myself to open my mouth.

"You think you could be pregnant?" he asked me.

It was as if I'd been doused in a bucket of ice water. I stared up into his handsome face, wide-eyed, and blinked stupidly.

He nodded to himself.

"We're pulling off at the next exit," he shouted for everyone to hear over the rushing traffic. "Get Red here some ginger ale."

And we did. We pulled off at the next exit and stopped at one of those 24-hour drugstores that had just about everything. I huddled miserably in the passenger seat of my car and wiped tears from my eyes. Everett sat silently beside me in the driver's seat.

"Is it possible?" she asked. I had told her when we were safe in the bubble of my car, away from Zander overhearing.

"Yes." I sounded miserable even to myself. "Please don't say anything!" I pleaded as Zander climbed off his bike and headed our direction.

"I got you, sis," Everett said. Zander opened my door and crouched beside me.

"Hey, how you doing?" he asked me. I didn't exactly have to lie to cover my tears, I only had to tell half of the truth.

"I'm so sorry," I said mournfully. "I'm holding all of us up and making everyone so miserable and some of them are getting angry and it's all my fault!"

"Ohh, hey no. Nobody's mad at you, Sugar. You can't help being carsick."

He kissed my forehead and gave me a watered-down version of his usually-phenomenal smile. He was tired, from a night spent too long drinking, from getting up early for the funeral procession, and from a long ride fraught with stops.

"Hey, girl," Cutter came up behind Zander and handed him a soda bottle of ginger ale. Zander cracked the top and held it out to me.

"Sip on this, Sugar."

"Gotcha some saltines too. Might help settle your stomach," Cutter remarked. I took the bottle from Zander; It was cool but not cold, and I sipped gratefully.

"I gotta hit the head, you sit tight, okay, Baby?" I nodded, and Zander kissed my forehead. Cutter crouched down, taking his place.

"Good. Now here, you take this." He reached around behind him and pulled a white paper bag out from the waistband of his pants, under his cut. I handed the bottle of ginger ale to Evy and took the bag, my hands closing on a cardboard box inside. I looked. Cutter had bought me a pregnancy test. I looked up from the bag in my hands.

"Thank you."

"No problem, sweetheart. Better to know than not. We'll get you taken care of as soon as we get to the house. We got an hour or two more."

Everett handed me back the bottled drink and took the pregnancy test, shoving it down between her seat and the driver's door of my car as Zander came back out and headed for the car. Cutter put a box of saltine crackers in my lap.

"Thank you," I repeated. My hands trembled. I was scared. What if I was pregnant? Zander had commented a few times now about hoping I was up on my birth control pills. I was. I mean I thought I was. I agonized for the hour and forty minutes it took for us to reach our destination, realizing, horrified that I had forgotten to take a pill – the day of the shooting – and that Zander and I had made love, without any other protection.

I closed my eyes.

I was pregnant. I had to be. I was sure of it, but I would hope against hope. I would pray it wasn't so and I would take the test.

We pulled into the drive of a very nice, very big, old house that sat right on the beach. The front drive was lush with foliage and private from the road.

Zander opened my door and I got out. It was warm. I was too warm and I stripped off my cardigan. The black of my funeral attire needed to go, even though it was well past sundown by this point.

"Go get cleaned up and lay down, babe. I'll bring in your bags." I nodded and Everett pulled my overnight bag with a nightgown and my robe out of the back seat. We'd decided it was a good idea for our first night, so we didn't have to go fish through all our luggage. We were well aware we were all going to be here for a very long time. Months. It would take that long for things to resolve with the police still investigating. No move could be made until then. At least, not by our men. We didn't know what the Suicide Kings would and wouldn't do.

Everett and I went into the house. Cutter showed us to our rooms and I changed quickly and quietly into my nightgown. Everett met me in the hall in her own version of sleepwear, a ribbed tank top and a pair of men's boxers. She ushered me into a bathroom, thrusting the box into my hands and shut the door behind me.

I stood for a long while staring at the little blue and white box, sitting on that bathroom sink like an accusation. I felt like it was taunting me for my monumental stupidity and as I tore it open, tears sprang to my eyes. I was terrified that Zander was going to be so hurt, angry, and disappointed with me. I swallowed the lump in my throat, read the directions and peed on the stick's felt tip. I capped the damned thing, set it on the counter and washed my hands.

I opened the door and Everett slid in. She sat cross-legged on the floor and I sat nervously on the closed lid of the toilet, my knee bouncing in agitation.

"How long do we have to wait?" she asked.

"Any minute now." I looked at my watch and watched the seconds tick by. Finally, I let out my breath, and, with a glimmer of hope, stared down at the stick. Everything crumbled around me.

It was positive.

Revelator...

"Dude, Rev, you better get in here! Mandy's having some kind of a meltdown," Ghost shouted from the doorway of the house. It was dark out here, the golden rectangle of light behind my brother cast him in deep shadow. I couldn't see his face, so I couldn't read him, but his words, in combination with the strain in his voice, had me dropping the bags I'd been pulling out of Ashton's Jeep, and running for the door. Ghost turned sideways in the frame and I barged past him.

"What happened?" I shouted, as I made for the sound of my girl's noisy, wracking sobs. She was through the living room, past the stairs, sounded like she was in the kitchen. I found her sitting on top of a kitchen stool, Everett holding her and rocking her. Ashton, Shelly and Hayden stood nearby, and they were all three huddled together, wide-eyed. Cutter leaned against one of the counters nearby, his hands stuffed into the little front pockets on his cut, his mouth puckered and twisted in consideration as his eyes roved across the scene going on in front of him.

"What the fuck happened to my girl?" I demanded, and his eyebrows went up.

"I think she needs to tell you that, friend," he said gently. But Red was inconsolable.

"Everett, what the fuck, over?" Everett looked at me over Mandy's head, a desperate look on her face like even she'd never seen Red like this before.

Red unburied her tear-stained face from Everett's shoulder and looked at me from across the kitchen as I stood there helpless and feeling like a jackass. I needed to know who to punch before I could make it better.

"Please, don't be mad at me!" she cried, and took several short hiccupping breaths. My brows crushed down in confusion.

"Babe, why would I be mad at you?" I went to her and knelt on the floor in front of her. I put my hands on her knees and tried to urge her to calm down.

"Shh. It's okay, Sugar, tell me. You can tell me anything, you know that." She quieted and swallowed hard.

"Promise you won't be mad," she demanded and I was confused as fuck.

"Baby, I don't think I'll be mad, but I can't promise anything until I know what's wrong!"

She stared down at me, debating, for a really long time before her face twisted with the oncoming fresh round of tears.

"I'm so sorry, I'm so sorry, Zander..." she sobbed, and I was beyond fucking confused.

"Babe, Baby you gotta calm down..." I tried, and that failing, I barked out "Will somebody clue me the fuck in?"

"I'm pregnant!" Mandy shrieked in response to my outburst and I fucking froze. I stared up at my girl, who looked like she was going to hyperventilate and the moment crystallized and I hyper-focused.

I asked very calmly, very quietly, "You're what?"

I was vaguely aware of the girls' faces behind her breaking into smiles as my Red whimpered and repeated herself.

"I'm pregnant."

I felt myself break into the most beatific smile ever, and Red instantly calmed.

"You're not mad at me?" she asked meekly.

I stared at her, stunned as her words sank in. My Red, my girl, was pregnant with my kid. Holy shit.

I took her hands in mine while I processed this information and tugged gently. Everett let her go and backed away, and Red slipped off the stool and to her feet. I looked up at her, my hands went to her waist and I stared at her stomach. I felt tears start in my eyes and I didn't even fucking care that I was supposed to be some big fucking tough guy

"Let me get this straight, we're having a baby?" I asked her and stared up the length of her beautiful body. She wore the cream satin nightgown I liked on her so much, her green robe edged in its fiery autumn leaves hanging open. I stared into my girl's autumn-colored eyes, framed by her fiery autumn hair, as her calm returned. She nodded and repeated her question, her soft voice filled with wonder and hope.

"You're not angry?"

I turned my head and put my ear to her stomach, my arms going around her and holding her firm, holding her close. Her hands drifted from my shoulders, her fingers tangling in my hair and I heard a bunch of 'awww's' and a smattering of applause.

"No baby, I'm so ridiculously fucking happy right now... Oh my God... I'm gonna be somebody's daddy, all! With the woman of my dreams!" Out-and-out cheering went off then, and Red closed her eyes, tears gone from panic and fear to ones of gratitude and joy coursed down her cheeks.

"I love you so fucking much," I said to her and climbed her body, struggling to my feet from my knees. I pulled her mouth down to mine and kissed her savagely.

"I love you so fucking much!" I whispered fiercely and she cried a little, but it was ruined in the most perfect way by her laugh.

"I love you too!" she cried, and held onto me tightly, while the women of the Sacred Hearts, the men of the Kraken, and my brother Ghost all clapped and cheered. I looked at Sunshine over my girl's shoulder, her face lit like her namesake and full of happiness and I looked to Shelly, her hands covering her mouth, her jewel-bright eyes lit with happiness and joy.

Finally I looked at Hayden, whose face was slicked with tears, sure, but even she was smiling, and I felt some constriction around my heart ease. I pulled back and cupped my girl's face in my hands and stared into her eyes for a time before I kissed her.

My club had just experienced such heartache, such excruciating pain, and death. I was so proud that it was my girl that would bring life to it again, breathe happiness into my brothers and sisters, even for this small moment. My woman, my goddess of autumn, would be the one to really put us on the path to healing again by giving us something to believe in, to remember that good things were out there, that good things happened, too.

"I love you until forever." I told her, and she smiled, her face crumbling with yet more tears as she nodded between my hands.

"I love you until forever, too."

Forever never sounded so good.

EPILOGUE

R ed-XIII...
Back in early November...

I stood by a dude named Rowdy, just inside the door to the Suicide King's clubhouse and sniffed like it weren't no thang while their VP eyed me.

"What the fuck did you say your name was?" he asked.

"They call me Thirteen," I answered with a shrug.

"What the fuck kind of a name is that?" he asked. He was a tall, burly motherfucker, probably six-foot-three, with long dark brown hair in a pony tail that stopped between his shoulders. He looked at me with a shrewd brown gaze and by all accounts had more than a little evil in him.

I couldn't –and wouldn't– resist yanking his chain a little, "Well, you ever hear the one about the horse in the bar with the pot of money?" I asked.

"What, you some kind of fuckin' clown?" he demanded, crossing his arms over his chest, his leather cut strained over the shoulders of his black tee shirt. He planted his booted feet shoulder-width apart and he had on some hardcore motorcycle boots, the kind you wouldn't want to be stomped into the asphalt by. They rode under dirty jeans, the blue of 'em faded and stained light brown with both dust and too many wears without washing 'em, which is where this shithead probably got his name from. 'Pig-Pen' was emblazoned on the flash over his chest on the left side of his cut. Dude reeked of marijuana and dirt but, thankfully, not B.O. At least he had that going for him, because he had a shitty personality to go along with the shitty look on his face.

I gave a one-shouldered shrug, and he rocked back on his heels with a gusty grunt. "Fine, fuck, tell me the damned joke, and you better make me fucking laugh, or I'ma have your ass beat," he growled.

"So, dude walks into a bar and down at the end is this fuckin' horse with a pot of money in front of him. Dude takes a seat at the bar, and after his second beer, his curiosity gets the better of 'im, and he asks the bartender 'Dude, what's up with the horse?' Bartender shrugs and says, 'It's easy, bro, you put a dollar into the pot, and if you can make the horse laugh, you get to take what's in it home.'"

"So, the dude eyes the horse and has another beer, and finally gets up, walks over and puts a dollar into the pot, which it's totally overflowing. He looks the horse in the eye, leans forward and whispers in the horse's ear, and the horse just starts fucking dying, man! The horse is laughing so fuckin' hard it can't breathe, and the dude, he picks up the pot of money, nods to the bar keep who's standin' there, fuckin' jaw hanging, and he leaves the bar."

Pig-Pen does not look amused, but I ain't fuckin' done, so I keep going. "So, a year or two goes by, and the dude blows back into town and stops at the same bar. Same barkeep, same horse, new pot of money, and he asks the bartender, 'So, what's the deal now? Same thing?' and the bartender, looking smug, crosses his arms and leans back and says 'Naw, this time you gotta make the horse cry!' and the dude shrugs like it ain't no thing and goes over to the horse and whispers in the horse's ear, and the horse starts cracking up again."

"The bartender raises an eyebrow, and the dude turns his back on the bar and faces the horse and does a little something, and the horse stops laughing and just starts bawling, man! This horse just starts weeping these massive fucking tears and the barkeep, man, he's fuckin' stunned, and the guy picks up the pot of money and the barkeep yells, 'Hey! Stop! What the fuck did you do to my horse?'"

"The dude stops at the door and turns and says to the bartender, 'First time, I told him my dick was bigger 'n his. The second time? I showed him."

Pig-pen blinks at me and starts fucking laughing a deep belly laugh and I sniffed and undid my belt. He stopped and his eyes bugged a bit.

"What the fuck are you doin'?" he demanded.

"You wanted to know how I got my name." I brought myself out of my pants and let fly. Pig-Pen looked. I mean, shit, I knew what I was packing, and how could you not?

"I take it that's where you get the Thirteen," he said, and he wasn't laughing no more.

"Yep," I said dryly, and tucked myself back into my jeans and zipped back up. Pig-Pen looked me up and down, considering, and finally broke into a broad grin.

"You got a brass fucking pair to go along with it! So you wanna hang around and see if the MC life is for you?" He put an arm around my shoulders and led me deeper into the Suicide King's compound.

"Oh, I know it's for me..." I said, and smiled one evil fucking wicked grin on the inside. This had been way too fucking easy.

ALSO BY A.J. DOWNEY

The Sacred Hearts MC

1. Shattered & Scarred

2. Broken & Burned

3. Cracked & Crushed

3.5 Masked & Miserable (a novella)

4. Tattered & Torn

5. Fractured & Formidable

6. Damaged & Dangerous

The Virtues

1. Cutter's Hope

2. Marlin's Faith

3. Charity for Nothing

The Sacred Brotherhood

1. Brother to Brother

2. Her Brother's Keeper

3. Brother In Arms

4. Between Brothers

5. A Brother's Secret

6. A Brother At My Back

Indigo Knights

1. Her Thin Blue Lifeline

2. His Cold Blue Command

3. A Low Blue Flame

Paranormal Romance (with Ryan Kells)

1. I Am The Alpha

2. Omega's Run

3. Hunter's End

ABOUT THE AUTHOR

A.J. Downey is the internationally bestselling author of The Sacred Hearts Motorcycle Club romance series. She is a born and raised Seattle, WA Native. She finds inspiration from her surroundings, through the people she meets, and likely as a byproduct of way too much caffeine.

She has lived many places and done many things, though mostly through her own imagination...An avid reader all of her life, it's now her turn to try and give back a little, entertaining as she has been entertained.

Stalker Information:
www.ajdowney.com